HIS HIGHLAND BRIDE

HIS HIGHLAND HEART SERIES BOOK 3

WILLA BLAIR

OLIVER
HEBER
BOOKS

PUBLISHER'S NOTE: This is a work of fiction. Names, characters, places, and incidents either are the product of the author's imagination or are used fictitiously. Any resemblance to actual persons, living or dead, business establishments, events, or locales is entirely coincidental.

Copyright © 2017 by Linda Williams

Published by Oliver-Heber Books

0 9 8 7 6 5 4 3 2 1

HIGHLAND TALENTS SERIES
HEART OF STONE

"...Fast paced and well written with passion, charismatic characters and romantic, thrilling storyline. Perfectly wicked and dangerous! Simply put, WOW!"

— MY BOOK ADDICTION AND MORE

"...you'll pick up to read again and again."

— READING BETWEEN THE WINES BOOK CLUB

"With a little highland magic, anything is possible. I loved this story. A must read and now amongst my favorites."

— TIMELESS LOVE AND ROMANCE

HIGHLAND HEALER

"This is a great novel. Lovers of Hannah Howell's highland novels will love this."

— ROMANCING THE BOOK

"*This story is action-packed and full of twists and turns that will keep readers on their toes. It is fast-paced and has a sweet romance that will warm your heart. Well written and full of imagination, this story is a must read for historical romance fans!*"

— THE ROMANCE REVIEWS

"*...a rich, enjoyable read.*"

— SATIN SHEETS ROMANCE

THE HEALER'S GIFT

"*A Highland romance with a truly great hero...the story is compelling...*"

— IND'TALE MAGAZINE

"*A story of mystery, regret, hope, danger and trust... The characters are endearing, the story is fulfilling, and the set up for the remainder of the series presents an open invitation to dive right in. THE HEALER'S GIFT is a highly recommended read.*"

— FRESH FICTION

HIGHLAND SEER

"*...this is different enough from other Highland romances to stand out from the pack. Ms. Blair's writing style is natural and evocative...*"

— ROMANTIC HISTORICAL REVIEWS

"16th-century intrigue, muscled men with claymores and a doomed romance — is it any wonder I was reluctant to leave the rich, riveting world of HIGHLAND SEER?"

— USATODAY HEA

WHEN HIGHLAND LIGHTNING STRIKES

"Ms. Blair is a consummate storyteller...Can't wait for more from this magical author."

— MY BOOK ADDICTION AND MORE

"Ms. Blair has an easy to read talent for bringing a story to life."

— LONG AND SHORT REVIEWS

HIGHLAND TROTH

"Scottish romance at its best!"

— IND'TALE MAGAZINE

"...an exciting, romantic, historical tale full of angst, action and searing hot passion...With plenty of adventure and the twist of an old murder, HIGHLAND TROTH by Willa Blair, kept me hooked from beginning to end. A wonderful Highland romance."

— FRESH FICTION

HIS HIGHLAND HEART SERIES
HIS HIGHLAND ROSE

"Masterfully and brilliantly written Scottish Romance...!"
My Book Addiction & More

HIS HIGHLAND HEART

"The plot was honestly a masterpiece. It was well thought out and orchestrated. Right out the gate I was hooked! The hero had immediate book boyfriend appeal."

— LONG AND SHORT REVIEWS

"Willa Blair knows how to make a story come to life and sweep you away on a beautiful journey into the Highlands...This is a Scottish adventure you won't want to miss!"

— BOOKS & BENCHES

HIS HIGHLAND LOVE

"Beautifully written and masterfully executed!"

— MY BOOK ADDICTION AND MORE!

"Fiery passion burns bright in HIS HIGHLAND LOVE! Readers who enjoy Highland romance should definitely try Willa Blair's books."

— BOOKS & BENCHES

"If you love romantic highland stories of warriors and danger, love and honor, you'll find this story intriguing as well as enjoyable."

— THE READING CAFE

HIS HIGHLAND BRIDE

"Ms. Blair has delivered a wonderful and captivating read in this book where the chemistry between this couple was strong; the romance hot..."

— BOOK MAGIC, UNDER A SPELL WITH
EVERY PAGE

"This is a very enjoyable and well-written book to satisfy any historical romance lover, especially one who enjoys forbidden love!"

— IND'TALEMAGAZINE

CONTEMPORARY ROMANCE
WAITING FOR THE LAIRD

"Willa Blair spins a beautiful romance set in the Scottish Highlands full of suspense, history and mystery... I highly suggests you pick it up and enjoy."

— NIGHT OWL ROMANCE

"About 3:00 am I finally had to force myself to stop... yes, it was that good. Give yourself a treat and grab this book..."

— THE READING CAFE

"A contemporary romantic tale with a touch of history—and ghosts...Waiting for the Laird by Willa Blair is a delightful romance and unexpected adventure set in Scotland."

— BOOKS AND BENCHES

WHEN YOU FIND LOVE

"When You Find Love is a beautiful romance filled with combative personalities, a family curse and a love that can't be quenched. Character-driven plot with supernatural undertones make this a must-read. The ending was so fantastic, I didn't want it to end. If you love fantasy romance, you'll be smitten with When You Find Love."

— N.N. LIGHT'S BOOK HEAVEN

SWEETIE PIE

"Willa Blair is known for her Scottish historical paranormal romance. She changes genres with a modern Scottish lass who escapes to the Big Island of Hawaii. SWEETIE PIE is a delicious pupu - Hawaiian word for appetizer. Blair delivers a sweet novella that captures the Aloha spirit of the island."

— K. LOWE

To all my fans, you've made my writing journey a joy. Here's to the next chapter!

CHAPTER 1

SCOTLAND, LATE AUGUST, 1411

*A*s her father's chatelaine, Mary Elizabeth Rose never knew from one day to the next what challenge she would face, but a servant summoning her to her father's solar never boded well. When she entered, the room had the look of evening, not late morning. Her father was seated at his desk reading a document by fire and candlelight while a storm pelted the keep's walls and blew in through an open window. "Ye sent for me?" she demanded as she rushed to close and latch the shutter. He'd been forgetful lately, but being unaware of the rain blowing in was something new.

Finally looking up, he waved the document in his hand. "Indeed, daughter. I have received good news this day. Prepare yourself to travel to Strathspey to visit Lady Mhairi Grant."

After Mary wiped a few raindrops from the seat opposite the Laird's desk, she sank onto it. "The woman ye met at Annie's wedding?" Her middle sister had married the Brodie laird months ago.

"Aye, the same. We are invited for a visit."

Mary thought back. She recalled the woman—easily close to her father's age and handsome, if faded. While

1

the three sisters saw to the wedding arrangements, Lady Grant and her father kept each other company at Brodie. Mary hadn't seen her father so cheerful or talkative since her *maman* died. During the wedding visit, she and her sisters thought little of the encounter. He'd gone years without remarrying, so they'd assumed he never would. If her father now intended to wed Lady Grant, Mary welcomed the news. The lady would relieve her of her responsibilities to Rose.

Yet Mary could see no reason for her father to insist she accompany him on this trip. "Da, I canna go. I canna leave Cameron Sutherland. He is still unwell."

Cameron had helped escort Mary's youngest sister home across Scotland from St. Andrews during the summer. When they were still two days away from Rose, he had been wounded by a rogue Irish gallowglass mercenary. The wound needed better care than was possible while they traveled, and it had festered within a day of their arrival. Cameron had hidden how bad it had gotten until he could no longer bear the pain of the infection. He'd spent weeks in and out of fevers, too ill to know where he was. Only lately, to Mary's great relief, had he spent more time awake and aware. But he was by no means well.

"Pah," her father spat, jerking her attention back to him. "Sutherland's in nay danger. The healer can care for him without yer help. Ye have been spending too much time with the man as it is. Now that he's getting better, 'tis best if ye avoid him. I'll no' have yer reputation ruined by too much association."

Mary's mouth fell open. Though he was the Sutherland's youngest son, Cameron was two years older than she, which made her father's concern for her virtue legitimate, if insulting. "My reputation? If my reputation was in danger, I would be ruined already. The entire clan kens what I've been doing. I promised

Catherine to care for him in her stead, and I have. And, Da," she appealed again, "he is no' yet strong enough to leave us."

"But he will be soon enough. Perhaps even before we return from Grant."

Nay, Cameron wouldn't go without saying goodbye. Mary lifted a hand to her throat and let out a long, steady exhale to slow her breathing. She had to remind herself that losing her temper with her father would not improve the situation, nor would it get Cameron the care he needed. "I promised," she insisted, keeping her gaze averted. Her father, like any predator, felt challenged when you met his gaze, especially in the midst of an argument. "I am duty-bound and honor-bound to see him well enough to travel."

When her father failed to respond, Mary looked up. He stared off into space, unmoving. Then he gave a little jerk and nodded. "Make plans to leave in a three-day. I have a few things to take care of here before we go."

Mary sucked in a breath and shook her head. Had he even heard a word she said? About her duty and honor? Apparently when they conflicted with his plans, they didn't matter to him. She got to her feet, tempted to argue, when another reason occurred to her.

Had he been daydreaming about Mhairi Grant? She should be glad to see him happy.

Instead, a low rumble of thunder made her shiver.

❧

OTHER BUSINESS AROUND THE KEEP KEPT MARY occupied until early afternoon, when she finally found a few minutes to stop by Cameron Sutherland's chamber. Her father could not be right, saying Cameron no longer needed her. And how would Da know? Had the servants been talking? To the laird? That would be most unusual.

In answer to her knock, Cameron called out, "Come."

She opened the door and paused against the frame, relieved to find him sitting in the chamber's lone chair, looking out the open window. The breeze wafting in carried the scent of the recent rain, but the morning's storm had given way and now the sun peeked through tattered clouds.

Cameron glanced at her and smiled, then went back to watching something outside.

"I'm surprised to see ye up," she said, crossing her arms. "Mayhap ye are ready to get out of this chamber and come to the hall for yer meals?"

"I considered doing that but the maid Janie brought me a tray, so I stayed here." He glanced around at her again and grinned. "I hate to disappoint a pretty lass." Then he turned back to the window.

His grin made Mary's pulse leap, which she attributed to her pleasure at his progress. He must be feeling better to care what Janie thought. "What is so interesting?" She moved to stand behind Cameron's chair, where she, too, could peer out.

"Just the younger lads, practicing at arms in the mud. I think any of them could take me down at the moment."

"Certainly no'. Ye could best any of them," she assured him. "Ye'd only have to fall on those wee lads to put them out of the fight."

Cameron snorted. "I'm pleased ye have so much faith in me."

"Always, Cameron. Always." She raised a hand. "May I?" Since he was awake, she felt the need to ask his permission to touch him. At his nod, she laid a hand briefly on his forehead. His skin was warm, but not hot.

A good sign. She nodded to let him know, then shifted around him to perch on the wide stone windowsill. "Look how far ye have come. What ye accomplished to get here. Ye brought Catherine safe through an army from St. Andrews."

He shook his head. "With her handfasted husband, dinna forget."

Mary stared off into space for a moment. "How that lass has loved Kenneth Brodie, ever since she met him. She didna give up hope, even when he disappeared for two years into France, and only God kens where else or what he did there. Fate must have led her into finding him again in St. Andrews." Mere weeks ago, over their father's strong objections, Catherine had handfasted with Kenneth, the Brodie second-in-command. Mary was happy for both of her sisters, yet sad at the same time. Here she remained, the oldest daughter. Unwed, and without prospects as long as her father insisted she remain with him.

"They wouldna have made it here without ye," she added and met his gaze. "I owe ye my sister and her happiness." Cameron glanced down and her gaze followed his, noting the inherent strength of his hands, like a banked fire, waiting to burst to light again. The scars across his knuckles were reminders of countless fights, and she was sure the long one on the back of his hand had been made by a blade. She'd traced them hundreds of times while he lay trapped in fever. His strength would return. The scars would be with him forever. And someday, she hoped he would tell her the tales they represented.

Cameron pursed his lips. "What about yer own happiness?"

She heaved a breath and glanced out the window, surprised he'd asked such a probing question. The subject pained her too much to discuss face to face, but resentment made words come, nonetheless. "My father ruined my chances when he delayed responding to the MacBean betrothal offer I welcomed. The man I loved, Dougal MacBean, gave up and married someone else." She stopped speaking, her throat tight with emotion. She cleared it, then added, "He abandoned me as surely as Da betrayed me. I no longer expect I'll ever find the kind of happiness ye mean, not this late in life."

Nor had Dougal, it seemed, or not for very long. Nearly a year ago, she'd heard the sad news that his wife had died, though not the reason why. For a few months, she had held out hope he would come for her and renew their romance. But he never made contact at all. That part of her life was truly over.

Cameron studied her, as if at a loss for a way to cheer her.

"Anyway," she said, pulling herself from her morose memories, "I came to tell ye I will be away for a few days. Da received an invitation from Lady Grant, and he insists I go with him."

"Do ye wish to?"

She shook her head. "Nay. I dinna wish to leave ye, but the healer will take good care of ye until I return."

Cameron laid a hand over his heart. "I may die of longing for yer smile before then."

She slapped at his arm. "Cameron Sutherland, dinna even jest about dying. Ye willna die. Ye mustna."

"Very well, I willna." He cocked his head, teasing her.

But she saw a question in his eyes. "I've worked too bloody hard to keep ye alive, man. I'll be *fashed* if I return to find ye gone." *And I'd miss ye.* The thought stabbed into her gut like an unseen blade. She'd spent hours reading to him while he thrashed in fevered dreams. But she'd said more. Somewhere along the way, he'd become necessary to her, though he could not know it. Her sisters were gone, and she couldn't complain to the servants. Knowing he could not hear her, she'd seen no harm in unburdening herself to him about whatever bothered her that day, often something her father had said or done.

"I willna go anywhere before ye return," he promised. "No' even if only to Sutherland and certainly no' to the grave. But lass, yer da takes shameful advantage of yer sense of duty to the clan. Why do ye no' simply tell him nay? Ye are a strong, brave lass. Stand up to him. Refuse to go."

"If only I could." She bit her lip. How had Cameron formed that opinion? Maybe he hadn't been as deeply asleep as she thought. "But I have to keep Da out of trouble, too. And Lady Mhairi Grant could be trouble aplenty." She lowered her voice to keep it from carrying out the window into the bailey. "She clung to him at Annie's wedding as though they were years-long friends, or even husband and wife. But they'd just met. It wasn't unseemly, exactly, but she did monopolize his time."

"I see nay harm," Cameron argued. "He left her behind, so perhaps they only enjoyed a flirtation during the celebration. Have they corresponded since?"

"Until this invitation arrived, I had no' been aware of any letters, and I didna ken about this one until Da waved it at me."

"Could it be an invitation to an event that will be attended by other clans as well?"

"Perhaps." She shrugged. Da hadn't said.

"*Dinna fash*, Mary, my love. All will be well."

Mary sucked in a breath. "Cameron! What did ye call me?"

"Mary?" His eyes glinted with humor.

He was teasing her. "Nay, there was more. Mary... my love." She could barely say the words.

7

"Only to make ye feel better, lass. I'm no' used to seeing ye so unhappy." Cameron grimaced. "Now, if ye would, help me to the bed. I am suddenly in need of lying down."

Mary castigated herself for getting so wrapped up in her own worries, she'd failed to notice Cameron's growing pallor. "Aye, ye must rest. Perhaps by suppertime, ye will feel strong enough to come downstairs." She got him to his feet and with an arm around his waist, across the small chamber the few steps to the bed, where he settled with a sigh. Mary pressed the hand she'd wrapped around his waist to her hip, uncomfortable how the flex of his muscles aroused such longing in her breast. This visit had not confirmed her father's assertion that Cameron no longer needed her, but it had convinced her she needed to get away from him for a while. He was becoming too important to her.

Then he reached up, squeezed her hand, and released it. "Go, and thank ye, lass. Dinna think any more on leaving me behind today—or at all." His smirk softened the implied scold.

"I'll try," she promised, though she knew her words rang hollow. She could not refuse her father's demand, no matter how much she might wish to—or why.

❧

THAT EVENING, CAMERON MADE HIS WAY DOWNSTAIRS before Mary or one of the maids had a chance to bring him a tray. He wanted to spend some time out of his chamber, with other people, hearing talk and laughter and seeing more than the four walls he stared at every day. He'd counted every stone, every crack, every cobweb, until he thought he'd go daft.

Surely that meant he was getting well.

Some of the clan had already gathered and taken seats at long trestle tables. The high table was still empty and Cameron wondered when Mary and her father would arrive. The day he and Kenneth Brodie had returned Mary's youngest sister home, he'd briefly met the man, but knew more about him from Mary than from that brief encounter.

Cameron glanced around. He should have waited for her, he supposed, but if the maid had brought him a tray, he might have thrown it against the wall once the lass left his chamber. When Mary arrived, she would not have been pleased.

She entered the hall from a doorway on its opposite side, and Cameron's breath caught in his throat. He'd tried to quell his rising interest in her, but she'd done so much for him, he supposed falling for her was a natural reaction. She was beautiful and kind and wise, but so were other women he knew, and thoughts of them did not fill his nights as she did.

Cameron headed toward her.

"Cameron!" The surprised pleasure in her voice was unmistakable. "I didna expect to find ye here. I was just coming up..."

"I was ready to come down, so, here I am."

She gave him a brilliant smile and took his arm. "Let's sit down, then. The meal will be served soon." She steered him toward the high table. "Da is busy and willna be here, so the meal will be more informal than usual."

He stopped her. "In that case, may we sit down here, so I can meet some of yer clan?"

Mary's hand lifted to her chest. "Ach, Cameron, of course. I'm sorry, I didna think. Ye've been in that chamber much too long."

She chose the last two empty two seats at a table

near the hearth and introduced him. "If ye will, go around the table and tell Cameron a bit about ye."

Cameron smiled and nodded as each person introduced themselves, committing their names to memory.

When everyone had finished making themselves known, one of the lasses, Annag, spoke up. "We kenned the healer and Mary were caring for someone ill. That was ye?"

Cameron ducked his head disarmingly and smiled. "It was, Annag. And as ye see, they took good care of me. I'm much improved." Annag had straightened and smiled when Cameron said her name—it was a device he'd often used. Most people never expected anyone to remember names in a group, but Cameron had made a point to develop the skill.

"Where is Sutherland?" one of the lads asked.

"To the north, across the Moray Firth" Cameron told him. "And ye are...Edan, aye?"

"Aye," the lad answered and sat back, looking pleased.

"We heard ye were stabbed by a gallowglass man," Annag announced.

Cameron nodded and glanced at Mary. How much had she told her clan about him?

"They ken what happened to ye," Mary told him softly. "And how sick ye have been since. But like me, they ken little about ye."

"There's little to tell," Cameron answered with a lift to his eyebrows, sweeping his gaze around the table as he spoke. "I have four siblings, all older. I'm a merchant's factor, so I travel a lot, lately to St. Andrews, where I met Lady Catherine through her cousin, Abigail Duncan."

"We heard how ye brought Cat home," another lass said. "It must have been very dangerous."

Cameron shrugged. "Kenneth Brodie and I helped her get home, Cailean. He took care of her. I mostly rode scout." The lass smiled at the mention of her name, as Cameron intended.

"What is Sutherland like?" Edan broke in.

"I've heard ye have a grand castle," another lad added.

"We do, Duncan," Cameron told him, earning another smile. "But 'tis where I grew up, so I tend to take it for granted." He turned his attention back to Edan. "Like Rose, 'tis also very near the sea."

"I'd love to see it," Annag said.

He felt Mary shift next to him. Her eyebrows lifted when he glanced her way, but he couldn't tell if she was surprised or amused by Annag's boldness.

Servants arriving with food and drink saved Cameron from extending an invitation. If he took anyone to Dunrobin, he would take Mary. She'd spent so much time caring for him, he owed her. And based on things he'd heard her say, getting her away from Rose for a while would do her a lot of good.

But he wasn't naive enough to think her father would allow him to take her anywhere. Given how much she thought her father depended on her, she would never agree, either.

He answered several more questions while they ate and managed to get in a few of his own. Since he'd been ill, he'd had little access to information on how things stood at Rose. Mary had shared the most, whether she meant to or not. Still, she had said little about what impact the recent trouble had on Rose between the Warden of Scotland—the Duke of Albany—and Domnhall of the Isles over nearby Ross territory. The servants mostly came and went from his chamber without a word, and the healer spent her time

11

inspecting his injury and making him drink noxious potions, then telling him what to do.

Before he left Rose, he must learn more. He looked around the hall while the others talked. It had filled for the meal, and given the number of lasses who sat with other lasses and their children, Rose had lost some men.

Enough to make them vulnerable to Albany or the Lord of the Isles? He turned his attention back to Mary. Would she be safe here when he left? Would anyone?

CHAPTER 2

"*W*hat are ye doing out in the garden, Cameron Sutherland?" Mary scowled at her stubborn patient, who sprawled on a garden bench, his back supported by the smooth trunk of a small rowan tree. After last night's supper, she thought he'd be exhausted and never expected to find his bed empty this morning. For a moment, her heart had stopped, then reason returned. Surely if something awful had happened during the night, the healer would have sent for her. She would not have taken his body away and not told the one other person who would check on him first thing in the morning. Nay, this disappearance was his doing.

Annoyed, she searched the great hall and the kitchen on the assumption he'd gotten hungry and again followed through on her suggestion yesterday to take his meals with the clan in the great hall. Not finding him any of those places, she'd gone to the stables. Not there, either. As she passed the garden gate, she spotted him where she least expected him to be.

Mary didn't usually frown so fiercely, but between her father and this man, she'd been doing that a lot lately.

13

"Ach, sweet Mary, my love. My angel of mercy." Cameron sat up and leaned forward with a wince. "I tired of staring at four walls. The sunshine revives me, and the scent of roses is most pleasant, even this late in the summer."

Mary tamped down on the thrill hearing him call her Mary-my-love had sent shooting through her belly. She knew better than to take him seriously. And she was annoyed with him, which was probably why he'd said it. Certainly not because he meant anything by it. "Ye have been ill for weeks. Yer side is barely healed." His pallor still contrasted with his hair, dark but with all the rich brown shades of a golden eagle. He was tall, with muscles honed to perfection—until his injury robbed him of strength. Still, Cameron managed to be proud and fierce. Too bad the wound in his side had clipped his wings. "If ye tear open yer wound, ye risk the fever returning, and ye are much weaker now than ye were when ye first came to us."

He lifted his arm on his good side and squeezed the big muscle between his shoulder and the crook of his elbow. "Aye, sadly, ye are correct. I've lost a stone or two. But lass, I must start to regain my strength soon, or I'll be of little use to anyone. This garden is a pleasant place to start. Come, sit with me and enjoy the day." He patted the seat beside him as he straightened. "Those dark clouds on the horizon won't arrive for hours yet."

Mary caught the hesitation in his movement and the grimace he quickly hid. His wound, despite his brave words, still pained him.

"Tell me what ye will do today, lass," he suggested as he made room for her. "Have ye heard from yer sisters or their husbands at Brodie?"

Mary pressed her lips together and chose to relent this one time. The reason she'd come to find him could

14

wait. "It is pleasant out here," she commented as she sat and arranged her skirts. A few varieties of roses were past their peak, but the rest still bloomed in a riot of pinks from pale blush to nearly red. The breeze wafted mildly around them, carrying not only the scent of roses, but the scent of the man beside her, and a faint hint of the storm to come. "Aye. They are well. I had a letter from Annie just today. Catherine asks after ye."

Cameron nodded, but he watched the clouds as she talked. The furrow between his brows slowly eased and finally disappeared as she filled him in on her sisters' news.

Mary had spent most of the last few weeks helping the clan Rose healer save his life, so she was glad to see some of the strain leave his face. There was nothing about this man's body she had not seen and did not know. He flirted when he felt well enough, and made their lives miserable when the fever took him, mumbling about battles and secrets that lent him an air of mystery and danger. Little of what he said during those times made sense to Mary, except to prove to her he had secrets and his duty lay elsewhere. Not at Rose. She pressed her lips together and exhaled.

He must have seen her tense, because he took her hand in his big one and sighed. "I would suffer this wound again and again, if I kenned it would end with me here, in this moment, with ye. Now, tell me, lass. What worries ye?"

She crumpled her skirt with her free hand while telling herself Cameron was only being kind. He must feel much better today to have ventured out into the Rose keep's walled garden. And to take her hand with such ease and continue to hold it. As many times as she'd touched him during his illness, to cool his fever or soothe his pain, he'd never reciprocated. Even when he felt well enough to tease her, he never presumed.

She shouldn't welcome the familiarity he now displayed, but she did. It made her feel like the connection she sometimes imagined between them could grow into something real.

But she also expected what she had to tell him might end it all. She hoped her news did not spoil his contentment, but she knew it would.

"I just found out Da has been writing to Earl Sutherland, keeping him apprised of yer condition. Yer progress."

Cameron snorted. "Currying favor, most like, in exchange for my care."

Mary should have felt insulted for her father, but Cameron was right. "That would be my father, aye. At any rate," she continued as she pulled a folded letter out of her pocket, "this came for ye a few days ago. I was waiting for the right time to give it to ye, but ye need to have it before I go away. The seal is unbroken."

Cameron dropped her hand, reached for the missive and ripped it open without bothering to verify it had not been tampered with.

While he read, Mary tucked away the hand he'd held. She missed the sensation of being enclosed, in at least some small way, in the heat of his body. Did his new familiarity mean he had a new awareness of her as more than his caretaker? She'd wondered for weeks what it would be like to be wrapped in his powerful embrace once he recovered. Now a chill skittered across her back as her hand cooled without his touch.

"Ach, Christ's bones, Mary. My father orders me home as soon as I am able to make the trip." He crumpled the letter in his hand. "He doesna say I have been neglecting my duty to Sutherland, but the implication is there. Now I am better, I must go."

Mary's heart sank, and she lifted her hand to her mouth. "Surely no' today!"

"Nay, lass, but soon." He smoothed out the letter again, folded it and tucked it inside his shirt, then stared toward the garden gate.

Mary turned to see what had caught his attention and shivered. The dark clouds had advanced to the edge of the sun's disk. In moments, they would hide the sunshine and steal its warmth.

Cameron shifted to face her.

He grimaced at the movement, but she bit her tongue and let it go. If pain kept him here longer, she would have to accept his suffering, and if that made her seem cruel, so be it. To survive the trip home, he had to be strong enough to fight.

"We've kenned this time was coming," he told her and pressed his lips together until the corners whitened.

Mary's heart swelled as he looked into her eyes.

The words were not what she had wanted to hear when he finally met her gaze with eyes clear of fever and pain. Yet they implied an understanding between the two of them neither had stated.

Then his gaze lowered. He took both her hands in his.

She took a breath to gather her composure before she spoke. "And I have dreaded it. But I must also be thankful for it, because it means ye are almost well." She didn't feel thankful at all. A distant rumble of thunder reached her ears like a heavenly rebuke for her lies—the words she'd said and the feelings she hid. Now finally faced with his departure, she wanted to burst into tears, to let them pour down like the rain those dark storm clouds, stretching to the horizon, would produce, angry and defiant. Instead, for his sake, she pulled her hands free, clasped them together and schooled her voice to mildness, as if the prospect of his departure meant less to her than his improving health—as any good nursemaid would. "So his letter means ye must regain yer strength as soon as possible. Ye must begin to walk more, and when ye feel up to it, to ride. Perhaps train—lightly—with some of the men, to build up your strength. But ye must be mindful. If ye open yer wound, we'll have to start over."

"Aye, I will do all those things." He leaned forward and rested his elbows on his knees, his gaze on the ground. "And I do have news—news I canna put into a letter—that I must tell my father before many more weeks go by."

Mary's heart sank and she stiffened her spine against her despair. There was no question Cameron would leave. She'd always known his time at Rose would be limited.

Just as she knew she must stay.

She stood, smoothed her skirts, and faced him. "I will do what I can to help ye get ready."

He surprised her again, standing and raising a hand to her cheek. When feeling well, he'd always been quick to flirt, but he'd never touched her so intimately before, though she'd touched him intimately—very intimately —when the fever took him and he could not assist with his care. She hoped he had been unaware of those times.

Mary leaned her head into his hand. She would not cry. Crying was for silly maidens her youngest sister Catherine's age. She was older and wiser—or she should be.

"Leaving ye will no' be easy, Mary Elizabeth Rose."

His gaze bored into her, a dark amber pool he tempted her to drown within. She took a breath and straightened away from his hand. "Then ye must return —when ye can. If ye wish to, that is. Later on..." The words left her mouth in pieces, like shards of glass.

They revealed too much about how she'd come to feel about this big, proud, difficult man.

❧

CAMERON HAD HATED BEING SICK. AND ALL FROM A WEE scratch by an Irish dagger. Hardly worth a mention. Until it became a fire in his blood—and not the kind of fire gazing at Mary Rose lit. He studied her, certain she was hiding her feelings as best she could. But he was a trained observer—his life had depended on his skill, and over their weeks together, he'd learned to read the nuances behind her expressions. Though his departure had been the specter on the horizon all along, the thought of him leaving distressed her. Before he went, he needed one important truth from her. "Why did ye care for me, Mary, my love?"

Her eyes widened at his question, and she pulled on her lower lip with her teeth, then dropped her gaze. "What do ye mean?"

Watching her mouth, he fought to keep from lowering his head and kissing her. Not yet.

Perhaps never.

He had to know if he meant anything to her. "Why ye and no' just the healer, or a serving lass like Janie?"

He didn't remember all of the last weeks, but he did recall the important things. Mary's hands cool on his forehead, the damp cloth cold as she washed the sweat from his body, leaving him shuddering with chills but grateful for the respite from the fires burning along his bones until he feared they would char and splinter from the heat. Her voice as she read to him, as she talked to him when she believed he couldn't hear.

He thought the Healer had taken care of his body's more basic needs. He hoped she had. But he couldn't deny Mary had been intimate with him in ways no maiden should. He'd like to recall more, but he'd lost much in fevered dreams.

Still, he knew more about Mary than she realized. She was beautiful, aye, but she was also strong and wise and compassionate—and trapped.

Such was their past. If he could, he'd repay her for her care with hours of passion and pleasure. Yet, he might as well dream to touch the moon. She was not the sort of lass to toss up her skirts, no matter how a man charmed her. Maybe with more time, Mary would come to think of him not as her ill Sutherland, but as a man she might enjoy being with—intimately.

Not today. Not tomorrow, either.

He was out of time. He'd avoided his duty far too long while he lay injured and ill. His father ordered him home—as soon as he could safely travel. For once, he was glad to be unable to comply.

Mary still pondered her boots, and Cameron wondered if talking about her care for him embarrassed her.

"I promised Catherine I would take care of ye," she finally said. She lifted her gaze to his. "How could I face my baby sister if I let ye die?"

His pulse stilled, then resumed more quickly. "Die? Was I in such danger?"

She let her head drop back, her eyes closed. Then she sighed. "Aye, ye were. I can speak about it now, but ye near scared the life out of me more than once. Despite the poultices the healer put in yer wound, and all the willow bark tea we made ye drink, and the cold water we bathed ye in, I feared ye would slip away from me...from us. Ye nearly did."

Slip away from *me*. Cameron heard the word Mary corrected, though she still refused to admit her feelings. He offered his hand, fighting to keep the stitch in his side from showing on his face. If he moved the wrong way, the scar pulled something fierce. "Let's walk a wee."

Mary gave him a worried smile and took his hand. "That still pains ye. Dinna deny it. I can see the way ye favor it."

He couldn't get away with anything around this woman. As easily as he read her, she read him. Yet they left so much unsaid, Mary the dutiful daughter of a controlling widowed father, and he, just as duty-bound. He nodded as they moved at a sedate pace across the garden, her hand on his arm. "Only a little."

"'Tis why ye grimace every time ye have to use the muscles on that side."

"We've already established 'tis no' entirely healed."

She nodded, her expression pensive. "I ken ye must leave soon, but ye mustna ride until the healer says ye may."

Cameron glanced at her while taking the next step and the one after that. As long as she guarded her feelings, he was reluctant to declare his. Maybe once she returned from Grant, things might change between them. He would remain here at least that long.

❦

MARY ASKED JANIE TO TAKE CAMERON'S MEAL TO HIS chamber. She couldn't face him again. Not yet. Not with what, to her, felt like a betrayal hanging between them. The fact that her father forced her to leave made little difference. In Mary's heart, she wanted to remain behind with Cameron and knew staying with him was the right thing to do. But her head argued for the duty she owed her father and laird.

She had just finished her own meal in the great hall with some of the clan, when Janie came running back and stopped below where she sat on the raised dais.

"He's acting *tetched* again, milady. I think ye need to come."

Mary jumped to her feet and hurried after Janie across the hall, past the concerned gazes of the people there. They all knew about Cameron, though few had met him yet. "Fetch the healer," she ordered when they reached the stairs. "Then bring cold water and cloths. I'll go on up."

"Aye, milady." Janie hastened away.

Mary ran up the stairs to his chamber and found Cameron sprawled in tangled sheets, tossing his head. She rushed to his side and put a hand on his brow. "Ach, nay," she muttered under her breath. His fever had increased again. "Cameron, 'tis Mary. It appears ye did a wee more than ye shouldha today. How do ye feel?"

He stilled. "Like hell." He turned his face away from her. "Sorry, lass."

"Apology accepted." She pulled the covers aside. His shirt was already wet and clammy with his sweat. What had happened between earlier today and now? "Cameron, let me pull up yer shirt. I need to see yer wound."

His eyes remained closed underneath a fierce crease between his brows, but his hands pawed at his waist. At least he wasn't so far gone in fever he couldn't understand what she said to him. Then she realized he was trying to keep a sheet over his lower half while he helped her with his shirt. It took effort, but she got it free just as the healer bustled in, followed by the serving lass.

Mary stepped aside to let the healer examine the wound. "I'll take those," Mary told Janie, who waited by the door with the water and cloths she'd asked for earlier. "I need ye to fetch some watered ale, too," Mary saw the concern written in the girl's wide-eyed expression and cocked her head.

"He'll no' die, will he?" Janie asked softly. "I like him. I wouldna want him to die."

"He willna die, nay. We dinna want him to, either." Mary gave her a reassuring smile and sent her on her way, then set what the lass had brought on the table by Cameron's bed.

The healer stood and beckoned Mary away from her patient. "I canna understand what set him off again," she said, speaking softly. "The wound looks to be healing well."

"So 'tis the blood fever again?" Dread slid down Mary's spine like cold rain. Had her thoughts about keeping him here ill-wished him into this fever? She shook her head, dismissing the notion. She wasn't a superstitious person.

The healer frowned. "I dinna ken. What did he do today?"

"I found him in the garden early this morning. We walked a while and talked. I canna think any of that would have harmed him." She wanted him well. She truly did, despite her thoughts this morning that she'd accept his suffering if pain kept him here longer. She wasn't normally a cruel person, either.

"Well, we'll resume the willow bark tea..."

"Ach, nay," Cameron objected, rising up on an elbow with a wince, clearly having heard at least the end of their discussion. "That bitter stuff."

"Twill save yer life, ye daft man. If ye'd stayed abed as I told ye, this might no' have happened."

"Ye told him to stay abed? When?"

"Just this morn. I found him in yon chair, soon after first light." The healer gestured at the wooden seat by the window.

"Bored," Cameron complained. "And now Mary will

leave me. More bored." He held out a hand. "I'm thirsty."

Mary rolled her eyes. "The maid is on her way with some watered ale. Ye are no' so sick as all that. I'll bring ye a book to read."

"I'll get the tea and be right back," the healer announced and left Mary to tend to her cranky patient, who had dropped back to his pillow and closed his eyes.

"For now, we need to cool ye." She put the cloths into the water pitcher to let them soak, then wrung one out. "This will be cold."

"I ken it. 'Tis no' like ye have no' done this to me before."

In answer, Mary laid the cold cloth on Cameron's chest.

"*Shite*! Could ye warn me?"

"Ye could open yer eyes." She spread the cloth across his broad chest, her fingers itching to trace its muscled contours. Instead, she stepped back and reached for another cloth. "Does the light hurt them?"

"Aye."

He'd frowned when he answered. Mary took pity on him and used the next cloth to wipe sweat from his face, then laid it across his brow and eyes.

Cameron nodded. "That feels better."

"I dinna ken why yer fever came back," Mary soothed, "but we will make it go away."

"I want ye to stay, Mary. No' to go with yer da. No one cares for me as ye do."

"Nonsense. Why, even the serving girl doesna wish ye to die, though I canna see why she likes ye when ye complain like this. Now, stop acting like a *wean*. Ye're no' three years old. Ye'll get better whether I have the care of ye or nay."

"So ye have made up yer mind to go," Cameron said softly, as though to himself.

He'd failed to respond to her teasing, making her frown. "I dinna have much choice, now do I?" Mary wrung out another cloth and stroked it along Cameron's neck and throat. It caught in the bristles of his dark beard and they teased Mary's fingertips with their rough texture. "We need to get the lad to shave ye again," she told him. He nodded and tilted his head, giving her better access. Then she got a fresh cloth and wrung it out. "Brace yerself. I'm going to put this one on yer belly."

"Ye dinna think yer da can take care of himself without ye?" Cameron challenged as she spread the cold cloth below the one on this chest. His only reaction was to tighten the muscles in his abdomen.

Mary was glad he couldn't see her face. She enjoyed looking at Cameron's muscles, and the trail of hair that disappeared under the covers. She knew where it led, of course, but that knowledge only made it more compelling. They were not wed. She should not even be aware of what the covers hid. She pulled her thoughts away from Cameron's generous anatomy. "Nay, I dinna think he can. I dinna ken what that Grant woman is planning or expecting to achieve with this visit. I'm sorry, Cameron. 'Tis my duty to him and to this clan."

The healer came back then with a cup of the willow bark tea in her hand. "Ye must drink all of this," she reminded him.

Cameron threw an arm over his eyes.

Though she couldn't see the upper part of his face Mary knew his expression had to be one of long suffering. He hated the taste of willow bark tea. "Let's sit ye up," she told him and stripped the damp cloths from his body, then tugged at the one he'd trapped between his arm and forehead. "So ye can drink it faster."

Janie returned then, too, with another pitcher. Her eyes widened at the nearly naked man.

Mary frowned and gestured for her to set the pitcher down, not liking the lass's reaction, so like her own, to seeing Cameron's chest. "Then ye can have some ale," Mary promised.

Cameron wiped his face with the cloth, then handed it back to Mary. With a grunt, he rolled to his side, swung his legs off the bed and sat up, tugging the sheet and woolen blanket along with him over his lap. Then he accepted the cup from the healer and tossed it back, wincing as he swallowed. "Ale...please."

The serving girl poured some into a clean cup with a shaking hand and gave it to Mary. Mary passed it to Cameron.

He tossed it back, then held out the cup. "More. I can still taste that bitter tea."

The healer nodded, so Mary let the girl refill the cup and gave it back to him. "Slower this time, aye?" Mary cajoled. He surprised her by obeying. When he finished, he handed her the cup.

"That's enough for now," the healer told him. "I'll check on ye in an hour. I expect to find ye asleep."

Cameron gave her a wry smile. "I'll do my best." Then he turned his gaze to Mary. "Will ye stay?"

"Aye, if only to torture ye some more." She gestured for Janie to follow the healer out. Mary reached into the water pitcher for another wet cloth. "Lie on yer good side if ye wish and I'll put some of these on yer back."

Cameron nodded and did as he was told, keeping the bedclothes over his lower half. Then he rolled to his belly, rested his head on his arms, and turned his face toward her.

Mary lost herself for a moment looking at the way the muscles of his back stretched like wings, then noticed the crease between his eyebrows. "Does lying like that pull at yer scar?"

"A wee bit."

"Stubborn man." She shook herself and wrung out a cloth, then laid it over this head, leaving his face uncovered, but pressing a corner of the cloth over his forehead.

Cameron sighed.

Would he sigh like that when he kissed her?

She had to stop thinking that way. After warning him, she placed another cloth on the back of his neck. He rewarded her with a groan of pleasure that reached deep in her belly and made her thighs clench.

She plunged her hand into the cold water to distract herself, then pulled out another cloth. She covered his back, though it took three cloths to span his shoulders and reach down to the swell of his buttocks. She longed to trace the dip in his lower back, but dared not touch him in any way not clearly meant to help him heal.

Instead, she asked, "Would ye like me to read to ye?" She knew her voice soothed him and the stories gave his mind something to focus on besides his discomfort.

His eyes opened long enough for him to answer her. "Aye, I would."

She removed all the damp cloths, pulled the covers up to his broad shoulders, but restrained herself from tangling her fingers in the hair curling along the strong cords of his neck. Instead, she crossed to the chair beside the fire and picked up the latest book she'd been reading to him. Eventually, his breathing slowed and the crease between his dark brows smoothed out, making him look younger, even sweeter. She set the book aside, bent over him and brushed her fingertips across his forehead. Cooler. Something had helped.

She left him to his rest. After she closed the chamber door behind her, she leaned against it. Cameron was a temptation she didn't need in her life. She could not hope for anything to happen between them. He owed duties to his clan and would soon leave her, so why did she allow herself to have these feelings about him?

She shook her head to rid herself of the unwanted longings and went to find the healer. After this relapse, Mary feared she'd spend the entire trip not just missing Cameron, but worrying for his life. She needed the healer's reassurance.

CHAPTER 3

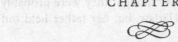

*M*ary awoke the next morning to the sound of someone knocking at her door.

"What is it?" she called, reluctant to leave her warm nest of blankets and the dream she'd been having about Cameron.

Her maid opened the door. "Yer father wishes ye to join him in his solar," she announced. "Do ye need my help getting dressed?"

Mary groaned and tossed aside the covers. "Nay. Stir the fire, if ye will, before ye go."

The maid complied and left her to her morning ablutions.

When she arrived at the laird's solar, her father sat at his desk, pouring over the same list Mary had seen him study many times—the names of the men he had sent in July to fight with Domnhall, Lord of the Isles, against the Earl of Moray's troops. Moray was the Duke of Albany's man. The battle between their forces at Red Harlaw, so called for the amount of blood spilled there in one day of fierce fighting, had solved nothing and resulted in many dead Highlanders, including men from Rose. Most of those still alive had returned by now. But even this late in the summer, a few stragglers had shown up at the gate, having wandered from town to village, doing God only knew what, until they decided to return to parents or wives and children. At least a dozen were still unaccounted for, a fact that obsessed her father. Mary thought they were probably buried in the field at Harlaw, but her father held out hope.

"Da, ye sent for me?"

When he set the list aside, Mary's tension eased. So he had not called her here to dwell on those men again.

"I'm thinking of sending to Domnhall for some warriors. We are undermanned. If we were attacked today and our walls breached, we lack the men to fight the size force any of our neighboring clans could throw at us. Perhaps some of those Irish mercenaries..."

A cold chill skittered down her spine. Their neighboring clans were allies—had he forgotten? As for gallowglass men, she shuddered. "Da, do ye no' recall what they did when Catherine and Kenneth were here?" Rose had taken in three of their wounded. The three hale warriors with them had assaulted Rose serving wenches and started a brawl in the great hall that had resulted in the lone Irish survivor of the brawl trying to kidnap Catherine. If she hadn't kept her head, and if Kenneth hadn't gone after her, she might have been ravaged and killed. But she fought off the attacker and Kenneth finished him. The next day, Rose had his men load the three wounded Irish into a wagon and send them off to Domnhall at Dingwall. "We dare no' let any of them inside our gates." How could her father have forgotten that day? His lapses worried her. She'd noticed his confusion before this, but to forget such events seemed more than distraction.

"Hmmmm, aye, I suppose ye are right."

But his frown told her something else bothered him. "If our manpower worries ye, are ye certain we should leave Rose right now?" she ventured. "Perhaps we should call on Brodie or another ally for men, and delay the visit to Grant until they arrive..."

"Nay! We will leave tomorrow, as I have said." He stared off into space, then shook his head and returned his gaze to her. "In the meantime, I called ye here about another matter. That crofter on the northernmost plot has failed to pay his rents these last three months. I tire of waiting. Send my arms master to collect what he owes. If he canna pay, I will throw him off the land."

"Ye mean Eanraig? Da, ye must recall the man's wife just had another baby. And an older child is sick as well. Their little coin has been given for medicine and for the midwife."

"So?"

"The harvest is just starting to come in. I already told him he had until after the harvest to settle his account."

"Ye did what? Ye are no' his laird. If I say they must meet their obligations, they must do so. Or leave, and I'll give the land to someone who will work it and make it pay."

Mary didn't like the stubborn thrust of her father's chin, but she had to tread carefully or she'd make things worse for Eanraig and his family. "What good will it do them or Rose to make a family homeless? Eanraig has been a good crofter since he took over the land from his father ten years ago. He's only fallen on hard times with this last bairn." Her father appeared unmoved, so she tried a more compelling argument and lowered her voice. "How will it look to our other crofters if ye do this to him and his family? If ye force them from their home to wander the countryside, the new bairn will die. When the rest of our crofters hear how ye treated Eanraig, they will be shocked. Do ye wish to lose them all?" She leaned forward, hands open, pleading. "Give him a chance to make good on his debt."

Rose leaned back and sighed. "Very well, he has until after the harvest. But ye must ensure he is able to pay his debt then."

Mary sat back, dismay roiling her belly. How did he expect her to do that? By growing the man's crops for him? Controlling the weather? How exactly did her father think she could ensure a good outcome? She shook her head, dismissing the foolish idea.

She quit the solar still stewing over her father's irrational order.

Soon after, the healer frowned when Mary repeated the conversation to her. "I dinna like it," the woman said. "But I dinna ken what to do about it. No' yet. Yer father will get better—or worse—and that may tell me what he needs."

"I hate the waiting," Mary admitted. "If he's ill, I want do something. If he's no' ill, I want to throttle him." She sighed. "In the meantime, it would be convenient if he forgot about Eanraig. I can do naught to improve his crop so he can pay his debt to the estate."

"Aye," the healer said and chuckled. "'Tis too late in the year for a Beltane fire."

Mary's eyes widened in surprise at hearing the healer mention the old superstition. The ceremony asked the gods for a bountiful harvest. "Surely ye jest..."

"Of course I do," the healer scoffed. "Though ye, my good lass, could do with a night by a Beltane fire, I'm thinking. And I ken just who would make a perfect partner for ye."

Mary felt the heat of a blush warm her cheeks. The rest of the ceremony had to do with bounty of another kind. One that required a virgin and a virile man. She qualified, but who did the healer have in mind to play her horned god? A vision appeared in her mind of Cameron, nearly nude, sitting on the edge of his bed, muscles rippling as he fought to keep the covers over his nether region. Warm tingles radiated from her chest. The healer's grin told Mary her thoughts were written on her face.

"'Twill no' happen," Mary warned her. "So dinna think I'll do anything so foolish."

MARY QUICKLY DISCOVERED HER DISCUSSION WITH HER father had set the tone, and this would be another of those days when she felt like one of the servants, always at someone's beck and call. Though she'd checked on him earlier, even Cameron sent a lass to fetch her. Mary ran a hand over her hair, smoothing it down and ensuring it hadn't come out of the braid she'd fashioned it into. It wasn't that she cared how she looked for Cameron; given her position as chatelaine, her father would be put out with her if she appeared disheveled. But she had to admit she'd paid extra attention to her appearance since she'd taken over the care of one handsome, but wounded and ill Sutherland, especially since he'd started getting well enough to flirt with her, and to take her hand and say things like it would not be easy for him to leave her. Still, she couldn't pin her hopes on him.

When she reached his door, she knocked softly and waited. If he'd gone back to sleep, she wouldn't disturb him.

"Come."

His voice sounded stronger, even irritated. That was good. She opened the door and stepped inside. The odor of sweaty male, too long fevered and confined, assaulted her nose.

Cameron sat up and shoved his covers aside, then swung his legs over the side of the bed. "I want out of this room," he demanded. "I'll go daft if I stay in here another hour."

Mary closed the door and regarded him. His wrinkled shirt twisted around his body, barely covering the top of his thighs and the long, thick outline of what rose between them. His dark hair was tousled and several days growth of beard shadowed his face, making him look disreputable and dangerous. He glared at her with eyes as piercing as the day he'd arrived, and his brow drew down into a frustrated frown.

"Has the healer said ye may…"

"I have no' seen her today, and dinna care whether I do. I want to dress and go outside again."

"Ye managed it on yer own once before. What is stopping ye now? Did ye do too much yesterday?"

Cameron shook his head. "Look at me. I'm no' fit to be seen. And after this last bout of fever, I'm weaker, damn it."

"Ye do need a bath." Mary wrinkled her nose, then grinned at Cameron's affronted expression.

"What do ye expect? Lying here in my own sweat for days, I have. And ye claim to be caring for me."

"Ah, so ye have enough strength to be in a foul mood again, do ye?" She laid a hand on his forehead. Warm, but not fevered. Just a cranky male. "Very well. I'll order a tub for ye and we'll see how ye feel after ye get cleaned up." She moved back to the door. "In the meantime, ye will stay in that bed. I dinna wish to have to call someone to pick ye up off the floor."

Cameron snorted, and she slipped out the door, unreservedly pleased with his foul mood.

When she returned, she led a parade of lads carrying a big tub and buckets of hot water. Serving girls brought bath sheets to line the tub, and towels. Mary oversaw the arrangements while Cameron looked on. Then the lasses left, but two lads stayed behind. "These lads will help ye," Mary told him.

Cameron shook his head. "Nay, they willna. I can bathe myself."

"Cameron, I dinna want ye to fall, or to drown in the tub. Someone must stay with ye."

"Nay!"

"Cam…"

"If ye insist someone must be here, then I want only ye to aid me."

Mary crossed her arms. "That's hardly proper."

Cameron pointed at his chest and shrugged. "Ye have seen it all before."

Mary pursed her lips and gestured for the lads to leave. "One of ye, fetch the healer," she told them. When Cameron started to object, she raised a hand. "I will have her here as well or I will leave." Then she turned back to the lads. "The other of ye stay nearby, out in the hall, in case I call for help."

The lads glanced at each other, their expressions stoney, and left. After a moment, she heard a snicker out in the hall.

Mary rolled her eyes. Perhaps her father had a point after all, and she'd become too familiar with this man. "Well, then," she said and gestured at the tub, steaming before the hearth. "Ye have gotten yer way, at least until the healer arrives. Let's get ye in."

Cameron hesitated.

Had the lads' laughter made him realize how his demand for her presence looked, and made him regret making her stay? Or did he suddenly feel shy?

"Ye may turn yer back, if ye wish," he offered. "I willna fall down between the bed and the tub."

Mary shook her head. "I've seen it all, is that no'

what ye said? I'm here to keep ye from falling. I'd rather stay close in case ye get dizzy when ye stand."

Cameron nodded and got to his feet. Spreading his legs, his gaze stayed on the hearth as he took a few deep breaths. Then he nodded. "I'll no' fall."

Mary heard him, but didn't believe a word. He'd gone a bit pale and shook ever so slightly when he stood. Then he steadied and his color returned. Likely he thought she hadn't noticed his lapse. Instead of backing away, she moved to him and took his arm. "Come on, let's get ye in. Lean on me." She wrapped an arm around his middle. He cooperated, walking with her to the tub. She knew she shouldn't, but she liked the weight of Cameron's arm draped over her shoulders, and the feel of his solid torso under her hand, muscles bunching and flexing as he moved.

He stepped into the tub without comment. Before he sat down, she tugged at his shirt. He took the hint and stripped it over his head, leaving him bare...and breathtaking.

Mary had seen him many times, lying in bed while the fever ravaged him, head tossing with delirium while she ran cool cloths over his body. Cameron ill and mostly unaware of her regard was one thing. Standing before her, close enough to touch, a wicked gleam suddenly in his eyes and a growing erection making known the direction of his thoughts, was quite another. His erection rose heavy and thick, his length much more intimidating than when he'd been ill and flaccid. "Sit," she commanded, fighting to keep her gaze on his face—and losing. Even with the weight he'd lost, he still had an impressive build. His arms and shoulders were generously muscled from training and fighting, his torso trim and solid, with rock-hard bulges and hollows of a well-honed fighting man. She covered her interest by inspecting his scar.

Cameron moved his arm away from his side and allowed her to look at it.

His wound had healed to a jagged pink line along his ribs. As she nodded, her gaze dropped. A dusting of dark hair covered his chest and arrowed down his belly to widen at the juncture of his thighs. She pulled her gaze from there, but not before he noticed and straightened, making what caught her attention even more prominent, thick and long. If she dared, she could wrap her hands around him. She knew he wanted her to, but doing so would change everything between them. Even if she did not expect the healer to arrive at any moment, she was not prepared to take such an irreversible step. Defiant, she continued her perusal. Below his rising manhood, heavily muscled thighs and strong calves completed the picture she would carry in her mind—forever.

"Like what ye see?" His voice rumbled low and gravelly with need.

Her body responded, her core clenching and turning molten, her heart beating faster. She bunched the fabric of her skirt in her fists, determined to fight the desire burning in her blood. "I'll like it more when it's clean and less whiff than it is at the moment. Now sit." Cameron grinned, and she suspected he knew full well what turn her thoughts had taken. He was a beautiful man. Powerful even now. He would be more powerful, more impressive, and harder to resist when he finally regained his health. "I'll no' tell ye again, Cameron Sutherland. The lasses brought up cold water, too. I'll toss a bucket full of that over yer head if ye dinna *sit down*."

Finally, Cameron complied. Despite the bravado he'd shown so far, his movement as he settled into the tub seemed careful, and a soft grunt caught in his throat. But he sighed as the warm water rose about him, and the wicked gleam returned to his eyes as he leaned back and rested his arms on the sides of the tub.

Determined to ignore whatever sizzled between them, Mary grabbed a cloth and dipped it in the warm water, then dragged it over his neck and shoulders. "Lean forward so I can wash yer back."

Cameron complied and she picked up a dab of soap in the cloth, then wiped it across the expanse of muscle and down his spine. It left a trail of suds as rivulets of warm water ran down his skin. She continued with his shoulders, then moved around to face him and handed him the cloth. "Wash yer face, and anything else ye can reach," she ordered, fighting a grin as his lips puckered in disappointment. She nodded at his side. "Be careful around yer scar."

"It feels better when ye do it."

"I'll wash yer hair. That will feel best of all."

He grinned and glanced down.

Mary followed the direction of his gaze. His erection still stood proudly below the surface, between his bent knees. "Or I could just get that bucket of cold water and pour it over ye right now."

Cameron dunked the cloth and applied it to his face, scrubbing harder than she would have. She watched, fascinated, as he dragged the rag down his throat and across his chest, then down his belly. When his hand went below the waterline, she turned her back and picked up the dish of soap, determined not to think about what his hand was doing. About how she wanted to touch him there. How she wanted everything that went with such intimacy—with him.

Where was the healer? If she stayed away, still thinking of Cameron as Mary's horned god, Mary would wring her neck.

After a moment, Mary heard the sound of water splashing as Cameron wrung out the cloth. She sighed and turned back to him. "Now I'll wash yer hair," she warned and took the cloth from his unresisting hand. She dunked it again and wrung it out over his head, several times, wetting his hair, turning all its shades of brown darker, black and slick. Then she took a palm full of soap and massaged it into his scalp.

His eyes drifted shut and he groaned as he leaned against the back of the tub. "Ye were right," he murmured, low and deep. "That does feel good."

His voice made her bones vibrate. "Then stay still and enjoy it," she replied, tunneling her fingers into his hair. A glance down his body revealed his erection had not subsided. It looked even larger and more insistent than before. More enticing. She wanted to slide her hands down his chest and across the rippled expanse of his abdomen to reach it. Instead, Mary looked away and concentrated on massaging Cameron's neck and ears, then ran her fingers across his forehead and back up into his hair. After a few minutes, he seemed nearly asleep, so she placed her hands on his shoulders and urged him forward. "Let me rinse yer head."

The bucket she'd threatened him with actually held more hot water, warm now that it had been sitting for a while. She poured a thin stream over his crown and watched the soap trail down his back and over his shoulders to his chest, a few small bubbles forming a barrier on the surface between her gaze and what rose beneath the water. When she'd rinsed his hair to her satisfaction, she used a towel to dry it. "'Tis time to stand and dry yerself," she told him. "Then ye can go back to bed if ye wish."

He rose from the tub like a god from the sea, water sluicing down his back and drawing her gaze lower than she should allow it to go. The tightly bunched muscles of his arse and the backs of his thighs flexed while she watched, fascinated.

"With ye?" he murmured and turned to face her, his erection again full and proud, straining toward her.

"Nay, Cameron." She handed him a towel. "Wrap that around yerself—if ye can."

He grinned and instead used it to dry his face and neck, leaving his body taut and exposed, tempting her.

She shook her head as he moved the towel aside to peer at her. "Step out of the tub, please. Put a hand on my shoulder if ye must. I dinna want ye to fall."

He lowered the towel and shifted his gaze between her and the bed. "I think ye'll have to help me," he teased and lifted one strong leg over the tub's edge to the floor, then the other. There he stood, feet spread, cock at full attention and sac dangling between his legs while the sight of him held her in thrall.

Mary could barely keep herself from reaching out and cupping him. "I'll get yer shirt," she finally managed to say, and turned away to the small chest. What was keeping the healer? She should have been here long before now.

"I have nay more clean shirts," Cameron told her, his voice a deep rumble that made her breasts ache. "I'll have to remain as I am, naked. And wanting ye."

Mary turned back to him and looked him up and down, an act more brazen than she'd ever done in her life, but he'd asked for it. "While I enjoy looking at ye as much as any lass might, I dinna wish ye to catch a chill, so here." She picked up a dry bath sheet and tossed it to him. "Wrap yerself in that and sit by the fire. I'll send for a clean shirt and a change of bedding."

She didn't know how she managed not to betray how much she wanted him. She felt molten and tight, her thighs tense and her breasts aching. But she forced herself to go to the door, and after a glance back to ensure he'd obeyed her and covered himself. She opened it and gave her orders to the lad still waiting there. Then she closed it again and leaned her heated forehead against the cool wood. Cameron Sutherland tempted her too much. By far.

&

"MY BACK IS COLD. IT MUST STILL BE DAMP. COULD YE dry it for me, please?" Cameron leaned forward in the chair and beckoned Mary closer. He didn't like her being across the room, by the door. He'd been wrong about her. She might not be the type for a quick tumble, but she wanted him. The musky scent of her arousal had filled his nose as she studied his body. And he couldn't hide how much he wanted her. He wanted her in his arms. In his lap, riding him, preferably. He wanted her to satisfy his raging need—for her. Only her. Surely she could see how she affected him by the way the bath sheet tented in his lap. He laid his hands over it. Perhaps if he played meek and ill, he'd arouse her nurturing instincts. He only needed her to come close enough for him to pull her into his embrace.

Mary cocked her head, then sighed and approached, picking up a dry towel from the stack the serving girl had left. "Ye are better. Yer body doesna lie. A lass will return in a few minutes, so forget what ye are thinking about. 'Twill no' happen."

"It could, if ye wished it to." He knew she'd never agree, but he couldn't help teasing her.

"Well, I dinna, so settle down." She scrubbed at his back dry. He was certain it must be reddened from the rough toweling. But she'd taken care and softened her touch when she moved the towel near the new scar on his side.

She had studied his body from head to foot when he stood in the tub, including every long and thick inch of him currently trapped beneath his hands. She couldn't hide that she'd liked what she'd seen. Her heightened color and fast, shallow breathing told him she wanted him, too. She'd clenched her hands rather than reach for him. He'd never been more certain of anything in his life.

But this was Mary, his angel of mercy. Suddenly guilt overwhelmed him. He'd forced her to stay while he bathed, and his actions went well beyond teasing, even beyond seduction. She would think him crude and unworthy of the care she'd already given him, much less what he wanted from her now he felt stronger. She deserved more than a tumble before he left for Sutherland. As she stepped away from his back, he sighed, weary again.

A knock at the door drew Mary even farther from him. The serving girl bustled in and handed Mary a shirt, then stripped his bed and remade it with fresh linens. He couldn't believe how inviting the bed suddenly looked. The serving girl, not at all. He shivered at that. Usually the sight of any comely lass's rounded backside bent over a bed or a table would rivet his gaze to her. But not now. Not since Mary Elizabeth Rose came into this life.

Mary brought him the shirt and he slipped it on over his head, careful to keep the sheet over his lap until the serving lass left the room. Then he stood.

Instead of moving away, Mary surprised him by stepping into his arms. He dropped the sheet, counting on the shirt to cover him. He wanted his hands free to touch her.

"Ye should feel better." She sniffed his neck. "Ye certainly smell better. Do ye still wish to go out or are ye tired again?"

"With ye in my arms? I could fight a dragon right now."

"Perhaps a small one." She studied him. "Ye are still

too pale. Rest for a while, aye? I'll walk with ye this afternoon."

Cameron nodded. "That gives me something to look forward to. No' what I most desire, but it will have to do for now."

Mary snorted a laugh and stepped out of his arms. "A lass always kens where she stands with ye, Cameron Sutherland, aye?"

He grinned and shrugged, relieved that she seemed to have taken no offense. "If that lass is ye, then aye. Why would I be anything but honest with ye, Mary? I've nothing to hide." He paused, then shook his head. "I owe ye an apology. I shouldna…"

Mary blushed prettily. "Dinna say it," she objected, holding up a hand. "We'll just forget this happened," she added and bolted for the door. "I'm going to find the healer and throttle her."

He let his soft laughter follow her out. Once the door closed behind her, he sank to the bed and rested his head in his hands, glad the healer had failed to arrive. This time with Mary had been illuminating. Teasing her was easy. Winning her would be much, much harder.

CHAPTER 4

The trip to Grant was barely underway when Mary's father glanced aside at the warriors riding escort with them and in a low voice told her she would soon have to plan a wedding.

"What?" Her heart immediately soared at the news and she straightened in the saddle. Had Cameron spoken to her father without telling her? He'd given her no hint he planned such a thing. Or had he? She closed her eyes as the image rose in her mind of Cameron standing before her in the tub, completely unembarrassed—even unconcerned—about her seeing his nudity and his arousal. She'd never forget that image. And never wanted to. He was a beautiful man, and when he regained his strength, he'd be even more attractive. She didn't know how she would resist him. He'd been right—she'd liked looking at him. Too much. And she wanted to touch him. Not the way a healer did, but the way a lover might. She twisted the reins in her hand, and her mount twitched its ears.

The wedding her father spoke of could be hers.

She turned to question him and reality set in. He wasn't looking at her. He was smiling, as if imagining they were already at Grant. Or he was up to something.

Mary knew her father well enough to suspect he probably had a very different match in mind for her. He'd warned her to spend less time caring for Cameron. He'd acted quickly to prevent their relationship going any further by corresponding with the Sutherland laird. And he'd warned her to keep her distance, as if he knew her interest in Cameron had grown into something beyond healing.

"Why so suddenly?" Her fist tightened on the reins. "Surely ye canna mean to try to marry me off, as ye did Annie and Catherine. And to a Grant I've never met. Who will take my place helping ye?"

Her father gave her a sly glance from the corner of his eye. "I'm no' thinking about ye. This wedding will be mine."

This time she did rein to a halt. Shock held her silent for a moment, then she burst out, "Yers! After all these years? Is that what this trip is about?" Her father's mount was less eager to stop. It carried on a few lengths while she scolded him. "Ye didn't mention an agreement when ye showed me the letter. Not one hint. So why tell me before we reach Grant?"

He waved their escort on ahead. "Because I knew ye might be upset by my marriage," he said as he turned his mount to face her, "and would argue about holding a wedding at Rose." He shrugged. "I have no' made a betrothal offer, but if this visit goes as I intend, I will make one before we depart."

Mary took a breath, trying to calm her racing heart. "How soon do ye expect a wedding to take place? There will be much to do to ready the keep for the wedding of the laird."

"I'll leave that to ye and to my future bride."

Of course he would. "And what do ye plan for me when ye have wed?" She might as well get that answer while he was in a good mood, enjoying his surprise.

"Married elsewhere," he smirked, "because I'll get a son."

Her father's words should not have shocked her, but they did. Despite wanting exactly what he'd described, she found they cut. Mary threw up her hands, hurt and confused about her future—and his. Her father was daft. Lady Mhairi Grant was close to his age, surely past her childbearing years.

"Whatever ye say, Da." She wouldn't argue with him. There were too many ears to hear if their voices rose. And while disagreements between a laird and his heir were inevitable, as were disagreements between James Rose and any of his daughters, Mary didn't wish to make this one quite so public within the clan.

He lifted his chin and kicked his mount into motion, making Mary struggle to catch up. When she did, he frowned at her. "The clan comes to you for most things, I ken that. But dinna plan to succeed me with that Sutherland invalid. I see how ye look when ye speak of him. Ye have spent so much time with him, ye have begun to imagine a future with him, though I canna see why."

Insulted for Cameron, Mary's ire rose. "He's no' an invalid. And I speak of him only as someone under my care." She swallowed, suddenly uncomfortable. Aye, she'd thought of him that way for weeks, until he'd started to feel better and his personality had come to the forefront instead of his fever-induced ravings and pain-filled irritation.

Her father might be mistaken about Cameron, yet he seemed deluded about the Grant woman. If her father wanted to marry, and if Lady Grant could make him happy, so be it. But if he wanted to believe that woman could give him a son, well, nothing Mary could say would dissuade him.

WHEN THEY ARRIVED AT GRANT, MARY HAD TO ADMIT the stronghold was impressive. Larger than the Rose keep and surrounded by wooden palisades topped with spikes, it looked formidable enough to hold off Domnhall and Albany combined. The steward greeted them and showed them to their chambers. Before he left, he advised them the evening meal would be served in an hour. Mary appreciated having a few minutes to rest before meeting new people and being judged as her father's heir. She spent part of the time exploring her chamber. Spacious and filled with fine French furniture, rich fabrics and a gleaming collection of small porcelain dogs, it was more luxurious than any she'd ever seen. She wondered what Lady Grant, once she became Lady Rose, would do to improve the furnishings at Rose. The tug-of-war between her notoriously tightfisted father and Lady Grant would be interesting to watch—if Mary remained there and her father didn't immediately arrange a match for her.

With Grant? She glanced around her spacious chamber again. Living here would be comfortable, but with a stranger? The thought made her shudder and she wrapped her arms around herself. Prospects at other Rose allies were no better. Rose was closest with Brodie, but with two sisters already wedded to Brodie men, a marriage there was out of the question. Since he was not favorably disposed toward Cameron, her father seemed intent on wasting the opportunity he represented, even when it brought Sutherland to her father's aid.

She couldn't think where else her father coveted an alliance. Until his surprising announcement on the way here, he'd been determined to keep her as his chatelaine. They never discussed her future beyond that duty.

A knock at her door roused her from her worries.

"Milady?" A lass's voice sounded from the hall.

Mary opened the door to a maidservant who announced, "My Lady Grant sent me to see to ye. I'm to unpack and prepare ye for supper. We must hurry. We haven't much time."

"Of course," Mary said and stepped aside to allow her to enter. "What is yer name?"

"I am called Jean, milady." She immediately set to work laying out Mary's dresses. She stowed everything else back in the trunks. "This one seems least crushed," Jean announced, shaking out Mary's fine, blue woolen kirtle. "Then I'll do yer hair."

Mary agreed and changed from her travel-worn clothes as quickly as she could.

"While ye are with the mistress, I'll see to yer dresses," Jean promised and chattered on as she undid Mary's braid and brushed out her hair.

Mary, unused to such treatment, relaxed and enjoyed the feel of Jean's ministrations. She was nearly dozing, dreaming about Cameron's touch on her face, when Jean finished and began twisting her hair into an arrangement Mary had never attempted on her own.

Someone knocked at the door. "Mary, 'tis time," her father announced as he pushed it open.

"Already?" Her heart thudded in her chest, surprising her. Suddenly nervous about what this meal might bring, she hesitated.

Her father smiled. "Ye look lovely, lass."

The unexpected compliment added to her nerves. "Thank ye, Da. I'm nearly ready." Jean nodded and stepped back, allowing Mary to stand. She smoothed her skirt and turned to her father. "Shall we?"

He held out a hand, escorting her from the room

and down the steps with uncharacteristic care. Had he, too, been entranced by their more luxurious surroundings?

Lady Grant herself greeted them at the entrance to the great hall. She hadn't changed much from the way Mary recalled her at Annie's wedding. Petite, with blonde hair going gray, thin features and pale blue eyes, she nonetheless had an air of command about her, assumed, perhaps, when her husband passed away and left her in charge of the clan. Her smile failed to reach her eyes as she chided Mary's father. "I did no' ken ye were bringing one of yer daughters. I thought ye had gotten them all safely wedded away by now."

"Nay, no' Mary. She is my eldest and serves as my chatelaine," he replied, then colored. "At least until I marry again. My future wife will take over those duties, of course."

Mary cringed at his gaffe. Of course Lady Grant would become chatelaine at Rose. And she hated to admit it, but from the look of the Grant keep, they'd be lucky to have her—if Rose could afford her refined tastes.

"Of course. Yer eldest. Yer heir then, too?" Lady Grant gave Mary a speculative glance.

"For now," was the extent of her father's reply. Mary stiffened, but let it pass. She dared not make a scene, though she was still annoyed with her father for refusing to tell her the purpose of the trip until after they were on their way. And for not admitting he intended to offer for Lady Grant.

When she saw who waited at the high table as she crossed the hall behind Lady Grant and her father, her belly sank.

"Here we are," Lady Grant announced as they ascended to the dining platform. "Laird James Rose, here is my son and heir, Kester, and his elder sister,

Seona. This is Laird Rose and his eldest daughter and heir, Mary."

The Grant heir, who looked to be about twelve years old, nodded to them, then looked away, apparently already bored with the niceties. Seona Grant looked like a younger version of her mother. Dark blonde hair coiled about her head, framing a high forehead and pale blue eyes. Thin lips and a long nose kept her from being beautiful, though prominent cheekbones made her face striking enough, Mary supposed. Then, as Mary's father bent over her hand, she simpered, revealing her true age. She couldn't be any older than Mary's youngest sister, Catherine.

Mary bit back a groan. A young heir and his older sister. Would Lady Grant bring them to Rose as well? Who would hold Grant for young Kester? Nay, that would never do. Lady Grant would not leave her son behind. Which meant what? Who would her father choose to marry? Did Lady Grant have a sister or cousin they'd yet to meet?

Lady Grant had them seated, Seona between Mary and her father, the lady and her son on his other side. After the meal was served, her father fell into conversation with Lady Grant. As far as Mary could see, Kester sprawled and picked at his food, only perking up when a pretty serving maid came near him. Mary was left to draw out the reticent Seona.

"Yer home is lovely," Mary began, hoping a compliment would get a conversation started.

"Ye can lay that at my mother's feet," Seona sniffed. "She has a taste for the finer things."

"And ye dinna?"

"Fine furnishings are well and good, but I prefer fine things I can wear—clothes and jewels. Compare my dress to yers, for example."

Mary swallowed, at a loss for how to respond to

such rudeness. She opted to take the high road. "Yers is lovely. Mine, sadly, is somewhat the worse for having been packed away while we traveled."

Seona sniffed and looked Mary up and down. "Ye would never be accepted at court in a muslin shift. Ye must wear silks, and jewels such as mine." She laid a hand at her throat, where pearls glinted.

Mary had no pearls. If her mother ever possessed them, Father had sold them to keep the Rose coffers full or to get the clan through hard times when crops failed or the fishermen were less than successful.

"I'll keep that in mind," Mary replied and turned her attention back to her meal.

"No' that ye are ever likely to be sent to court," Seona added.

Mary closed her eyes and thought about the likely consequences if she stabbed the haughty lass with her eating knife. Nay, that would never do. But she couldn't help considering it. While Mary contemplated murder, Lady Grant captured her daughter's attention and drew her into conversation with Mary's father. Mary sighed in relief. She had a few moments to eat in peace. Like the surroundings at Grant, the meal was sumptuous and to Mary's taste, excessive. Who needed so many courses? They were not at Court, and most Highland clans could ill afford to waste anything, food included. Her father's new wife would have to adjust.

She glanced around, studying the people in the great hall. If her father wed a relative of Lady Grant's, would the woman try to match her up with one of the men here? None of them appealed to her, though she knew better than to make assumptions based solely on looks. Some Rose men with the least attractive appearance were also some of the best at what they did, or the friendliest, and would likely make some lass wonderful husbands—if they had not already done so. No doubt, the same could be said for the men she saw at Grant. Not that it mattered. She wouldn't be here long enough to become acquainted with anyone.

And besides, Cameron Sutherland waited for her at Rose. He'd promised to remain until she got back. And Cameron swore he kept his promises. Given what Catherine had told her about him and what she'd learned in their time together, Mary believed him.

A match with Grant would be out of the question from her father's perspective, anyway. If he married a Grant, he would not need his daughter to wed into the clan, as well. He'd already been clear with Catherine about his reluctance to waste another daughter on Brodie after Annie married the laird, Iain. Catherine had managed to wed Kenneth Brodie anyway. In her father's mind, the same restriction would apply to clan Grant. Which left Mary right where she'd been when she arrived at Grant. Unable to foresee her future—and whether it included Cameron.

❧

THE NEXT MORNING, HER FATHER STOPPED BY HER DOOR on his way down to break his fast. "We are finished here," he announced. "We'll be leaving soon, so make certain ye have packed all yer belongings."

"So soon? What about yer betrothal plans, Da? Have ye…"

"Come down as soon as ye are ready," he said, interrupting her, and then closed the door.

Mary stared at the heavy oak, frowning. He hadn't answered her questions about his betrothal plans. At that thought, Mary's belly filled with buzzing bees. Maybe, since he'd spent more time with the lady and her family, he'd changed his mind about picking a bride at Grant. Which might leave him free to pick a husband from Grant for her.

She shook herself, not liking the thought one bit, and, with a silent apology to Jean, went to work repacking everything the lass had so carefully laid out. Where was she when Mary most needed her? Da would be eager to leave and would not be pleased if Mary delayed him.

At least they were leaving for Rose this morning. She laid aside the dress she had folded and crossed her arms, trying to contain the longing filling her. Eager to return to Cameron, she told herself she was simply worried about him. She didn't miss him. Or want him. Though she did.

Stop it!

She had to focus on getting her father away from Grant before she did something to embarrass him like murdering Lady Grant's daughter. With the image in her mind of being on her horse headed back to Rose and to Cameron, she hurried through the rest of her packing.

Downstairs, Mary entered the great hall, her belly sour with dread. If the meal went at all as yesterday's had gone, she'd be stuck trying to draw conversation out of Seona Grant again, and she had already exhausted her supply of small talk, not to mention her tolerance for being disparaged. Her father hadn't helped. He'd focused all of his attention on the lass's mother and barely glanced Seona's way.

Her father, Lady Grant and her heir were already at table. And so was Seona, on her father's other side, as usual. She saw no sign of any other Grant lass who might be a prospective bride. Perhaps there would be no betrothal and they had wasted the trip.

Mary nearly groaned aloud as her father noticed her entry and broke off the spirited conversation he

seemed to be having with Lady Grant. She frowned as
he indicated for Mary to sit next to the sour-faced
Seona. Only for a little while, Mary promised herself,
and then they'd be on their way. Given the glazed look
on Seona's face, the lass was barely awake and wouldn't
utter a word. Mary could tolerate her silence long
enough to get through one last meal.

"Good morrow," she offered as she took her seat.
She would be polite, even if Seona wasn't.

Seona shook her head and went back to staring at
the trencher before her, hands clasped in her lap. Her
rigid posture gave Mary pause. Was something wrong?
The lass seemed upset—and unhappy. Perhaps she'd
been told their parents would wed after all and
disapproved of whatever arrangements Lady Grant
intended to make for her brother and her. She might
have heard how Mary's father had treated betrothals
for her younger sisters. Seona would have reason to
fear how he'd control her marriage prospects

Mary suddenly felt pity for Seona. If she had a beau
here at Grant, chances were strong Father would never
allow her to wed the lad. Mary debated whether to
warn her, but decided this was not the place or time.
Seona would find out soon enough.

The smell of food restored Mary's appetite. She had
barely taken a bite of her own breakfast when her
father stood and took Lady Grant's hand on one side
and Seona's on the other. Seona gasped and paled,
making Mary glad she hadn't warned her what her
future might be like. She took Seona's other hand and
whispered, "'Twill be well," even though she hated that
she probably lied.

Seona shook her head as Mary's father lifted her
hand and pulled her to her feet.

The shimmer of tears in the girl's eyes shocked

Mary. Yet her mother, who now stood on the other side, wore a wide smile.

Confused, Mary frowned. Did Seona oppose the idea of her mother being wed again? She'd been widowed for years, as had Mary's father. The lady would be a good companion for her father, and an experienced chatelaine, which would free Mary to pursue her own life, if her father didn't immediately betroth her to a stranger.

James Rose waited until everyone in the hall noticed he and the Grant women were on their feet, and ceased speaking. Then he cleared his throat.

Before he could say anything, Lady Grant announced, "Laird Rose has some happy news to share with ye." Then she turned to him and prompted, "James…"

He nodded, but Mary thought he looked a trifle annoyed that Lady Grant had exerted her role as head of the clan and took control of the room before he had a chance to. Well. She would be an interesting partner for him. Another woman to stand up to his demands, as his younger daughters had done. Mary smiled to herself. He should be used to headstrong women. He'd married one in France and raised three equally determined daughters.

"Lady Grant and I," he began, then glanced aside until she nodded for him to continue. "Lady Grant and I are pleased to announce a betrothal between clan Grant and clan Rose."

Truly? Mary watched, fascinated, while the hall echoed with a rumble of voices. He had their attention now. Here it comes, she thought and schooled her features to polite interest. Why had her father not told her his plans before he told the gathered Grant clan members?

"The documents were signed this morning. I am

happy to inform ye," he continued with a glance toward Seona and Mary, "Lady Grant has agreed to betroth..."

He stopped and cleared his throat, making Mary tense. He should be happy, yet suddenly, he looked nervous, his gaze shifting around the room, lingering on her, then settling on Lady Grant.

"...Has agreed to betroth her daughter Seona to me."

Mary couldn't help it. Her mouth fell open. She looked from her father to the lass standing between them and back to her father again. On his other side, Lady Grant wore a smug smile, as did her son, who smirked at his sister. He must be happy to have his older sister out of his way, though the Grant succession stayed in the male line. Her absence, however, left him the sole object of his mother's attention and under her control until he reached an age to take over the clan. Mary wondered if he'd considered that in his eagerness to see his sister wed to an older man.

"The wedding will take place at Rose in a fortnight," her father added, as Seona collapsed into her chair, pulling her hand from his.

If Mary hadn't already been seated, she would have collapsed into hers, too. As it was, the gasps of the assembled Grants in the hall rolled over hers, and covered the soft whimpers Seona uttered.

Mary sat, frozen, while the noise died down, wishing for some of Annie's optimism or Catherine's brashness. Something that would let her react to her father's announcement with anything other than shock and dismay. Seona was the same age as her youngest sister, nearly nineteen, to her father's forty-two summers.

"I'm pleased my daughter will be instrumental in strengthening the ties between Grant and clan Rose," Lady Grant added, smiling at her people. Then she turned to Mary's father. "I look forward to being received at Rose in a fortnight for the nuptials." Her smile quickly turned to a frown as she regarded her daughter, now seated, pale and shaking, her hands clasped together on the tabletop and her head bowed over them as if in prayer. "Seona," she hissed. "Stand up."

The girl tried, but her knees would not support her. Mary put a hand under her arm and whispered to her, "Ye can do it. I'll help ye," then lifted. Seona must feel humiliated. Her new betrothed simply turned to frown at her. Far be it from him to add his support. Mary returned his frown with a glare, heedless of how it might appear to the gathered Grants.

Seona made it to her feet, but it was a near thing. Clapping and cheers suddenly filled the hall, and she looked up in surprise, pink staining her ashen cheeks.

Mary noted one well-built lad slam down his tankard. His table companion gripped his shoulder, but he knocked the man's hand away, jumped to his feet and bolted from the hall. She glanced at Seona. Her gaze was on the hallway where the man had disappeared, her brow and lips pinched with pain. So Seona did have a lad she cared for. Or one who cared for her.

This was awful. She'd been through similar upsets with her sisters and hated the prospect of another. Her father made Iain choose among the three of them then denied his choice. He'd also made three ill-advised matches for her youngest sister, Catherine, who loved the Brodie lad her father had refused. Each time she'd seen the misery on Catherine's face, she'd wanted to scream at their father. Not that screaming would have done any good. Not then, not now. As bad as what he'd done to Annie and Catherine had been, this was so much worse. How could he even think of taking a young lass like Seona to wife?

She shuddered. Of course, he wanted a male heir. His daughters were grown and gone, except for Mary, and with Catherine's departure last month, his thoughts must have turned with urgency to his legacy. Her father was smiling benignly at the gathered Grants, as if nothing were amiss. While she still felt sorry for Seona, she found the idea of a male heir suited her fine.

Mary patted Seona's hand, trying to soothe the lass. How embarrassed would she be if she fainted dead away in front of her entire clan? Her pallor told Mary it could happen.

But Seona as chatelaine? Surely the girl was as ill-prepared for that responsibility as she probably was for motherhood. She'd already said she didn't care about the things around her—just her clothes and jewels. How would she care for a clan, a keep and her own bairn? Mary knew full well on whom James Rose would lay the responsibility to see her readied for all of those.

Mary's hand froze over Seona's as she realized her tenure at Rose was far from over.

CHAPTER 5

Cameron heard a commotion out in the bailey and made his way to his window. Mary! He counted James Rose and eight Rose warriors in the bailey with her, and two stable lads who took charge of Mary's and her father's horses. Rose looked angry, but then he often did. Mary looked weary.

Cameron considered going down to the great hall to greet her and find out what had happened. He was stronger now than when she'd left nearly a week ago and had spent some of the time she'd been away wandering the keep. He enjoyed seeing areas he'd missed up to now, imagining her in them. He'd walked every day and even done some light exercise in his chamber. The healer had kept a close eye on him, happy that no more fevers had wracked him. Mary would be surprised, and he hoped, pleased.

Conscious of Mary's concern that he stay out of her father's sight as much as possible, he remained at the window, knowing she would come to him soon enough. He watched the bailey clearing of men and horses until he heard a soft knock at his door. "Come," he called.

The door opened as he turned, and Mary slipped

59

inside. "I'm back!" she announced toward the bed, then spotted him and gasped. "Ye are up and dressed." She made her way to him and gently touched his face. "How do ye feel?"

He wrapped her in his arms and inhaled the sweet, alluring scent that was all Mary, even after a long ride. "I'm better now ye are here, Mary, my love. How are ye? What happened at Grant?"

"Sit," she said, gesturing to the chair by the hearth, "and I'll tell ye." She took his place by the window as he settled into the chair, her arms crossed over her chest, tension in every line of her body.

She'd failed to react to his endearment. Cameron wanted to hold her, to ease whatever bothered her. But for the moment, he knew he could best help her by listening.

"My father has lost his mind," Mary began.

Cameron quirked an eyebrow. This was interesting. "Truly? What has he done now?"

Mary shook her head and started pacing. "He betrothed himself to Mhairi Grant's *daughter*, a lass Catherine's age."

Cameron fought back a chuckle that would incense Mary and nodded. The reason was obvious. "So he has decided to try for a male heir."

"So it appears. He and her mother were thick as thieves. I believed he planned to offer for Lady Grant. But nay. She is regent for her son. I suppose she could no' abandon that responsibility, no' if she meant to keep Grant power in her husband's line, and her son looks to be only about twelve. Once I realized that, I expected to meet a cousin of hers, or a sister, but nay. They made the announcement just before we left. Poor Seona was shaking like a leaf." Mary quirked a corner of her mouth into an ironic semblance of a smile. "I dinna think the lass is eager for the match."

"Or the marriage bed, I'll wager," Cameron muttered. When Mary's hand flew to her mouth, he added, "Sorry. I didna mean to make ye think of that."

"Ye jest." She clenched a fist over her belly. "'Tis nearly all I've been thinking about. I've barely eaten a thing since the announcement. The idea turns my stomach."

"Yer da is no' so old."

"He's too old for her."

"Apparently no', or her mother wouldna agree to give her daughter to him."

"Her mother is up to something. 'Tis no' the first time—or the last—that a daughter has been used as a pawn for her laird's purposes. I dinna yet ken what she has in mind, but I suspect we will find out eventually."

"Is that all that has ye *fashed*?"

"All? Is that no' enough?" She sighed and moved away from the window. She paced for a moment, then perched on the edge of his bed.

Seeing her there, Cameron sucked in a breath as images of what he would like to do with her flooded his mind. He clenched his fists, then forced them open. Now was not the time for such thoughts.

"Da was insufferable on the way home," Mary continued, her gaze on the window and apparently unaware of his reaction. "Full of himself and of ideas for things I must do to ready Rose for the wedding."

"He means to hold the wedding here?"

She dropped her head in her hands. "In less than a fortnight. I have little more than a week to arrange everything."

Cameron leaned forward, wanting to reach out and stroke her silky golden hair. "What can I do?"

She lifted her head and met his gaze. "Do? Nay, Cameron. Ye are a guest here, as much as the Grants will be and ye have been ill. I will no' put ye to work..."

Cameron stood and took her hand. Then he pulled her to her feet and wrapped her in his arms. "I can do this much, aye? To comfort ye when ye need it, as ye have cared for and comforted me. I owe ye that much and more."

She tilted her head back and studied his face while he traced lazy circles on her back with one hand. He could feel the tension leaving her body, and knew she capitulated when her arms went around his waist and she lay her head on his shoulder.

"Then ye'll be busy all the time," she told him.

"I canna imagine a worse fate," he teased and chuckled, resting his chin on the top of her head. When she didn't respond, he tilted his head to study her face. Her eyes were closed, her lashes damp. "Ach, lass, all will be well."

She gave her head a little shake against his shoulder, but kept her eyes closed. "'Twill no'. I must train my new step-mother in her duties—to take over my duties as chatelaine. If she's truly as lamb-headed as she seemed to be at Grant, I'll never be free."

"Lamb-headed?" His incredulous tone earned a chuckle, making Cameron's heart lift a bit, despite her obvious distress.

Mary met his gaze. "She barely speaks. She's timid, and her mother can direct her to do her bidding with a look. She stumbles around, looking lost and confused one moment, imperious the next. She can be rude and arrogant. I dinna see what made Da choose a lass like that."

"I do. He wants a son, and wants as little disruption to the rest of his life as possible. If she's no' assertive, she'll no' be demanding things like his daughters have always done, nor trying to change Rose—or him."

"Ye may have the right of it. But how can she run a

keep such as this?" she asked, stepping out of his arms and waving a hand.

Cameron let his hands drop to his side and managed not to clench his fists.

"If the servants willna obey her, Da will chew her up and spit her out." Mary paced to the door, then back again. "I fear she will make him very unhappy. If she ever manages to give him an heir, 'twill be a miracle."

He settled a hip against the wall next to the window while she walked out her worries. "Then let's hope for a miracle, aye? One that includes yer freedom." He hated the idea of Mary being trapped here for years more, raising her father's son and doing the work his wife should be doing. He wanted more for Mary than that.

"Ach, Cameron, dinna make me wish for so much. I dare no' think that far ahead. I must get through the next fortnight—and whatever comes after—before I can hope for anything like a life of my own. On my own terms." She turned back toward the door. "A male heir, ready to take control of the clan, will be years in the making."

"I ken that." Somehow, he'd managed not to growl those words.

"So, ye must focus on getting yer strength back, no' on me."

"I can do both, ye ken."

Mary paused with her gaze averted. "Nay, ye canna. All too soon, ye will be gone, back to Sutherland."

He sighed, hating the misery in her voice. This discussion was straying into the dangerous territory of promises expected that he was not free to make. He needed to find a way to help her, but first, to distract her. "Ye ken Domnhall will seek to expand his influence on Ross, and likely beyond. If something happens to yer da any time soon, Rose will be vulnerable to Grant or any other clan with designs on yer territory for

Albany or their own purposes." Such as using it as a stronghold to begin taking over other clans' territories along the south shore of the Moray Firth. Such boldness would fit with information Cameron had learned in St. Andrews about Albany's plans for Ross. "Perhaps yer da would be wise to name Kenneth Brodie as his heir, rather than ye."

Mary's gaze snapped up. "What? Ye ken he'll no' do that. He's too angry about Catherine right now. And it gains him nothing, since he already has an alliance with Brodie."

Cameron stood. "But if ye were no' his heir, would ye no' feel less confined? Less obligated to solve every problem in clan Rose?"

"I dinna!" She crossed her arms over her chest.

Cameron expected her to start tapping her foot at any moment. At least she no longer looked so world-weary. Her anger was an improvement over the defeated slump of her shoulders. "I've spent a lot of time staring out the window," Cameron told her, nodding toward it, determined to keep pushing her. "I've seen ye again and again, directing the servants, resolving disputes, even rushing toward the stable to help with a foaling in the middle of the night. Yer da takes great liberties with a lass he's determined to unseat as heir."

"I do those things on my own. He doesna tell me to."

"He doesna have to. Ye have a strong responsible streak in ye, for a lass."

"For a lass! Cameron Sutherland, I didna come in here to be insulted."

"Then think, Mary, and dinna give up on yer future before ye even have a chance to claim it."

MARY COULDN'T BELIEVE CAMERON WOULD SOONER SEE Kenneth and Catherine in charge at Rose than her. Instead, she hoped he'd irritated her on purpose, no doubt trying to give her an outlet for her anger and dismay at her father.

Or to distract her from how he cared for her.

She studied him, surprised by how much better he looked after she'd spent a week away from him. He looked different. Stronger, with more color in his skin and more fire in his eyes.

Cameron would make a her good husband. Her father should be thrilled to ally with Sutherland, one of the most powerful clans in the Highlands. But to him, Cameron was only a wounded and ill man in her charge.

They were friends—and perhaps more—but he was not her betrothed, even though having his arms around her made her blood heat and her insides melt. What would his nearness do to her when he was fully healed and well? "'Tis no' my place to claim my future, as ye say. 'Tis my father's to decide it."

"Ye dinna believe that."

"I do." She pursed her lips.

"Dinna lie to me, lass, no' after all ye have told me. If ye believed that, yer sisters wouldna be wed and happy. 'Tis yer turn. Ye must help yerself now."

Mary shook her head. Cameron was right, as much as she hated to admit it. To him, or to herself. "I dinna ken how," she murmured. "They had help."

"From ye, aye."

"And who is left to help me? I canna simply leave. Da would be within his rights to send men after me and haul me back. And where would I go? A woman alone?"

"Ye could do as Catherine did and go to family."

"Da kens that trick now. If he didna discover me missing in time to send men after me and find me on the road, they'd search in Inverness and St. Andrews and anywhere else a Rose might live across the breadth of Scotland. And all the while, he would think he did it to protect me. To save me from some horrible fate—death, or life as a fallen woman."

"Does he no' ken ye better than that? Ye would be prepared."

"Aye, I would. But what does it matter? As capable as ye are, look at what happened to ye. Do ye think I would have survived something similar?"

Cameron had the grace to look dismayed. "Ye are right, lass. Ye must plan and bide yer time. But I ken ye better than ye think. Ye will find a way to control yer own fate. I dinna doubt it."

If only her father believed in her as much as this man did. She couldn't help but hope some part of Cameron wanted her as much as he seemed to respect her. She could be happy with a man who treated her as he did. Still, for her father ever to see him as more than an invalid, Cameron needed to regain his strength. And as soon as he did, duty would call him away, and she might never see him again.

❧

HOURS LATER, WHEN MARY RETURNED TO CAMERON'S chamber after dinner, she found him seated by the hearth, reading by firelight. A tray with the remains of his supper sat on the nearby table.

He set the book aside when she came in.

"Ye ate, then," she commented, smiling. "Are ye well?"

"Well enough. Ye must be tired. Ye got home only a few hours ago."

"I am tired, but I couldna go to my bed without checking on ye."

Cameron stood and folded her in his arms. "Ach, Mary, my love. I spent my days and nights the last week looking forward to seeing ye, and to doing this." He pulled her closer.

Mary didn't know what to say to that, but she liked hearing it, and the way she felt wrapped in his powerful arms, safe and protected. "Tomorrow, we'll walk outside."

"I'll look forward to it." Cameron lifted her chin with one finger and met her gaze. "Ye are well?"

Mary's gaze settled on his mouth. His lips were so close. Would he kiss her? "Aye, I'm fine. Da had another headache at dinner and didna stay long, much to everyone's relief, I think. He's tossing out orders right and left, confusing everyone when he contradicts himself." She bit her tongue to stop the nervous flow of words.

"Anxious bridegroom?" The corner of Cameron's mouth tilted up.

Mary wanted to lick it. "Perhaps. Or just Da being Da. Though tonight he was worse than usual. I hope he'll be better tomorrow." She took a breath and lifted her gaze to his cheek, his hair, anywhere but his mouth or his eyes.

"Aye. Ye dinna need two of us to look after."

"I'd leave him to the healer, never doubt it," she replied with a desperate chuckle.

Cameron's regard and hands lingered on her longer than they should. But so did hers on him. She couldn't help thinking about leaving Rose with him, especially now her father planned to marry the Grant lass.

But the clan would fail without her.

She stepped out of his arms and went to the door before either one of them could say or do more. She might want him, and knew he wanted her, but she needed more. She needed a future with him, and so far, he'd said nothing to give her hope he had considered a future with her. She said, "Good night, Cameron," more to the door than to him, then slipped out without looking back and went to the healer's chamber.

The woman answered on her first knock. "Ach, Mary. Is aught amiss?"

Mary pursed her lips. "I'm sorry to bother ye, but Da complained of a headache at dinner. I think he's probably tired from the trip, but I'll feel better if ye have a look at him."

"I'll go now," the healer agreed.

Mary nodded and headed for her chamber, though her feet wanted to carry her back to Cameron's.

CHAPTER 6

*A*n hour later, the healer arrived at Mary's door. "I came to tell ye I took yer Da some willow bark tea. He seemed well enough. If ye are still concerned, perhaps ye should go speak with him."

"I'll do that, and thank ye."

The healer nodded and left her.

Mary pulled a warm shawl around her shoulders and made her way through the dim hallway down the stairs to his solar. The door was open, so she went inside. The low flames in the hearth illuminated her father bent over a document, seemingly unaware of her arrival. A lantern on the desk threw light on whatever he read.

"Da? Are ye well?"

He glanced up. "Aye, well enough. The healer just left, as I'm sure ye ken fine."

Mary smiled and moved forward. "Is yer headache better?"

Her father gazed off into the distance for a moment, then nodded. "Aye, it is."

"Ye are welcome, then."

He answered with a snort.

Mary peered at the document on the desk, but she

could not read it upside down. "Is that the betrothal agreement?"

Her father sighed and leaned back in his chair. "Aye."

"There's something I dinna understand," Mary told him, taking a seat across from him. "Ye seem to be great friends with Lady Grant."

"So why no' wed with her? That is what ye are asking, aye? At her age, if she even managed to get with child, do ye think she could carry it?"

"I'm no' daft..."

"Just answer the question."

So she and Cameron had been right. Mary shook her head. "Likely she couldna."

"Or survive birthing it?"

Mary shrugged. "'Tis hard to say, Da, but likely no'."

"Exactly." He waved a hand. "She'll never give me the son I need. But her daughter can."

"Are ye certain naught else going on here? Why would she willingly give her daughter to a man so much older than the lass? Do ye no' think Lady Grant has a goal of her own in mind?"

"I'm no' in my grave yet, daughter. And her goal? Besides making an advantageous marriage for her mouse of a daughter, ye mean?"

Mary couldn't disagree with his characterization of his betrothed. "So ye are willing to live the rest of yer days with that 'mouse' as ye call her. And to have her care for yer clan and its people?"

"Only if she gives me sons. She'll have time to learn our ways. If she does no' produce an heir, I'll set her aside and try again elsewhere."

"Da!" Mary clenched her fists, outraged, even if she didn't particularly like Seona. She couldn't believe her father would be so cruel.

"Dinna screech at me, daughter. There's no' a man

70

in Rose fit to be chief after me, and ye are still unwed..."

She spread her hands, palms up. "And whose fault is that? If ye'll recall, I had a suitor. Dougal..."

"No' one strong enough to lead this clan," he broke in. "For the good of Rose, I could no' accept him."

"I disagree. Ye didna ken him well enough, and ye didna give him a chance."

"I didna need to ken him. His clan is no' strong enough."

"So ye are left with nay alliance at all. Ye have only yerself to blame."

"See if ye still think so when I have a son on my knee."

She sighed. "I hope ye do, Da. I truly hope that comes to pass. If that's what it takes to make ye happy. Clearly, my sisters and I have no' been enough to please ye."

He frowned and glanced away. "That is no' true. I love each of ye."

"Then why..."

"Make it difficult for yer sisters to wed?" He pressed his lips together. "I couldna bear to lose any of ye. Can ye no' see that? Each time one of ye left, 'twas like losing yer *maman* all over again."

He held up a hand when Mary started to speak.

"When Iain showed up," he continued, "I thought giving Brodie the choice of the three of ye would confuse the lad and he'd leave without making an offer. Instead, he chose Annie, and though I tried to stop him, ye three went behind my back. Near to broke my heart."

"Why not simply tell him nay when he arrived?"

"And cause trouble between our clans?"

"Then ye betrothed Catherine three times, and never once with the man she truly loved."

"Three I kenned she would refuse, aye? But if they fought for her, if she didna refuse one who proved himself strong enough to gainsay me, any would bring an alliance that would benefit us. Yet, she had her heart set on another Brodie. What did that accomplish, save to satisfy yer sister? For the sake of the clan, for alliances, I had nay choice but to try to tempt her in another direction."

"And now I am left, and ye cling to me on any pretense ye can manage."

"For the good of the clan, Mary."

"Aye, and I'll go along with ye, but no' forever. Yer new bride had best have her wits about her." Not that she seemed to have any, Mary despaired.

"She'd best do more than that." Rose dropped his head in his hands, then looked up again. "As for her mother—Mary, ye are wiser than that. She is regent for her son."

"I realized that when I saw him."

"Then ye ken she would never relinquish such power in Grant to be the wife of a laird. I never considered her as my bride."

"What if she means to gain Rose territory for Grant? If something happens to ye, Seona's brother could claim Rose through her."

Her father shook his head and winced. "No' if I have a son. The lad would inherit, no' Grant. If she fails in that, well, I dinna need any more daughters to marry away from Rose. I'm no' a fool. A Rose must inherit, no' a Grant."

Disquiet prickled along Mary's neck. He didn't need any more daughters to marry away from Rose? He meant to keep her here for years more, perhaps forever, even though he was taking a wife? Mary's heart sank.

Then he grunted and rubbed his forehead.

Despite her dismay at her father's continued

stubbornness, she worried over his suffering. "Is yer head hurting again?" His headaches plagued him too often and seemed to be making him more querulous and confused as they progressed. Since he'd already had willowbank tea from the healer this evening, this one worried her more than most.

"Aye."

"I'm sorry. I upset ye." She stood. "I'll fetch the healer."

"Nay. She's already done what she can tonight."

"Then ye should go to yer rest, Da. Ye are tired. We've only just arrived from Grant today and the trip was long."

He nodded. "Ye have a right to ken why I've done what I've done these last two years. Annie's bairn got me thinking. I've wasted years since yer *maman* left us. I'm no' auld, but I'm no' getting any younger, either. I must leave Rose in strong hands."

A WEEK LATER, MARY STEPPED OUT OF THE KEEP AND took a breath of air redolent with horses and sweaty men. At least it gave her a change from the soap being used to clean inside the great hall and guest rooms. She wiped a tired hand across her forehead. Much to her relief, wedding preparations were well underway. Still, much remained to do before the bridal party arrived.

She didn't see Cameron among the men in the practice yard, but perhaps he'd already finished. He had been walking every day and getting stronger. Yesterday, he'd even picked up a dirk and done some light sparring with the Rose arms master. Mary had watched from her chamber window, glad to see him so improved, yet sad he would soon leave.

That's what men did, wasn't it? Leave. She shook

her head. Cameron Sutherland was not Dougal MacBean. Though she knew he had to return to Sutherland, she should not think him cut from the same cloth.

Mary moved to a sunny spot closer to the practice ground. Da was sparring today. He'd paired off with one of his favorite partners. She watched for a few minutes, thinking about Cameron's observation that her father wasn't very old yet. Barely into his fourth decade, he still moved well, and seemed not to be winded by his exertions. Yet a bit of silver glinted in his hair. How old was too old to take a bride Seona's age?

As Mary turned to go back into the keep, her father dropped his sword. His partner immediately backed off, but he wasn't what caught her attention. Her father's stillness did. He stood for long moments, head bent, looking at the sword, and flexing his hand. Eventually, he picked up the sword and stalked off the practice yard toward the stable, leaving his partner staring after him, eyes wide and mouth agape.

Mary kept her gaze on the stable door for a few moments longer, but he didn't come back out. Her father's odd behavior tempted her to follow him and ask what had happened, but he'd walked away under his own power and he would not welcome her fussing over him in public.

She decided to find him when she'd finished checking on the tasks she'd assigned the servants today. That should take long enough so he would not feel she'd run to his aid and embarrassed him in front of the other men.

All the rushes had been swept out of the great hall and carried away. Four lasses were on their knees, scrubbing with soapy water and stiff brushes at stuck food and God only knew what the dogs might have left on the floor. Mary glanced back at the practice yard, knowing when they were done, the men out there would head straight into the hall for an ale to quench their thirst.

"Ella," she called to a passing servant. The lass approached, russet head tilted in question.

"Please set up a table with cups and pitchers of ale outside. I want these lasses to finish the floor and let it dry before the men troop in here and track dirt everywhere. The men must remain outside until new rushes are down and I allow them back in. Or they must use another way to their chambers. They are not to enter the great hall."

"Aye, milady. I'll get one of the kitchen staff to help me."

"Good idea. Thank ye." Mary nodded and headed for Cameron's chamber. She hadn't seen him all day. He was pacing when she entered. "What are ye doing?"

He waved a hand. "Thinking about how far I've yet to go and how soon the information I carry may be of no use. Time is passing while I languish here."

Mary's heart sank. "Ye are anxious to get word to the Sutherland."

Cameron nodded and heaved a breath. "Aye, but I can do naught about it at the moment. Perhaps in a few more days…"

Mary's breath froze in her throat at the sudden reminder.

"Ach, lass," Cameron said and stepped toward her, reaching for her hand. "I dinna mean to upset ye."

Mary crossed her arms, determined to hide her feelings. Cameron needed to leave. She knew that. "Ye havena. Ye simply caught me off guard. I…I'm very busy today. And I saw Da have another of his spells out on the practice yard. I worry…"

"Let me hold ye, then," he replied, and pulled her into his arms.

She tried to step back, but he held her fast.

"I promised to help ye by holding ye when ye needed a minute, aye? Just rest, Mary, my love."

Mary gave in and leaned into Cameron's warmth. He knew how to soothe her, his hand tracing circles on her back as his voice rumbled against her chest. Finally, her shoulders dropped and she sighed.

He let go of her then. "Better?"

"Aye, thank ye. If ye'd like to get out of here for a while, come with me. I need to check on the chambers for our distinguished guests, then consult with Cook about the wedding feast before I find Da and see how he is. Ye can have something to eat while I do."

He brightened. "I like yer last idea best."

Mary chuckled. So Cameron was not a man to concern himself with his surroundings unless his belly was full. Nonetheless, Mary took him to the guest chambers she was giving over to the Grant party. "The largest is reserved for Lady Grant," she told him as she opened the door. "And the next largest, across the hall, for her daughter, the bride, Seona."

"What about the men they'll bring with them?" He leaned against the doorjamb, apparently reluctant to enter, and crossed his arms.

"Their guards will sleep in the great hall, where Rose warriors can keep an eye on them."

Cameron glanced around the room and nodded at the fine fabrics and porcelain washbasin. "Prudent for many reasons."

Mary gave the room a sharp-eyed once-over. It looked clean, the hearth swept and the drapes removed to have the dust beaten from them. A deep pink brocaded coverlet that had been her mother's topped layers of linen sheets and woolen blankets on the bed. Mary had put her mother's finest silk covers on the bolsters at the top of the mattress.

Cameron indicated the decorative vas
mantle. "French?"

"Aye. Each room has a vase I will fill
Anything for the comfort of our guests." A s
full of flowers would not make them as well
as the chambers at Grant, but the room was
the bed as comfortable as she could make it.

"Glad I'm no' a guest, then," Cameron te
is all too *pernicketie* for me."

Mary laughed at his use of the old term.
just to impress them, though ye shouldh
chamber at Grant. Rose has naught to appr
shrugged. It would have to do. "Anyway, ye
much more care than I will lavish on the Gr

Cameron sobered. "And I'm grateful for

Mary crossed her arms. "Ach, Came
think I would let ye die?"

"Never." He traced a knuckle down he
across her lips. "Ye have given me much to

Her pulse kicked up and something
twisted along her nerve endings. It seeme
Cameron touched her, he touched her mo
than the last time. "I'm glad," she told him,

Cameron grinned. "Me, too."

Mary knew if she didn't distract him,
in his arms and kiss her, right here in M
guest chamber. "Hungry?"

"For ye, aye."

She stepped aside, torn but determin
herself from his allure, and from the d
coursing through her veins, making he
prickles broke out across her chest and d
She wanted him to kiss her, she did, but
encourage him. He was too accustomed
with her. And the rest of the clan, as we
nothing of her spending time alone

amber. Where anything could happen, now he felt
tter. "Flirting comes as naturally to ye as breathing,
es it no', Cameron Sutherland?"

"Given the proper incentive, aye."

"Sorry, I'm no' on the menu." She closed the door
d stepped past him across the hall. She gave Seona's
amber a cursory glance while she got her racing
lse under control, then turned back to Cameron. His
ze had not left her. He looked hungry, indeed. For
r. She forced herself to ignore his gaze and said
ightly, "Let's go to the kitchens and see what
licacies Cook has prepared for us to taste. Then I
st check on Da."

Cameron's lips twisted into a rueful smile as he
pitulated. "Aye."

*

JR DAYS LATER, MARY STOOD IN THE BAILEY WITH HER
er. An hour before, a messenger had warned them
wedding guests would soon arrive. Now they were
e. Following a pair of guards, Lady Grant and her
ghter rode through Rose's gates with heads held
h, barely glancing at their surroundings. Their
ds and a cart loaded with boxes and bags trailed
ladies. A guard force made up of another dozen
followed and gave the keep a short inspection, no
er than necessary to ensure they were not under
ck. Mary watched with interest as her father
ted Lady Grant, taking her hands and helping her
n her mount. He escorted her into the keep,
ing poor Seona to fend for herself. Mary glared at
retreating back and went to greet her future
her-in-law, striving for the courtesy her father had
ed. Seona looked wan and pale. Tired from the
ney, no doubt. Mary escorted her straight to her

chamber, leaving the steward to settle everyone else. The bride's brother, it appeared, had remained at Grant.

Seona took one look at the chamber Mary showed her to, shook her head and refused to enter. "'Tis smaller than my chamber at home!" she complained.

"'Tis temporary," Mary reminded her, clenching her fists in her skirts where Seona would not see them. "After the wedding, ye'll move into the laird's chamber with my father." Mary found it hard to believe the girl could get any more pale and remain upright, but she did.

"I must have my own chamber," Seona announced. "Larger than this one. I am unaccustomed to sharing. I canna sleep with someone else in the room."

"No' even your maids?" If Seona and her mother insisted on private quarters, Mary would have to find the maids sleeping arrangements nearby.

Seona crossed her arms. "I prefer solitude."

Mary wished her luck with that. Seona would have much to adjust to, it seemed, in her married life. Clan Rose was less formal than Mary had observed Grant to be. "In any event, supper will be in an hour. If ye like, ye may rest here until then. I will send a bath, if yer maid will be here soon to help ye dress."

To Mary's relief, Seona relented and entered the room with a sniff. "Rest well," Mary told her. She meant to take her leave, but remained at the open door when the steward led her father and Lady Grant to the chamber across the hall.

"Ye will let me know if anything is no' to yer liking," Rose said to Lady Grant.

Mary closed Seona's door and rolled her eyes while her back was to her father. To all appearances, he remained smitten with the mother. Then she turned to them and nodded. "Welcome, Lady Grant. Yer daughter is just here. I was about to see a tub sent up to her. Would ye like one as well?"

Lady Grant sniffed and turned her gaze to the steward. "I am dismayed to find it is not already in place awaiting me."

"It will be brought in minutes," the steward assured her, then hurried away down the hall. Mary watched him go, angry at being ignored and jealous of his easy escape.

"I'm sure my daughter can see to everything else," Rose announced with a frown at Mary.

She fought down her irritation and nodded. "Ye have only to tell me what ye need and I will see it brought to ye," she promised Lady Grant. She knew her smile looked forced, but what did they expect such arrogance to achieve? She wasn't a servant. As the laird's eldest child and heir, she deserved some respect.

The Lady sniffed again and entered her chamber, then closed the door on Mary and her father.

Rose frowned at the door, then rounded on Mary. "I thought ye had everything prepared for their arrival. Ye promised me..."

"I did, Da. I do. But what sense is there in readying a tub in their chambers until after they arrive. Naught, aye? Unless they wish to bathe in cold water."

Rose crossed his arms over his chest. "They are here now, so see it done."

Mary sighed and held her tongue as her father stalked down the hall in the same direction the steward had taken.

He had to flatten himself against the wall to allow lads carrying a large tub to pass. The steward, followed by servants, brought up the rear. They carried bath sheets, towels, and buckets of steaming water from the large cauldron in the kitchen. Mary had ordered it kept full and hot hours ago.

She raised an eyebrow at her father, who tipped his head, then went on his way. Mary pursed her lips, then knocked on Lady Grant's door. "Milady, yer bath is here."

The door flew open. Mhairi Grant stood in the way, hands on hips. "And about time, too," she said, looking past Mary to the lads with the tub. "Bring it in, then see to the same for my daughter." She paced to the window on the opposite side of the chamber and stood with her back to the room until the servants finished filling the tub.

"Do ye require assistance with yer bath?" Mary asked as sweetly as she could manage. She didn't like that the woman turned her back on the servants as though they were beneath her notice "Or with dressing?"

"Nay. My maid will be here with my things shortly. In the meantime, I can take care of myself. Get out. All of ye."

"As ye wish." Mary followed the servants out and closed the door, then leaned against it for a moment with her eyes shut. When she opened them, she nodded a silent apology to the steward and the others. "Fetch another, please. The bride is there." She indicated Seona's door. "And make sure their maids bring whatever they will need, quickly," she added for the steward.

When the servants and steward hurried off to do her bidding, she decided against waiting for their return. Instead, she went to Cameron's chamber and knocked softly. She doubted he'd be asleep so close to supper time, but he'd walked a lot today and might be tired. She sagged in relief when she heard his deep, "Come," filter through the door. She entered, closed the door behind her and leaned against it. "'Tis going to be a long week."

Cameron stepped toward her. "I saw them arrive. Troublesome, are they?"

"Ye have nay idea." Mary spread her hands, palms up. "And right from the beginning. They've made nay attempt to be civil." She sighed and planted her hands on her hips. "Lady Grant has taken arrogance to a fine art. Seona is intent on remaining alone. She must have her own chamber, even after the wedding," she parroted. "I canna wait to hear what my da has to say about that."

Cameron wasted no time wrapping his arms around her. "Ye are aware sleeping separately is common in marriages," he murmured. "No' that I would encourage such behavior." He grinned. "And making an heir doesna require they spend every night together in the same room or bed."

"Dinna remind me." Mary rested her head on his shoulder. Cameron started rubbing her back, making her melt against him. "If only ye could rub my feet, too," she murmured. "I've walked this entire keep a hundred times today, making certain all is prepared."

Cameron laughed. "I'll do that later, Mary, my love," he promised with a wink and wicked grin.

Mary tingled all over. If only he meant the endearment. And if only later, he would take her away from here.

CHAPTER 7

Two days later, after dealing with more demands and displays of arrogance than she'd ever faced in her life, Mary stood in the kirk and watched her father wed a lass his youngest daughter's age. He seemed distracted rather than pleased. Less the eager bridegroom and more...what? Was he having second thoughts? She couldn't tell, but if he was, she wished him well of them. It was much too late for cold feet when he stood before the priest with his young bride by his side, her Grant guards lining the kirk's walls and posted at the door. Mary's hackles had risen at the way the guards positioned themselves. Keeping trouble out or the Rose clan members in?

Since they hadn't been invited, she'd written Annie and Catherine to tell them of the wedding, but was glad they weren't here. Da was still annoyed at Catherine's and Kenneth's handfasting, and Annie's second pregnancy made travel uncomfortable for her. Mary expected they'd be scandalized by the bride's age and worried by the *entente* between their father and the bride's mother.

What the Grant guards might do to her father—and her—if Lady Grant was of a mind to take Rose for her son concerned Mary more. Her father's certainty that there was nothing amiss only served to make her more anxious. The wedding could be an elaborate ruse—but an effective one.

Cameron Sutherland stood by her side, which gave her more comfort than the presence of one man should, despite the long looks he got from some of the clan who'd yet to meet him. Their companions from the supper he'd attended made up for the rest. Edan and Cailean had greeted him on the way in, and Annag all but swooned at his feet when he bowed over her hand.

Mary didn't care what anyone else might be thinking at seeing him standing beside her. Surely his situation was common knowledge by now. Where else would he be, but standing with her at her father's wedding?

She'd tried to talk him out of attending, but her father had insisted on having him witness the ceremony, suddenly a convenient representative of the powerful Sutherland clan rather than an inconvenient invalid. Cameron felt he had no choice but to comply. "Besides," he'd told her when she brought her father's *request* to him, "my father would want a Sutherland recognized in an official capacity. If he were here, he'd surely attend. So must I."

At the kirk, Cameron pointed out the array of Rose guards. "Inviting me," he told her softly, with only a trace of irony in his voice, "and including his men in numbers to match the Grant guards, tells me yer father may no' be as certain of the Grants as he professed to ye. Ye can take comfort. He is being cautious."

Mary hoped he was right. She also hoped Cameron could remain on his feet through the entire thing. Fortunately, her father had instructed the priest to keep the ceremony short. Da wasn't a particularly religious man, and he often said he didn't see the sense of allowing a priest to drone on and on, the only one enjoying the sound of his voice. Mary had smiled at that, but hidden her expression behind her hand. The priest had been displeased, but clearly took the laird's orders to heart. He presided over the shortest kirk ceremony of any sort that Mary could recall. She held her breath once the vows were said and the wedding recorded in the kirk's bible over her father's and Seona's signatures. If Lady Grant planned anything, this would be her first opportunity.

But Cameron must have seen Mary pale and realized what she was thinking. He shook his head. "*Dinna fash.* There are too many Rose warriors present for Grant to cause trouble here."

Soon enough, they were back in the great hall, everyone seated at long tables except the Grant guards, who took up positions near the doorways along the wall. Mary tried to ignore them and made sure to seat Cameron near the hearth. She didn't want him to get chilled, in case his health was still at all compromised. She stayed by him, at the opposite end of the long table filling the center of the hall, well away from the wedding party. Her father didn't object, but she didn't think he would. He was too busy laughing with the bride's mother while the bride sat on his other side, ignored.

During the wedding supper, there was no lack of ribald jests directed at the laird. Mary cringed at each tasteless comment and the rowdy laughter that followed. Seona's face went from pale to red and back again, depending on whether she heard—and understood, Mary supposed—the comments directed at her and the jests directed at her new bridegroom. Mary felt sorry for Seona and frustrated by the entire display. Once tables in the middle of the room were pushed aside and dancing started, Mary muttered, "I wish I could leave."

Cameron took her hand under the table. "'Tis naught any bridal couple hasna gone through," he reminded her.

Mary gestured toward them, still seated at the high table, watching the festivities. "Look at Seona and tell me this isna worse."

"Aye, well, 'twill be over soon," Cameron replied with a yawn.

Just then, Lady Grant approached Seona and bade her stand. "'Tis time to prepare ye," she announced to her daughter in a strong, clear voice that carried above the musical instruments and across the room. Hoots, clapping, and laugher answered her.

Seona paled, but rose at her mother's bidding. The women left the hall, followed by their maids and the Grant guards.

Mary breathed a sigh of relief as the Grant guards left the hall. She had feared a few would stay and take part in the drinking, leading inevitably to trouble.

Since she had no experience to offer, she had left putting the bride to bed to the Grant women. But seeing them go brought a tear to her eye. If her time ever came, who would see her to bed? Her mother died many years ago. Her sisters, married and living at Brodie, might be with her, but she might be alone.

Cameron leaned toward her, concern written in the crease between his brows. "What's amiss?"

She shook her head. "Naught, really." She wiped away the tear and faced him. She'd be stuck here as host even after da followed his new wife to bed. "Should ye go upstairs? I can get away for a few minutes to help ye get settled for the night." She shouldn't really leave, even for a short time, but she didn't want him to run into trouble. There were too many drunk lads in the keep. She feared Cameron could not yet to defend himself in a fight. With only the wee blade in her skirt pocket, she could do little to defend him, but her presence should dissuade any Rose from harassing him. Even without such a confrontation, she worried Cameron would get overtired.

He shook his head, refusing. "I'll stay with ye." He nodded at some of the louder lads halfway down the table. "That lot could cause trouble, and yer da is no' of a mind to do anything about it."

She appreciated his gesture. He was right—her father was too drunk and too busy with his cronies to care what happened in the hall. Likely Da assumed she didn't need protection since, for the most part, she ran the keep. Still, Cameron's presence kept the other men at bay. Even when not at his best, he intimidated by being big, well-muscled and looking capable of mayhem.

His presence failed, however, to keep the Rose lasses at bay. Several came by to meet him. They had no lack of questions about his convalescence, his role at Sutherland, and his relationship with Mary.

One particularly bold lass asked the question Mary had been dreading. "Ye have spent so much time together, surely there might soon be another wedding at Rose...?"

"Alia!" Mary objected. "Ye are being rude."

"I only ask what many are thinking," the lass replied with a smirk for Mary and a smile for Cameron that could not be mistaken for anything other than an invitation. "If no', perhaps ye would like to spend time with me. I'm certain I could make ye feel better."

"Thank ye, nay," Cameron told her. "Mary and the healer are treating me well enough."

"And that is *quite* enough," Mary said, standing and

putting some teeth in her tone. "I'll thank ye to go on about yer business."

Alia huffed and strode away.

Cameron grinned at her back. "The lass kens what she wants. Does she always go after it so openly?"

A moment later, Mary saw her tittering behind her hand with Annag, their gazes fastened on Cameron. What were the two of them up to? Mary frowned. "I apologize for her behavior. Likely she's had too much to drink."

Had her invitation piqued Cameron's interest enough for him to take her up on it?

"Well, she's safe from me, Mary, my love." He turned to her. "And so is Annag, and any other Rose lass. I like the one I'm with."

So he had noticed the two staring at him. Mary let out a breath, suddenly feeling lighter than she had all evening. She'd never taken his pet name for her seriously, but she appreciated that Cameron chose to stay with her, and to use it while other hungry gazes devoured him. Though he could act the frivolous youngest son, teasing her and flirting with her, tonight the term frivolous didn't seem to fit him. His continued presence by her side gave her hope.

❦

A FORTNIGHT AFTER THE WEDDING, MARY ROSE EARLY AS was her habit. She went down to the kitchen to break her fast, taking some sorely-needed time to herself. Cook and her staff knew to leave Mary be unless she asked them for something. Today, she sat in a corner, lost in her own thoughts. She still worried for her father. Though marriage should have made him mellow, he remained testy and quick to anger, and his headaches continued. The healer remained puzzled, with no solution to offer. And then there was Seona—but she refused to dwell on that lass while she ate.

The bright spot in her day was the time she spent with Cameron. To build his strength, he sparred with the other Rose warriors every morning. She enjoyed the glimpses she got as she moved around the keep doing her chores. Every afternoon, she walked with him, determined to do her part to help him regain his stamina. Her clan was accustomed to seeing them together, and people often stopped to greet him and exchange a few words. Cameron seemed to enjoy meeting everyone—his mood improved with each person who spoke to him, which pleased her.

Mary finished her simple repast with a smile on her lips that faded as headed upstairs. She needed Seona to accompany her if the lass was ever going to learn her duties—no matter what time of day they occurred. Yet she had become reluctant to wake her step-mother too early. The lass was always irritable in the mornings and refused food until midday. Breaking her fast before she fetched Seona was the best compromise she could manage.

Until the wedding party arrived at Rose, Mary had conceived of a faint hope Seona, despite the awkwardness of their ages and respective positions, would become a friend. Mary missed her sisters and longed for close female company—company Seona seemed loathe to provide, even when they were together. Mary expected developing anything akin to friendship would be difficult, if not impossible.

She had quickly become convinced her new stepmother was not only painfully shy, she was not terribly bright, and when cornered, reacted with her mother's arrogance. Mary did her best to school her, but was not optimistic the lass would ever comprehend the variety of things that needed to be done to manage a keep this size. Nor did she seem to care about how to address the servants and Rose warriors to ensure her orders were carried out without angering them.

Though Mary had been glad when Lady Grant took most of her retinue and left the day after the wedding, in hindsight, if she'd been willing to help with her daughter, Mary would have welcomed her assistance. On the other hand, unless she'd left the lass in the care of some hapless nursemaid, she'd had the care and training of Seona from birth, and had ill-prepared her for life as a laird's wife. Mary shook her head. There was no getting around it. She needed to have a stern talk with her new stepmother. One that inspired the lass to take on her duties, and that did not anger her father.

As Mary approached Seona's chamber, she saw the remaining Grant guard who worried her the most. After the wedding day, once she had gotten a good look at him, she realized he was the man who'd stormed out of the Grant great hall when Lady Grant and her father announced his betrothal to Seona. Mary nodded to him as she approached, not comfortable addressing him. She feared what might come out of her mouth. Had Seona chosen him for her guard, or had her mother? Why on earth had Lady Grant left him behind with the lamb-headed lass? Worse, the guards had taken up station outside the chamber Seona had chosen for her own private use, rotating duty during the day—and night. Seona's favorite usually had the night shift. Questions about whether he spent his nights outside her door or inside her chamber filled Mary's mind. About how long he and Seona had been lovers. All things she had no right—and no solid reason—to ask him. Standing guard outside Seona's door was innocent enough on the face of it. But his proximity to the lass worried

Mary after the way he'd reacted to the betrothal announcement.

She decided to wait to rouse Seona until another guard stood at her door. This one inclined his dark head as Mary passed, but did not speak. As she continued down the hall, she couldn't help wondering how recently he had been inside that chamber with Seona. Mary gave herself a shake, little more than a shudder, trying to drive out the notion. She prayed they had not done what she feared. Seona's wedding vows were barely uttered. It was much too soon for her to take a lover, or to resume a dalliance with one. Or at least Mary hoped so, for her father's sake. He counted on the woman giving him a son.

Mary paused at the corner and glanced back. The man had not moved from his position by the door. His gaze was on the wall opposite, but shifted to Mary for a fraction of a second, long enough to give her chills and get her moving again, out of his line of sight.

It mattered to her that any son Seona bore was her father's and not this guardsman's. Yet there was no sense borrowing trouble. For the moment, the man seemed content to watch over her. Surely, at some point, Seona would become convinced she would not be harmed at Rose. Or her husband would finally insist she send her mother's men home to Grant. With that thought, Mary put all Grants out of her mind and went on about her business.

Later in the day, she was doing needlework with some of the Rose lasses and a sullen Seona in the ladies' solar when word came that a courier arrived from Sutherland. He had four men in escort, and asked for Cameron Sutherland. Mary's heart sank. There could be only one purpose for the visit. Her time with Cameron might end today. She set aside her stitching and went down to the great hall where the men waited.

Cameron was already speaking to the courier while the other four stood aside, near the hearth, their gazes roving around the room as they warmed themselves from their travel. Cameron's frown told Mary how the conversation had gone. He gestured for the courier to join his fellows by the fire, then sought Mary out and confirmed her fears.

"I am being called home. These men will escort me and ensure my safe arrival. Can ye offer them hospitality for the night? We will leave on the morrow."

"Ach, nay." Mary's chest filled with ice. She reached a hand out, but pulled it back, mindful of where they were, in full view of everyone in the hall. Her belly twisted at the news and at the restraint she must exercise. She wanted to throw herself into Cameron's arms. "That's so soon," she managed to utter, somehow putting all of her dismay into those three words.

"Ye need no' worry. I am fully recovered and those Sutherlands are all braw warriors. I will be well."

Mary hung her head, devastated. He thought she still worried about his health, not that she didn't want him to leave. "Why now? Why send those men now?"

"Ye canna guess?"

"Aye, I can." Anger flared, hot and biting, from her belly to her throat, displacing the cold that had settled there at Cameron's news. "Da must have sent yer father another letter."

"Aye, he did. Claiming I have recovered well enough to travel, and fearing for yer virtue if I remain any longer. He left Sutherland nay choice but to send these men after me."

Mary huffed. Sadly, her virtue was just fine. After that memorable bath, other than holding her when she needed it—his way of repaying her care with his own—Cameron had remained a gentleman. They'd never even kissed. "Can ye no' send them away and stay?"

"Ye ken I canna. I am no' eager to leave ye...yet."

His slip made Mary's eyes widen, and her pulse leapt in her throat.

"But yer da is right. I am well enough—or nearly so —to travel." He pursed his lips and glanced toward the waiting men. "I must do as Sutherland bids."

She crossed her arms. They felt weighted with lead. "And I must do as my father bids and continue to school his new bride. We both have our duty." She sighed and turned away from Cameron to look at his escort. "This is an awful day."

THE NEXT MORNING, CAMERON AROSE EARLY AND MADE ready to travel. Despite his reluctance to leave Mary, the courier's arrival was well timed. He needed to get to Sutherland before the information he gleaned in St. Andrews was overtaken by events. He could also fill his father in on what he'd learned from Domnhall's men while riding scout for Iain Brodie on the way back to Rose. The healer had examined him again last night and pronounced the rest of his recuperation up to him. It didn't matter where he did it.

Mary's pain yesterday had been plain for him and everyone else to see. If he'd told her in private he had to leave, he could only guess what would have happened next. She had reached for him, but she'd quickly withdrawn her hand. Would she have stepped willingly into his arms, or done as she did in the great hall and turned away? The difference between Mary when they were private and Mary in public could not be more stark than she'd demonstrated in that wrenching moment.

When he joined the other Sutherlands in the bailey,

Mary was already there, waiting. She gave him a brave smile, but he could see her fighting back tears.

"Are ye truly able to travel? I dinna wish to find out ye have fallen ill again because ye left too soon."

Her concern about his health seemed the safest ground to stand on at the moment. "*Dinna fash*, lass. I will be fine." He traced her cheek, trying to memorize the softness of her skin, the dewy pink of her lips, every feature, every expression he'd ever seen her wear. She'd cared for him in his illness, and come to have feelings for him. He had them for her, too, more than he ever believed he could. More than he knew how to handle, or tell her.

She'd been so kind to him, he didn't want to see her hurt, and definitely didn't want to be the one hurting her. The courier had confirmed James Rose kept Sutherland informed of his progress. Rose always intended for him to leave—without Mary. That didn't mean he wouldn't eventually return. But since he didn't know what his father would have him do once he got home, he might never get the chance. This was a good time to leave, before Mary got more attached and he broke her heart. And his.

Not that their feelings mattered at this moment. As she'd said, they had their duty. And his called him north. The others had mounted up, and so he must, too. Though he wanted to tease out one last smile to remember, teasing words failed him. Instead, he simply told her, "Dinna forget me, Mary."

"How could I?" She reached for his hand and this time she didn't hesitate.

He took hers and kissed her knuckles, imagining the heat of the skin under his mouth came from her lips. He wanted much more than to kiss her hand, but in the bailey, in front of all these people, hers and his, more was not possible. Now he was leaving, more might never be possible—and would be cruel. He released her hand, turned away and threw himself onto his horse, wincing at the unexpected pain in his side. Without looking back, he flicked his reins. His side hurt less than the shards of glass filling his chest. He heard the other Sutherlands' mounts fall into line after his, but he didn't turn his head to see them as he passed through the Rose keep's gate. He might catch a glimpse of the pain on Mary's face, and that would surely stop his heart.

CHAPTER 8

$\mathcal{M}$ ary fought for composure, aware that every gaze in the bailey had shifted from the riders departing the Rose keep to her. Many knew what Cameron Sutherland had come to mean to her. They'd protected her and kept the truth of her feelings for him from her father. They knew how losing him would affect her.

She turned away and forced her legs to move, to carry her into the keep, through the great hall and up the stairs to her chamber. No one stopped her. No one offered her sympathy. She would not have been able to tolerate a kind word, or even a sympathetic look.

She lifted the knuckles Cameron had kissed to her mouth, pretending his lips were meeting hers. Her blood heated at the same time as her heart plummeted into her belly. Would she ever see him again? He'd become her best friend, and she'd lost him. Her sisters were gone, and now Cameron, too. She was alone, more alone than she'd ever been in her life. The pain in her chest brought back memories of the grief she'd felt when her mother died, doubling her pain. Only now she was older, more mature, and would be expected to handle it better. She would not be able to cry and scream and pound her fists on the table as she'd done as a child. She could not even go to his chamber—being found there would make her seem pathetic. And Cameron had once told her she was a strong, brave lass. She needed to be both of those things. She had a new stepmother to train.

Her window looked toward the keep's gate, but Cameron and his escort were already out of sight when she reached it. She would be denied even that last glimpse of him. Her friend. Her treasure. Or so she'd hoped.

The healer barged in without knocking. "Here ye are, as I expected, already mooning over the lad, and he's just left. Now, lass, he'll be gone for weeks, so ye'd best straighten yer spine."

Mary knew she'd come to comfort her, prompting tears she'd fought to hold back. "He could be gone forever."

"Ach lass," the healer murmured, patting her shoulder, then pulling Mary against her chest.

Mary let her head drop to the woman's shoulder and allowed the tears to come while the healer murmured nonsense. Finally, they slowed and she raised her head. "Thank ye. I needed that."

"Ye did and ye are welcome. Now, dinna ye give up on Cameron Sutherland. There is more to that lad than flirtation. He's got a good heart—and a good head on that braw body."

Mary snorted. If she'd meant to make her laugh, she'd almost succeeded.

"He'll be back," the healer predicted.

"Ye are going to make me cry again." Mary wrapped her arms around her middle. She hoped the healer was right.

"Nonsense. Ye are done with that. Now comes the hard part." She patted Mary's hand. "Waiting. But never fear, when he returns, it will be because he returned for ye."

Mary shook her head. "Nay, he'll no' return. 'Tis no' his way. He has nay need of a wife. Nay wish to be tied down."

The healer held up her index finger. "Mark my words, lass. Ye will see."

Hours later, she made her way to her father's solar. She'd given her situation a lot of thought. With her time as chatelaine coming to an end, she needed to do as Cameron urged her and take control of her own life.

"I wish to visit Auntie Jane in Inverness," she told him without preamble.

He shook his head. "Ye canna leave until my new wife knows her role. Ye've only had the training of her for a short time. I canna believe ye have taught her all ye ken about running Rose."

"My lifetime may no' be enough, Da. She doesna care to learn."

"Then make her. I raised ye to do yer duty. Now is no' the time to think to shirk it. The clan depends on ye, as do I."

❧

MARY DRAGGED HERSELF OUT OF BED LATE AGAIN, dreading another day with Seona—and without Cameron. He had been gone only two days, but Mary missed his smile, his chuckles, the warmth of his arms around her. She even missed the bad moods that plagued him while he'd suffered from his wound and the fevers that overtook him.

As she dressed, she told herself she should be grateful she had to work with her father's new wife—almost. That responsibility kept her from barricading herself in her chamber and moping. Instead, she spent an hour each morning and another in the afternoon with her new stepmother. Mary had finally conceded that Seona's attention span seemed to be good for only an hour, and she couldn't stand trying to pour wisdom into the silly girl's head any longer. So the arrangement suited them both as well as could be expected.

When not in her chamber or tutoring Seona, Mary moved around the keep like a wraith. Though the healer scolded that keeping to herself was bad for her, for now, solitude suited her.

This morning, while she broke her fast, Cook mentioned she couldn't find a jug she favored using when she made cider. "I think I saw it...somewhere," Mary told her, tapping her chin while she tried to remember. "Ach, I ken where to look. If 'tis there, I'll bring it to ye."

"I can send a lass..."

"Nay, I'm no' certain, so let me look for it."

Cook nodded and Mary went on her way, happy to have a simple errand to divert her. The storage area was full of odds and ends. Mary had searched it days ago, looking for bone buttons she recalled her mother saving. She hadn't found the buttons, which vexed her, so she couldn't be sure, but she pictured Cook's jug on one of the shelves.

She turned down the little-used hallway leading to the storage area and gasped. Her stepmother gazed with longing at the young Grant guard she favored, while he held her hands against his chest. Mary imagined Seona could feel his heart beat under them.

Mary stood frozen, watching them. They hadn't noticed her yet, and she feared if she moved, they would. Lady Grant may have left the guardsmen to ensure her daughter's safety and well-being in her new position, but this one seemed intent on seduction, and Seona looked more than willing.

The guard and Seona leaned close together, gazes locked, their voices low and intimate. Then the man straightened and seemed irritated by something Seona whispered. His shoulders tight and muscles bulging with emotion, his expression changed to wistful when he reached out to cup her cheek. Seona tilted her head into his hand. When she did, she saw Mary. Her eyes widened, then narrowed as she stared. The guardsman turned to see what had caught Seona's attention. He straightened and stepped away from her, his hands clenched at his side.

"Ye will say naught," she hissed.

Mary, shocked at Seona's unexpected boldness, clutched her belly and backed away, suddenly sick for her father. His new wife had already decided to take a lover. There could be no doubt Seona was in love, and not with her husband. Mary's father was ill. What might happen to him if she gave him this awful news?

CAMERON WAS GLAD TO BE HOME. STILL NOT AS STRONG as he'd hoped to be by now, he arrived exhausted from the brief trip on horseback to the coast and the voyage across the Moray firth to Dunrobin. But when his father came out to greet him, he suddenly felt better.

"Where are my brothers?" he asked when his father released him from a bear hug.

"Away at other Sutherland holdings," the older man answered. "I dinna ken when they'll be back, but soon."

Cameron had looked forward to seeing them, and his father's definition of *soon* could be slippery. They might return before he had to leave, or they might not.

At the evening meal, he greeted everyone and explained what had kept him away so long. In answer to catcalls about his somewhat diminished appearance, he showed off his scar, earning him feminine gasps and, after the meal was done, offers from several of the lasses to care for him. Normally, when his older brothers were home, they got the majority of the lasses' attention, though he'd had his share. Now, he didn't want them. His emotions were still raw after leaving Mary behind. Bemused, Cameron bid them good evening, then joined his father in the laird's solar.

"I see ye have no' lost yer touch with the lasses," his father chided.

His grin took the sting from the comment and put Cameron at ease.

Then he sobered. "And I heard what ye told the clan. Now tell me the rest," he demanded as he poured whisky for both of them.

Cameron had no doubt that was the laird speaking. He lifted his cup in silent toast to his father. "There is, of course, more to tell," he acknowledged. "Domnhall will no' remain at Dingwall. I learned in St. Andrews if he doesna return to Islay of his own volition by Samhain, Albany plans to force him out. I learned that before Red Harlaw, but I doubt those plans will have changed."

"That's three weeks from now. I'll send ghillies toward Aberdeen—if Albany's men are headed west, we'll ken it soon."

"I'll go." Observing and gathering just such information as this had always been his role.

"Nay, ye willna. I have something else in mind for ye. And Albany may no' wait. He could attack Dingwall any day now. I dinna want ye in the middle of that."

"Aye, he could, though we had no news of an army moving near Rose. He then plans to return south before winter sets in. If Albany succeeds, he'll control all of Easter Ross, south of Sutherland."

"And be sniffing at our borders when the weather

improves in the spring, with his supporters in MacKay at our backs to the north." Sutherland drummed his fingers on the arm of his chair.

"Unless he gets caught up in chasing Domnhall back to Islay to finish what they started at Harlaw," Cameron said with a shrug. "A lot of good men's deaths on that field accomplished exactly nothing for either side."

Sutherland frowned. "Were ye there? Is that how ye came by yer injury?"

"Nay. From a gallowglass straggler on the way to Rose. We arrived near Harlaw two days too late. We heard about it from Brodie men who fought and survived."

Sutherland compressed his lips, then spoke. "No doubt Albany would like to strip Domnhall of his holdings on the mainland, along with as many of the isles as he can take."

"That should keep his attention well south of us."

"If it comes to pass. If no', Domnhall is the one we'll have to deal with. He will have an eye to expanding Ross territory east or north—if no' this year, then the next."

Cameron nodded. "Likely east, rather than north. If James Rose dies, and Brodie and their other allies aren't strong enough to help them, Rose will be ripe for the picking. His heir is his eldest daughter, Mary." He turned his cup in his hands, hesitating to make his interest in Mary Rose evident just yet.

Sutherland grunted.

"Unless Rose names another," Cameron added, "or manages to get a son on his new, much younger bride." He outlined the situation there, all the while remembering Mary's voice, her touch, the way she melted against him. All things he already missed.

"And if she weds?"

The twinge in Cameron's chest had nothing to do

with his wound and everything to do with the image suddenly filling his head of Mary standing beside another man. He took a breath. "Depending on what her father does about the succession before he's gone, and with a husband to support her claim, she could become Laird."

His father frowned. "No' a Sutherland husband, if that's what ye're thinking," he said, narrowing his eyes at Cameron. "There's nay connection between our holding and theirs, save across the firth. And must I remind ye of our tie to Clan MacKay?"

Cameron's blood went hot, then cold, but he kept his expression neutral. He'd never seriously expected his father to honor a betrothal agreement made between the clans when he and the lass were toddlers, and his brothers not much older. The agreement didn't specify which Sutherland brother would wed the MacKay lass, only that one of them would. Eventually. Surely his father would not try to marry him off now, and certainly not to a MacKay. "Indeed?"

"Clan MacKay finally wants to end the feud between our clans with this marriage. 'Twould be a good match for ye and for Sutherland."

And while that decision, he thought with a groan, might be important in its own right, likely, his father would want him to report back with everything he could glean about clan MacKay. Its laird, his current political leanings and anything else that might affect Sutherland in the ongoing trouble between Domnhall and Albany.

For the last century, MacKays had killed Sutherlands and Sutherlands had returned the favor. Recently, MacKay had supported Albany when Domnhall set his sights on Dingwall earlier in the year. Sutherland supported Domnhall, who had soundly defeated MacKay forces. Cameron didn't think the feud would end so easily. "Do they plan to murder a Sutherland son in his bed, I wonder? Did they ask for me specifically?"

His father hesitated, then smiled. "I could tell ye aye, but I would lie. Nay, lad, they asked for a match with Sutherland, but no' with ye or any of yer brothers by name. No' even Ian. Ye are best equipped to enter their keep and leave it again, both alive and with useful information."

"Why did they no' ask for yer heir, I wonder?"

"Perhaps they thought that would be reaching too high."

"Or perhaps they think the potential alliance is valuable enough not to care with whom it is made. They simply want to hold the kirking here, be welcomed into our keep, and murder all of us in our beds." Cameron shrugged.

"Mayhap their usual allies, Sinclair and McLeod, are planning something that's making them nervous."

"If I were the MacKay, I wouldna trust them."

"Nor would I." Sutherland emptied his cup and set it aside. "I also willna trust MacKay without proof of their intentions. And I'll take their arms from them as they enter the keep."

"They willna like it, but that's wise."

"The lass, Mariota, would be a good match. I hear she's comely enough to please any man. And I'm no' getting any younger. Ye lads must marry soon and give me more heirs."

Cameron furrowed his brow, then tossed off the rest of his whisky. He was accustomed to roaming at will. Marriage had never been part of his plans—at least not until he met Mary Elizabeth Rose. Now, the notion intrigued him—as long as she was the bride. But he knew what his father wanted to hear. "I'll give it some thought."

"Ye must ken what yer choices are in life, lad, never more so than when ye are picking a wife."

"The lasses rarely have a choice. Why should I?"

"Do ye wish for me to add yer name, sign the betrothal agreement and send it off to Laird MacKay today? 'Tis easily done."

Cameron's belly clenched. "Nay, I dinna want that."

"This lust ye think ye have only for the Rose lass may turn to fire for another in another's arms."

Cameron had a sinking feeling James Rose had told his father more in those letters than the state of his health.

CHAPTER 9

nowing a reaction last evening would not have swayed his father, Cameron slept on the news about the betrothal offer. The next morning, he lay in bed, thinking about it. He had not changed his mind—such an alliance was not for him, even though Sutherland saw it as a more valuable alliance than one with Rose. Wedding a woman he'd never seen, from a clan his had feuded with for over a hundred years seemed to make little sense.

Neither alternative fit the way he expected to continue living his life, but of the two choices, he'd prefer to stand at Mary's side, even if that meant he became consort to the Rose laird. Still, Mary's father's recent marriage and the possibility of a male heir made it all too unanswerable. Unknowable. He just knew he already missed Mary, which surprised him. He'd had plenty of lovers, but none ever filled this thoughts after he left them the way Mary Rose did.

His body tightened as he recalled the way she felt, wrapped in his arms. Her warm, sweet scent, and the gentle touch of her fingers on his fevered brow. The memory made him harder, then filled him with remorse. He now regretted teasing her and trying to tempt her, standing bare and rampant in the bath before her. Other lasses had been more easily conquered, but to Mary, he was only a difficult patient, a flirt, even a comfort, but never a lover. She'd still thought of him as her wounded and ill Sutherland and resisted him easily. That memory dampened the desire coursing through him. She deserved a better man than him. She deserved to wed an older son, an heir who could give her the kind of life and the kind of position she was accustomed to. As the youngest son, he never would.

Perhaps his father was right—he should give Mariota MacKay a chance. But it didn't feel right.

He rolled out of bed, still favoring his side. Clangs and shouts in the bailey told him some of the lads were practicing at arms. Joining them would improve his mood—and rebuild his strength.

He dressed and donned his weapons, then headed outside. Scanning the men on the practice yard, he spotted his oldest friend, Malcolm, who was intent on demolishing the clan's arms master. "Enough," Cameron heard the arms master say. "Go mangle someone else."

Malcolm grinned and stepped away, then spotted Cameron. "Perfect timing. I find myself in need of a new partner."

Cameron grasped his forearm. "Ye'll have to go easy on me. Ye heard what happened, aye?"

"Got yerself stuck by an Irish mercenary, aye," the arms master interjected with a clap on Cameron's shoulder. "Ye used to be faster."

"Well, we thought he was already dead. I learned my lesson the hard way."

The arms master grinned. "And it's a good one to share with the lads." He stepped away.

Malcolm hefted his blade. "Now then, what's yer pleasure?"

"Nothing too strenuous. Ye'll find my strength and stamina are no' up to my usual standards."

"Let's see how weak ye are, then," Malcolm replied, stepped back, and brandished his sword.

He let Cameron take the lead, for which Cameron was grateful. Malcolm matched him, thrust for thrust, but didn't push any harder than Cameron did. When Cameron planted the point of his sword in the dirt and bent over it, Malcolm called a halt.

"That's enough for yer first day back, aye?"

"Aye. Tomorrow, then?"

Malcolm nodded and grinned. "If ye'll have an ale with me now."

"There's an idea I can get behind," Cameron told him and straightened with a wince. Malcolm eyed his broadsword, but Cameron lifted it onto his shoulder rather than let his friend carry it for him. He wasn't that tired, or that weak. They left the practice ground together.

Over an ale by the hearthfire, Cameron told his friend what Sutherland was considering.

"Ye lucky bastard," Malcolm said and laughed. "I hear she's bonnie."

"As long as she's no' murderous." Cameron swallowed a mouthful of ale. "But twill no' be me. One of my brothers will get the honor of mending the feud."

"If her da is intent on honoring the betrothal agreement, she'd best no' be."

"I'm glad enough no' to be the one."

"Ach, left a lass behind, did ye?"

Cameron shrugged and lifted his cup in silent toast. Malcolm wouldn't press, at least not right away.

Cameron looked around the great hall, noting the people moving through it, the tapestries and banners gracing the walls, the swords displayed over the hearth. All comfortably familiar. He was glad to be home. To see Malcolm and the rest of his old friends. And truth be told, mildly curious about the MacKay lass. Yet, something Mary had said before he left Rose had plagued him on the trip here, and bothered him still. She had predicted he'd return home and forget about her. He shook his head. Forget Mary? He knew now that he never would.

THE NEXT MORNING, WHEN MARY WENT TO FETCH Seona, the guard usually outside her door was missing. Mary knocked but got no answer. She took a breath and opened the door, fearing she'd find Seona and her guardsman in her bed. But the chamber was empty.

Seona was never up and about this early. Had Mary seeing her with the guardsman led her to spend the night with her husband? Her father was in his solar when she checked there.

"Have ye seen Seona?" she asked.

"No' this morning," he replied.

Mary's nerve failed her at the thought of asking if she'd spent the night in his bed. Instead, she continued her search. Finally, she spotted a guard outside the tiny Rose kirk. Surprised, she brushed past him and found Seona sitting on a bench at the back. Whether she was praying or just thinking, Mary didn't want to disturb her and turned to leave, but her boot scraped on the stone floor.

Seona turned at the noise. "Stay with me," she said quietly.

The request shocked Mary. Seona usually did her utmost to avoid her and her never-ending lessons.

Mary never expected to be invited to keep her company.

"Of course," Mary replied and took a seat on the bench next to her. "Does something trouble ye?" Like the affair she appeared to be having?

Seona took so long to answer, Mary feared she'd been mistaken in the invitation she thought she'd heard.

But Seona finally took a breath. "I am trapped here."

Mary fought not to laugh. Seona had no idea what being trapped at Rose meant. "I, too. 'Tis the burden we women bear, to live where and how and with whom men decide."

"I'm tired of it."

"Ye have barely arrived. And ye may soon have a bairn on the way. Does the prospect of the *wean* no' make ye a wee bit happy?"

Seona gazed at the cross hung on the wall at the front of the kirk. "It should. I hope it will, when it comes."

"I do, too." Mary didn't know what to say to console the lass. For all any of them knew, the future of clan Rose lay within her. She should have been pleased and proud but all she felt was trapped.

Mary realized the same applied to her. As eldest and heir, at least until Seona provided a son for the clan, Mary was also the future of clan Rose, and should be pleased and proud. Still, she'd spent years feeling trapped and resenting her father. Despite Seona's many faults, Mary could sympathize with her a little.

"I wish to make a bargain with ye," Seona said.

Mary had an idea what was coming and didn't like it.

"In exchange for yer silence, I'll make ye this promise," Seona said. "I will convince yer father to wed ye away, and soon. Yer presence here is a distraction."

"A distraction? Ye mean a danger to ye, and to yer position as my father's wife."

Seona laid a hand on her belly. "As soon as I give yer father a son, even before, when I am carrying, my position will be in nay danger."

"Even if Da finds out what ye have done?"

"What if I told ye we have done naught save what ye saw. We are two who cared for each other at Grant, but were denied the chance to be happy together. What ye saw was a moment of weakness."

"If ye thought anyone would believe that, ye wouldna offer to see me sent away."

"People will believe what they wish, no matter what the truth may be."

Mary stilled, thinking back over what she'd seen. The encounter was damning, but not conclusive. She'd debated long into the night whether she should tell her father, but in the end had decided hearing this tale would do him more harm than good. "At Grant, were ye lovers?"

"Ye try my patience, Mary. I have made ye a fair offer."

"And I must think on it. My father's happiness is important to me. If your heart is given to another, he will be displeased."

"What he doesna ken canna hurt him."

Mary didn't like the implied threat. "Aye, it can."

"Ye say ye, too, are trapped here. I can free ye."

"Only my father can do that." Her father and the right man.

Mary's heart swelled at the idea of being able to marry a man she loved. Seona's offer should please her, but it also worried her. She liked being a distraction if she stood in the way of whatever Lady Grant wanted her daughter to accomplish, or Seona's own goal of betraying her husband with her guardsman. There were so many possibilities. Keeping Seona off-balance might keep Mary's father alive.

In addition, she and Cameron had developed such a rapport that Seona's promise to convince her father to send her away soon could be disastrous. With Cameron gone to Sutherland and God only knew where else, she feared what her father might do. Yet, before he left, Cameron had not promised to return. He'd merely asked her not to forget him, and she didn't know what he meant.

"Think on what I have said," Seona told her.

Mary heard the warning for what it was. "I will think of little else," Mary promised and left her to the peace of the kirk.

Seona didn't fit in at Rose. She'd done her best *not* to adjust to her new home. And if Mary was right, she'd brought her lover with her from Grant and refused to give him up. Mary's father was ill and unhappy. Mary, ever the dutiful daughter, could not imagine leaving Rose any time soon.

❧

A SOFT KNOCK WOKE CAMERON. TROUBLE? HE ROLLED from bed and pulled on a shirt, then picked up his dirk before answering. "Who is it?"

"'Tis I," a woman's low voice penetrated the thick oak. "I need to speak with ye. Let me in before someone sees me."

Nan—he recognized her voice. She was one of the women who'd regularly watched him practice at arms. A distant cousin visiting Sutherland from another of his father's holdings, she often flirted with him, but she'd also flirted with other men. He'd believed she meant nothing by it.

Cameron debated for a moment. Whatever she

hoped to accomplish at his door in the middle of the night could not be good for him. At least his shirt covered him to his thighs, but if they were caught together in his chamber and she made it appear Cameron had dishonored her, they could be forced to wed and Mary would never be his.

Yet, Cameron's curiosity burned. She might have information he needed, or there might be trouble in the clan that she, an outsider, had noticed. He opened his door a crack. "What is so urgent ye must see me in the middle of the night?" Cameron peered down the dark hallway in both directions.

"Let me in," she demanded, hands on hips. "I willna discuss this in the hall."

"Ye canna be in my chamber, especially no' in the middle of the night."

"Would ye rather I screamed?"

With a sense of doom, Cameron regretted not fully dressing nearly as much as he regretted opening the door. He stood back and let her enter, but left the door open.

She closed it. "I've seen ye notice me while ye practice," she allowed, turning back to him. Her gaze lingered on his body before she added, "Ye seem kind, so I thought ye worth spending some private time together, aye?" Stepping closer, she placed a hand on his chest, studied him for a moment, then nodded, apparently having come to a decision. "My heart is given elsewhere. My father wants me to be sure before he agrees to any match I prefer."

Cameron relaxed a trifle. She wasn't here to trap him into marriage. That left one possibility, one he knew very well how to manage.

Cameron trained as hard as he dared during his time at Sutherland, fully expecting his father to send him on another mission soon. His side no longer bothered him, and his strength was nearly what it had been before his injury. The lasses noticed his improvements, as well. While the men's practice always garnered a few who paused to watch when their chores brought them near, lately there were more, laughing and cheering and commenting to each other behind their hands. The lads liked the attention.

Cameron did, too, but not when it led to midnight visits. He wasn't surprised when she added, "Yer brothers caught my eye, but yer father sent them away." Her hands slid down his chest to his belly and paused, her gaze on his, as if asking, or even daring him, to allow her to continue lower. "They're no' here, and ye are."

Cameron frowned, insulted, but also amused. "So, I'll do?" He laid his hand over hers, then took a step back. Though tempted to play along, she wasn't worth the trouble she could cause, especially if she pursued one—or both—of his brothers when they returned. The sooner he got her out of his chamber, the better. "Ye dinna need to do this, lass." He didn't want to hurt her feelings or anger her. But he must convince her to leave.

"What if I want to?"

"What will yer future husband think? The man ye say ye have already given yer heart to."

"He and I have already..." she said and shrugged, then lowered her other hand to the hem of his shirt.

Cameron caught her fingers before she could lift it or reach beneath, and clasped her fists together in his larger hands. He could only take so much. His blood heated at the promise of her touch. What she offered, his body wanted. Only he didn't want it from her. "There is a reason, lass, and a good one, for both of us to refrain. I find myself in a similar situation." He released her and moved to the window. Let her think he regretted refusing her, so long as she kept her distance. He needed a moment to let his blood cool. "In truth, I have noticed ye. 'Twould be hard no' to notice such a bonnie lass." He held up a hand as she took a step toward him. "And I thank ye for yer honesty, but my heart is also given elsewhere." The moment he spoke the words, Cameron felt the rightness of them. He'd avoided admitting his feelings to himself, convincing himself he wanted Mary, aye, but not that his heart ached for her. To now realize he cared for her in that way? The shock had him grasping the top of the shutter hard enough to crush the wood beneath his fingers.

"I dinna ask for yer heart."

To his relief, her voice still came from across the room, but her words dismayed him. She was far from chaste, it seemed, and intent on seducing him, despite his attempt to give her an honorable way out. Perhaps he'd been wrong and she wasn't simply bent on seduction.

He turned to face her. "Does yer father ken? Did he order ye to come here to catch the eye of a laird's son?" Was she setting him up?

"Of course, no'."

"Or to keep ye away from the man ye want?"

"Nay." Her voice sounded tinged with ice this time.

Misgivings flooded Cameron yet again. He winced. "If ye are found here, yer hope of marrying him is gone. Ye risk ruining any accord between yer da and mine. Ye must leave my chamber."

"No one kens I'm here."

"Ye and I do." He could see her growing annoyance in her stiffening posture. He had not behaved as she expected.

"Ye men are all the same, worried about alliances

and wars. I am offering ye a few hours of respite, a small measure of passion for us both."

Cameron crossed his arms. "I must be able to face my father on the morrow." To spare her feelings, he hoped he sounded regretful rather than rueful.

"I could scream." She took a step closer.

Apparently not. He frowned. "That threat got ye in here. But think, lass. Ye'd be forced to wed me, and ye dinna want to." Unless her story of another love was as false as the rest of her now seemed. She could be bent on trapping him.

She threw up her hands. "Naught I say will make ye want me, will it? My God, I've stumbled upon an honorable man. "

"Only just barely, lass, and ye're straining my control. Now, ye should go. 'Tis best for all."

Nan nodded and moved to the door. "Ye are as stubborn as I am. I'm impressed."

Cameron followed and opened it slowly. He checked the hall. Nothing moved. The silence felt heavy, for all of being empty. He gestured for her to leave.

Nan gave him one last regretful glance that slid down his body and lingered before she stepped out.

Cameron closed the door softly behind her, torn between pure male satisfaction that a lass had tried to seduce him and anger that she had while claiming to love another. He sighed and rubbed the back of his neck.

He needed to speak to his father first thing in the morning, then leave. If he stayed, as long as Nan bided at Sutherland, she might continue her efforts. Though he'd only touched her when he must to keep her from seducing him, she could run to his father even now with a story about him ravishing her, and he'd be wed by morning. Cameron clenched his fists. The more he considered it, the more convinced he became that she might fit in perfectly with his father's wishes to see his sons wed.

Alas, she didn't fit his plans—only Mary could do that.

CHAPTER 10

After a fortnight without Cameron, Mary thought she had become accustomed once again to being on her own, with no one to confide in. She and Seona had come to an uneasy accommodation and Mary had not caught her and the guardsman in a compromising situation since that first morning. Seona had never again mentioned the bargain she'd offered. But Mary could feel Seona watching her, much as she watched Seona. Carefully, quietly. And with no little malice. Still, life had taken on a comfortable, if not comforting, routine. Not quite what it had been before Seona's arrival, or even before Cameron's. But predictable enough that Mary had started to let down her guard.

When her father stood and called the clan to attend him at the end of the midday meal, Mary was only mildly curious. A glance at Seona made her straighten. The lass looked pleased and satisfied, even before Mary's father started speaking.

"Clan Rose is an old and powerful clan," he began.

Mary frowned, suddenly certain where this was leading. Her father was not usually given to exaggeration, nor was he one for making speeches.

Rose might have been a powerful clan, but its influence had waned along with its strength.

"Some have said its future is in doubt, but doubt nay longer." He turned to Seona and smiled. "Yer new lady is with child."

Mary clenched her jaw as he raised his glass to his bride of only a few weeks. Seona had warned of this. Whether she was truly with child or not, she was consolidating her position, and weakening any argument Mary might make against her.

"To Lady Seona, may ye give me, and Rose, a strong, healthy son." He took her hand and pulled her to her feet as the clan members in the hall cheered their new lady.

Mary forced a smile to her lips. She wanted the same as her father, after all. A male heir—but of his line, not the guardsman's. Though either, if her father claimed the lad, would eventually free her from her responsibilities to Rose. She would have choices. Poor Seona would have none. If she birthed a son, Da would want another as a spare. As many sons as she could give him. Lads to ensure the posterity of James Rose's line. His eldest daughter would serve no purpose in the succession. Her only value would lie in forging an alliance through marriage. At least her father would no longer need her to remain at Rose. So she smiled and nodded to her father as he reveled in this moment. For reasons of her own, so did she.

Two hours later, a lad brought her a summons from the healer to come to her father's chamber. The lad looked scared and sad. Concerned, Mary hurried to the door. Could Seona already have lost the babe she claimed to be carrying? So soon after her father's prideful announcement? She feared it would break his heart. If the pregnancy was real, she couldn't guess what Seona's reaction would be. But in any case, the loss of the bairn would be a loss for the whole clan.

Her father sat in a shaft of light from the open window on the edge of his bed, pale and shaking. He wore his linen shirt, a plaid and a fur throw draped over his legs. The healer stood over him, holding his left wrist in her capable hands. His new bride sat in a tufted chair near the hearth. Wrapped in a rich brocaded robe and woolen shawl, she remained still and silent as a wraith, her expression no more revealing than usual. Mary could guess what they'd been doing, but she didn't want to know.

"What happened?" Mary asked, entering the chamber. "Is the bairn all right? Da, why are ye…"

"'Twas a wee tremor, naught more," Da replied. "Likely from too much whisky. They shouldna have sent for ye. I am well."

Mary gasped, at once relieved Seona had not lost the baby and concerned at her father's sudden illness.

"Are ye?" the healer responded. "Make a fist for me, then."

"Let go of me, ye daft auld woman."

"Make a fist and I'll let ye be."

He made a fist with his free hand and swung it just under her nose, but stopped before he hit her. "Release me," he snarled.

She didn't budge, merely looked down at his left hand. She'd set it on the bed when he swung at her with his other hand.

She pointed. "Ye didna feel that, did ye?" He inhaled and she held up a hand to silence his denial. "Ye have developed a terrible palsy in yer left hand and lower arm. Ye didna feel the difference between it being held in my hand and lying on the bed. I could cut off yer arm below the elbow and ye'd no' ken it 'till ye saw the blood spurt. Now will ye listen to me?"

Mary sank into the other hearthside chair, her knees suddenly weak. "What does this mean?"

"It means yer da is getting older than he'd like to admit, wed to a lass who could be his youngest child. Pah!" She spared a frown for Seona, who stared at the low flames in the hearth and, except for a slight narrowing of her brows, didn't seem to notice she'd been disparaged. "Wearing himself out, most likely. A strain he can scarce afford, keeping up with a lass her age."

"Silence, ye auld witch," her father snarled. "I'll no' hear this in my own chamber, certainly no' before one of my daughters."

"I helped the auld healer birth ye," the healer responded. "I dinna plan to wash yer body before they plant ye. But if ye have more of these episodes, I may have to. 'Tis a good thing she's carrying," the healer continued, matching her laird snarl for snarl and gesturing toward his silent bride. "Now ye'll have to leave her be. Ye could use the rest."

Mary couldn't believe what she was hearing. Her father was that ill? Then she noticed a lift at the corners of Seona's mouth. Not quite a smile...yet.

Her father pushed the healer's hand away. "I dinna need..."

"Ye *are* ill, James. Face it, and take care of yerself, or worse may happen."

Suddenly terrified, Mary couldn't remain still. She stood while her father objected to the healer's demands.

"Canna be ill," he muttered. "Must no'." His gaze slid from the healer to Seona, then to Mary. "I canna leave Rose in the hands of a pregnant young wife or in Mary's alone."

Seona's gaze cut to him. She frowned, then quickly smoothed it away.

A shiver ran down Mary's spine. What had Seona planned? Mary found herself willing to consider the notion that her father's new wife was poisoning him. Yet it made no sense. His headaches had started before the trip to Grant. "Ye'll be fine, Da. Just rest. Seona will be a good wife to ye and give ye sons. Just be patient."

Seona settled back in her chair and crossed her arms, looking satisfied. A cat replete, with cream still on her whiskers. Seona's mask was slipping.

"Ye will stay at Rose," he demanded, his gaze skewering Mary, dark and fierce until he blinked. "Ye will no' leave me until the babe comes and the succession is settled. I'll let ye go then, make whatever match ye wish. I willna argue *then* if ye dinna argue *now*."

Her father had to be frighted to bargain with her. The revelation sickened her. She hated to see him vulnerable and weak, no matter how much of a tyrant he could be. Mary shook her head. "I wouldna leave ye ill and worried, Da. Ye ken me better than that."

Yet with that promise to her father, she knew in her bones she'd sealed her fate. After this, even if her father recovered fully, he'd depend on her more than he had in the past. He didn't trust Seona's competence to run Rose, and with good reason. Mary knew she'd have to be more involved to help raise and train any male child, any brother, she thought with a shiver, when, or if, he came along, no matter who sired him. She considered again whether she should have told her father what she suspected, but one look at him now and she knew she could not add to his burdens. Not now. Perhaps never. To protect her father, she might be forced to accept another man's child as the heir to Rose.

Still, she would not leave her father at Seona's mercy. Seona's expressions, subtle as they were, worried her.

Her father had first gotten ill before the wedding, even before the trip to Grant, but that didn't prevent Seona from doing something to make him worse. Her father's life—and perhaps, her own, might be at risk, as she'd feared before the wedding. The Grant guardsmen within the keep would do Seona's bidding without question. And what Mary could do against her father's lawful wife, she didn't know. Watch and wait, and hope for the best, she supposed. She crossed her arms over her chest and indulged for a moment in wishing Cameron was here. His powers of observation were better honed than hers. He might notice things she missed.

MARY WAS IN THE KITCHEN DISCUSSING THE EVENING meal with the cook when a lad ran in, calling for her. She turned to the lad, heart in her throat. Was her father worse? "What's amiss?"

"Visitors at the gate. The guard told me to fetch ye," the lad replied, then ran out again.

Mary took a breath and traded a look with the cook.

"That lad canna stand still," the cook reminded her. "Everything is urgent around him. But what I'd give to have his energy!" She laughed, then sobered. "So, ye will send the lad back to tell me how many more mouths I'll have to feed, aye?"

"Of course." Mary smiled and took a breath of air thick with the comforting scents of baking bread and bubbling stew. Cook had been trimming a venison roast when Mary entered. That would go on the fire soon. Despite the cook's concern, they would have plenty to feed unexpected guests. "Perhaps some apple tarts, as well, then?"

"I'll check the larder. I believe the lads brought in a basket of new-picked apples this morning."

"Thank ye." Mary took her leave and headed outside. It wouldn't do to leave visitors waiting at the gate. Unless they were Irish gallowglass men. But the lad's summons didn't include any hint of concern from the guard. Likely he just needed her approval to allow the visitors into the bailey.

"Who is it?" she asked when she got the guard's attention.

"MacBeans, my lady. Asking for ye."

Mary's breath froze in her chest. MacBeans? For a wild moment, she imagined Dougal, her former hoped-for betrothed, at the gate. But surely not. Dougal had abandoned her and married another. So why would MacBeans be at Rose gates now?

"Let them in," she commanded, then returned to the steps leading into the keep to await their arrival.

The gate swung open and four men rode in, Dougal in the lead.

The ground tilted below Mary's feet and she dragged in a breath to steady herself.

He dismounted and approached the steps where she stood rooted. He stared up at her but stopped before he reached the lowest step. "Mary Elizabeth Rose, I'm so pleased to see ye."

Mary studied him, surprised at how much he'd changed. Glints of silver shot through his hair, and lines creased the skin around his eyes. He looked tired. "I am surprised to see ye, Dougal. What brings ye to Rose?"

"As ever, ye do."

Mary's head jerked back and she clasped her hands together to keep them from shaking. She'd given up on Dougal long ago. Seeing him now—how could he think she would welcome his return?

Dougal gestured toward the door behind her. "Can we talk inside? And perhaps get some food and drink for my men?"

"Of course," Mary replied. "I'm forgetting my manners. The lads will care for your horses in the stable. Come inside and get warm." She ascended the last few steps and entered the great hall. Stopping the first serving lass she reached, she requested ale, bread and cheese for the MacBeans, then led the men to the hearth.

"Ye have ridden a long way," she said as she gestured them to pull a bench over and place it near the fire. "Ye must stay the night."

"Thank ye," Dougal answered. "We will have more time to talk. Is there somewhere we could be private?"

A frisson tingled along Mary's nerves. "Follow me." Reluctant, she led him to a room off the hall and gestured to a seat by the small hearth. "Why are ye here, Dougal?"

For a moment, he looked flustered, then he straightened and met her gaze. "I'm here to see if there's still anything between us. If ye have forgiven my youthful impatience. I was younger then and frustrated with yer father. I married in haste."

Mary stiffened, not liking the implication, and needing to confirm the rumor she'd once heard that he was widowed. "Ye are nay longer wed?"

"She died in childbed a year ago. It took so long for her to get with child, we were elated, but in the end..." He shook his head. "I never loved her as I loved ye, but she was good to me, and she died trying to give me a son. I do miss her."

Mary supposed his sentiment spoke well of him, despite what he'd done to her. Tragedy sometimes matured men. Dougal, it seemed, had seen his share of sorrow. "But now that a year has passed, ye are ready to wed again, is that it?"

"I wouldna put it so baldly, but aye. I've held ye in my heart all these years, Mary. I never heard ye had wed, and given yer father, I believed ye might still be an unwed maiden, so—here I am. Can ye forgive me? Can we try again?"

Mary's head felt light. Could she? Cameron had gone to Sutherland, perhaps never to return. They'd become close, and while more attraction seemed to sizzle between them than she'd ever felt for Dougal, they'd done little to act on it. He'd never asked her father for her hand. He was accustomed to going where his father sent him, gathering information. He probably considered marriage something for his distant future, if at all. While he'd been determined to defend her claim to be the Rose heir, which they both knew might become hers someday, he'd never even suggested he might want to stand at her side as her consort if it ever came to pass. If Seona failed to produce a son.

"I dinna ken," Mary finally said. "A lot has happened since then."

"Did ye wed after all? Are ye a widow?"

"Nay, I didna. I am no'."

"Then allow me to remain and court ye. Once we get reacquainted, I hope ye will look upon me with fondness—and more. A chance to offer for ye would make me most happy."

"My father is no' well," Mary told him. "He may be little disposed to hearing offers, as he depends on me." Mary knew how stiff and formal that sounded, but she needed to slow things down. To make Dougal realize he could not simply come here and offer for her and expect to be wedded and bedded so easily.

"But I was told he recently married."

"He did, to a much younger wife, who is slow to

accept the responsibilities of her position. I fear the burden remains mine for the foreseeable future."

Dougal took her hand. "Are ye trying to discourage me, Mary?"

Cameron's *Mary-my-love* echoed from her brain to her heart and back again. But he wasn't here, and while Dougal's betrayal had proven him unreliable, since then, he'd married and lost a wife he cared for. Perhaps he'd grown up. If she ever hoped to have a family of her own, what choice did she have? She had thought herself in love with Dougal years ago. Despite the way he'd hurt her, could she learn to fall in love with him again? "Nay," she said, throwing caution to the wind. "I am no' trying to discourage ye. Ye may stay. But if I ask ye to leave, ye must agree to go without argument. If ye canna agree, ye may only stay this night and must be gone in the morning."

"I accept yer terms."

"Very well. I'll take ye back to yer men, then see to having chambers made up for ye."

"I appreciate yer offer of a chamber for myself. The men will be fine sleeping in the hall."

His comment shouldn't have bothered her. It was a common practice but it seemed callous. And in addition to Grant guardsmen, she'd have MacBeans in her hall. Rather, her father's and Seona's hall. It still seemed strange to think of it that way. Even stranger to be overrun by men of other clans.

CAMERON ACCEPTED HIS FATHER'S INVITATION TO GO riding with some trepidation. He'd listened to Cameron's tale of Nan's midnight visit with a frown, then suggested they leave the keep. Cameron worried the old man might try to push him into a betrothal with her. But perhaps he only wanted to spend some time together before Cameron left Sutherland again. Time they had missed in the last weeks, and, if Mary and the Rose healer had not worked their magic, time they would not have had at all.

They left the keep and headed north into the forest at an easy pace, a dozen Sutherland guards at a discreet distance behind them. The escort surprised Cameron. "Since when does the Sutherland chief need an escort on his own land?"

His father glanced around them. "Since Domnhall of the Isles started stirring up trouble. I am pleased ye have returned without harm from Rose."

"Well and healed, thanks to them, aye." Cameron inclined his head.

His father waved his gesture away. "I've given what ye learned a great deal of thought. Domnhall may be busy consolidating his hold on Ross, or he may take it into his head to use all those soldiers he gathered to overrun other territories. Like Sutherland. No one leaves the keep without an escort until we learn where Domnhall is and what he's up to. No' even to return to Rose."

"Ye are that worried?" The subject surprised Cameron. He took a moment to consider, letting his gaze sweep the gaps between the trees around them. He saw nothing to concern him, but remained vigilant.

Sutherland nodded. "As ironic as it sounds, weak neighbors are dangerous to us."

Cameron agreed. "But Domnhall is no' the only one with an eye on someone else's holding."

"Aye?" Sutherland's gaze finally cut to his son.

"I think 'tis highly likely Lady Grant intends to usurp Rose for her son before moving against the other southern Moray clans' territories."

"Has she become so bold?" His mount got a little

ahead of Cameron's, so he threw his question over his shoulder.

Cameron waited to reply until he caught up with his father. "With Albany's backing, of course. If aught happens to James Rose, with or without a male heir, Grant may claim Rose through his new bride, Seona Grant."

Sutherland laid the reins he held loosely over his mounts neck and regarded his son. "How likely is that?"

"'Tis hard to say." Their horses settled into a companionable, side-by-side pace, making it easier for Cameron to continue. "James Rose had his own agenda in marrying the Grant lass. That's true enough. He wants a male heir, even this late in life. But his real connection is with the lass's mother. Now, Mhairi Grant doesna strike me as one to waste an opportunity. She certainly convinced James Rose to her way of thinking, and sacrificed her daughter to achieve her goals."

Sutherland barked out a laugh. "I'm acquainted with Lady Grant. I'd say ye have described her—and her avaricious nature—verra well."

"Then I must ask, are ye willing to stand by and let Grant take control of the south side of the firth?"

His father's gaze shifted to Cameron. "Why should Sutherland care?"

Wasn't it obvious? "Because the more holdings she amasses, the more wealth and power the lady will have. And potentially the more influence with Albany. She'll strengthen Albany's hold north of the Tay. Since Sutherland is known to ally with Domnhall, what effect do you think such an alliance will have on us?"

His father nodded and gave him a brief smile. "Ye confirm my faith in ye, in sending ye out as my eyes and ears. Ye have assessed the situation, and our danger, verra well."

Warmth suffused Cameron at his father's praise. "Then perhaps ye will be more amenable to a match with Rose. I have given some thought to the idea of wedding Lady Mary Rose."

Sutherland snorted.

"Mary is the eldest daughter, the titular heir," he continued, ignoring his father's reaction. "If Rose fails in his quest to sire a son, Mary's husband will be the one to hold Rose and keep it out of Grant hands."

Sutherland reined in and regarded his son. "A wee convenient, would ye no' say? Since ye are besotted with the lass."

"No' besotted, father. In love with. There is a difference."

"Or ye have taken yer sense of obligation for her care of ye and turned it into something else entirely."

Cameron felt his temper rise and controlled it. "Ye ken me better than that. Aye, I am the youngest and have done my best to stay as far away from the responsibility of yer position—and Ian's when the time comes—as I can. So aye, 'tis ironic to hear me plead to wed a lass who will, for all we ken, one day be laird. Or she may no'. Her da may succeed in getting a son on his new bride. I find myself willing to take the chance, either way. Though I'd prefer to bring her back here, she is worth the risk of remaining at Rose."

"Aye, ye always did ken yer own mind. And were an excellent observer of others." Sutherland tightened his grip on his reins and kicked his horse into motion. "So ye love the lass."

Cameron hurried to catch up, relieved his father seemed to understand. "I do. I have nay doubt, and it surprises the hell out of me. I love the lass, not her prospective position in the clan."

"Then why are ye here?"

The question seemed so out of character, Cameron

didn't know how to answer. Then he thought back to the way his father had brought up the betrothal offer. "Wait a minute. Was this business with MacKay your way of testing my interest in Mary Rose?"

Sutherland threw back his head and laughed. "Ye always were a bright lad." Then his expression grew serious. "Not the only reason, but an important one. Go to Rose. Win yer lass. I will support ye in this. I willna let Grant make Albany's control of the north unassailable. If that can be accomplished without bloodshed, so much the better. If her father objects to yer betrothal, as ye say he has done with the younger daughters, remind him of Sutherland's might, and of our alliances. If he's as ambitious as ye say, ye should be able to convince him."

"I hope ye are right. James Rose can be difficult when it comes to his daughters."

"Then use yer keen powers of observation and discover why. Or, if ye think ye can get an answer without getting tossed in the Rose dungeon or getting yer head removed from yer shoulders, just ask the man."

Cameron snorted. "I'll keep that in mind."

Sutherland flicked the reins. "Do that," he said as his mount cantered forward. "And keep me apprised," he added over his shoulder. "I dinna want to hear what ye have done in another letter from James Rose."

Cameron nodded as his father got out ahead of him. He was content to let him take the lead. He'd done what his father asked. It was time to do what he needed.

CHAPTER 11

The next morning, Cameron turned his face into the freshening breeze, enjoying being back at sea on a Sutherland *birlinn* despite the storm clouds gathering on the horizon. The ship had sailed smoothly this far, but now it bit through the increasing waves, its sails bowed like full bellies, ready to burst. He didn't care if the deck tossed beneath his feet. He was on his way to Mary, finally, and if the storm-driven wind got him there faster, he'd ride it out and thank the saints for it.

He would make a life with her, whether Laird Rose approved or not.

He thought back over his father's praise of his intelligence and sense. High praise, indeed, from Laird Sutherland. And a balm to Cameron's damaged ego. It made him proud. After their discussion, he found himself even more determined to do anything necessary to stand at Mary's side and be an asset to her. He thought about how he would approach James Rose and ask for Mary's hand. He had only himself to offer her, weakened, yet determined—and Sutherland, powerful and strong. He hoped that would be enough for her father and her.

Would Mary accept him? Would she welcome him back to Rose? After his conversation with his father, after he declared his love for Mary, he could not return to Sutherland without her.

He would stay as long as it took to win her. What happened after they wed would depend on her. He would remain at Rose with her if she remained the Rose heir. Or, if she wished it, though the consequence of abandoning Rose seemed dire, he would return with her to Sutherland as soon as he could get her away from her father, his seemingly lamb-headed wife, and any bairn they might produce. If she became laird, his answer would be the same—he would remain by her side.

If Mary had missed him half as much as he missed her, all would be well. If not, he would convince her. A vision of her filled his mind, blonde, laughing, eyes snapping at some clever remark one of them had made, then coming toward him, gaze locked on his, until his lips met hers and he lost himself in her kiss. Just thinking about her made him hard and hungry for her.

"Ho, Cameron, a moment of yer time," Malcolm called, interrupting his thoughts.

"Aye?" Cameron glanced around, surprised at how dark it had gotten while he woolgathered.

"Storm's coming on fast," Malcolm said, pointing. "Help me take down the sail."

Cameron leapt to the ropes. He and Malcolm made fast work of securing the sheets. The pull and tug bothered Cameron's injury only a little today, so he took one of the rowing stations and helped steer the *birlinn* closer to shore.

"Have we reached Rose territory yet?" Malcolm, sitting opposite him, asked over the rising wind.

"Nay. Brodie, I think." He studied the storm clouds. "'Tis time to put ashore and seek shelter with them."

"Do ye ken them?"

"Aye. They're friends."

"Any port in a storm," Malcolm quipped as the rain suddenly pelted down.

They beached safely and made their way up the bluff to the Brodie keep. Cameron's name got them inside the gates without delay and into the hall where a newly rounded Catherine Rose rushed to meet them.

"Cameron Sutherland! I never thought to see ye here."

He held her away from him, studying her and smiling. "I'm returning to Rose for Mary," he told her, "but the storm forced us ashore. Ye look well...and happy."

"I am!" She laid a hand on her belly. "But ye are wet and ye must be cold. Let's get ye warm and dry, aye?" She glanced aside as her husband entered the hall. "Kenneth, see who has turned up."

Kenneth Brodie joined his wife and offered his hand. "Sutherland." He glanced Malcolm's way. "And ye are?"

"Another Sutherland. Malcolm," Cameron said, introducing his friend.

"Welcome to Brodie," Kenneth told them. Catherine signaled for food and drink and led them to the hearth, where the fire quickly took the chill from them and dried their clothes.

"Once the weather clears, if ye'd loan me a horse so I can continue to Rose. Malcolm can sail back to Sutherland."

"Of course," Catherine answered.

Kenneth's eyebrow went up. "Have ye yet returned the three we borrowed from yer friend on the coast near Aberdeen?"

Cameron laughed. "No' as yet. He'll no' *fash* over them. He owed me."

"Rather a lot," Kenneth agreed.

"We have visitors? Why did no one send for me?" Another woman's voice rang out in the hall. Cameron turned to see a lovely honey-haired and also pregnant woman headed their way.

Catherine jumped to her feet. "Annie, ye willna believe who is here." She made the introductions in time for Annie's husband, Iain, to join them.

"Laird Brodie," Cameron said, "'tis a pleasure to see ye again."

"And ye." Iain gestured. "Ye have met my wife, then?"

"Indeed."

"What brings ye in out of the storm?"

Cameron told them about his trip to Sutherland and that he had his father's approval to offer for Mary Rose.

Annie smiled. Catherine squealed and threw her arms around his neck. "That's wonderful news!" Then she sobered. "Ach, wait. Ye have no' yet spoken to Da about this, have ye?"

Everyone laughed, although the prospect of the interview with Laird Rose did not make Cameron feel the least bit jovial. "Nay, no' yet."

"He'll be difficult," Catherine warned.

"I understand. But he has a bride of his own now. 'Tis time for him to let Mary live her life as she sees fit."

"Aye, aye," Annie proclaimed, slapping her hand on the tabletop for emphasis. "'Tis past time."

"As long as ye ken what ye are up against," Catherine allowed.

"I learned from ye."

"Ye ken our da well, then," Annie added.

"I do. And if we must, we'll do as ye two did to get around him."

That elicited more laughter. They talked until the meal was served, then they bedded down in a chamber

Annie had the servants prepare for them. The next morning, the sky was clear of cloud, as if the storm had never happened. Malcolm took his leave to return to Sutherland. With a Brodie escort, Cameron headed toward Rose on horseback, full of stories and good wishes from Mary's sisters and their husbands. And even more determined, after getting their enthusiastic approval, to make Mary his bride.

⁂

MARY SNEEZED AS SHE STEPPED OUT OF THE BUTTERY into the bailey. The kegs tended to trap dust on their surfaces, so she spent as little time in there as she could, or brought a lad with her to fetch what she needed. The lad had already carried the cask she selected to the kitchen and Mary turned her thoughts to her next task. She hadn't gone far when she crossed paths with Dougal.

"Is something amiss, Mary? Can I help ye?"

His question made her realize her skin must still be blotchy and her eyes red. "I'm fine," she said. "Just stirred up a lot of dust. It makes me sneeze."

"In that case, rather than return to the keep, perhaps some fresh air would do ye good. Will ye walk with me?"

She wanted to tell him no, but she'd agreed to let him court her and she'd spent very little time with him since he'd arrived. So she nodded. He led her into the garden, all the while chatting about nothing in particular. Mary found him easy to ignore and wondered what she had ever seen in him. Opportunity, perhaps, to get out from under her father's thumb. Now, Dougal did nothing but remind her he wasn't Cameron. He wasn't as big or as strong or as forceful or as tempting or…she pursed her lips. She had to stop torturing herself, recalling a man she might never see again. She'd already been through that kind of pain once—with Dougal.

His voice, and the rising intonation of a question, finally pulled her attention back to him. "I'm sorry, what did you ask me?"

"Nothing of importance, it seems. Only which is yer favorite rose. Or if ye favor another flower." He took her hand. "I'd give ye a cartload of whatever ye like if I could."

"That would be sweet of ye, but isna necessary." She stopped and faced him. "I am fond of ye, Dougal, but…"

"But no' as fond as ye were before I abandoned ye. Ye are still angry and hurt. I understand. And I hope to make my past mistake up to ye."

"Yer past *mistake*?" Did he see how he'd betrayed her as a mere mistake? Mary pulled her hand out of his and crossed her arms. She tried not to dislike Dougal, and she felt sorry for his loss, but his comment didn't help his suit.

He cleared his throat. "I didna mean…" He held up a hand.

Mary told herself he'd had a difficult time since she'd seen him last. But so had she. And despite her father's marriage, she still wasn't free to look for a man to wed. "'Tis ironic," she told him, "that before, I wanted to go to ye, but my father wouldn't let me and ye got tired of waiting. Now I need to stay. I am still responsible for Rose. And ye must wait—if ye can." More so now than when she'd known Dougal all those years ago.

He dropped his head, but kept his gaze on her. "I have learned my lesson, Mary. I will wait for ye this time."

He sounded sincere, but something in his eyes made her wonder. "Ye promised me if I asked ye to leave, ye would go without argument." Suddenly, she was heartily tired of his company. Was there anything he could ever do or say—or be—to endear himself to her as much as Cameron?

"Ach, Mary, dinna ask me that. Give me more time with ye."

He reached for her, but she stepped away. His expression was so anxious, so remorseful, she took pity on him. "Very well, I willna. But ye must excuse me now. I must check on my father."

"When will I be able to speak with him?"

Mary shrugged. "When he is strong enough for visitors, only then."

Dougal ran a hand through his hair. "When will that be?"

"I dinna ken." But she did suspect his ability to be patient was less than he claimed.

"If I were a suspicious man, I would think ye are keeping me from him."

"Nay, Dougal." She sighed and shook her head. "He truly is ill. I dinna want anything to upset him."

"Speaking to me would upset him?"

"He feels guilty for ruining our betrothal. So aye, it would. And an offer for me at this time, when he is not at his best, could harm the progress he has made toward regaining his health. He canna foresee the day I leave Rose as anything but a problem for him. He must grow stronger before such a decision has to be made."

"Will his wife never accept her role and free ye from it?"

Mary sighed. "There are days when I despair of it ever happening."

WITH HER FATHER REMAINING OUT OF SIGHT OF THE REST of the clan for the past week, Mary knew all was most definitely *not* well. Seona and her guardsman spent more and more time together as the days went by, more brazen—or less careful—about being seen. Rumors were starting to rumble among the clan, making Mary feel even worse for her father than his infirmity had. Assuming Seona was truly with child, would she present him with his hoped-for Rose heir, or the guardsman's bairn? Mary dared not speak her suspicions aloud, not even to the healer.

Too restless to sit with the other ladies and do needlework where she'd first gone to hide from Dougal and his fawning attention, she dressed for riding and crossed the bailey, intent on saddling a horse and getting some distance from her thoughts and fears. Then she heard a familiar voice hail the gate guard.

She froze, then spun toward the guard tower. Could it be?

The guard called out a welcome.

Mary broke into a run toward the gate as it swung open and Cameron rode in with four Brodies.

He reined to a halt, swung off his mount, and caught her in his arms.

"I canna believe ye are here!" she told him as she flung her arms around his neck, her blood singing in her veins. Dimly, she became aware of cheers and clapping all around them. Embarrassed, she pushed at his chest, but he kept her pressed against him for another moment. Finally he loosened his hold and she opened her eyes, only to drown in his dark amber gaze. "Have ye missed me, then?" she asked after she had a moment to catch her breath.

He laughed, picked her up and twirled her around to the sound of laughter filling the bailey. "Every moment of every day and twice as often at night," he replied, then set her on her feet. "We'd best go in. I think we're attracting an audience."

They had indeed attracted an audience, but thankfully most were smiling. Then Dougal stepped forward from the back of the crowd, a scowl drawing down his brow, his eyes glittering with anger. Mary's breath froze in her chest, fearing what he might do. But Dougal's approach was blocked by the crowd. While Cameron responded to calls of welcome and the people who surrounded him and clapped him on the back, Mary glanced toward where she'd last seen Dougal. He had disappeared.

Once she'd made sure the Brodie guards would be taken care of, and people started to move away, Mary asked, "Why are ye here, Cameron?" She tugged on his arm, eager to get him inside, away from any trouble Dougal might cause.

"To see ye, of course," he said, wrapping an arm around her waist and turning her toward the entrance to the keep. "And to ask yer da for yer hand."

Mary's heart thundered in her chest, and she couldn't seem to make her feet move. Had she heard him correctly? His tone had been too mild for such momentous words. "Ask my da..." She turned and faced him.

"To let us marry, aye." He took her hands in his. "Ye heard me right. I love ye, lass. I missed ye more than..." He waved a hand. "More than the air I breathe. I missed ye more than I ever thought possible to miss anyone. But ye must tell me. Do ye want me, too? Is being my wife something ye wish for? Or should I leave without seeing Laird Rose?"

Dear God, had Dougal heard Cameron's declaration? Mary needed to look, but couldn't tear her gaze away from Cameron's earnest one.

"Nay!" Mary fought for breath.

Cameron studied her, paling slightly.

She held up a hand. "Nay, dinna leave. Let's go inside." On trembling legs, Mary led Cameron into the keep.

Cameron stopped her just inside the door. "Ye didna answer me, lass," he told her, his voice low and intimate. "Will ye marry me?"

Mary swallowed, conscious of the people in the hall, watching them. "I would like nothing better than to become yer wife, Cameron Sutherland. Today, if possible. But first I must explain..." God, she was babbling! As much as Cameron's return thrilled her, she worried about how she would explain this to Dougal. And explain his presence to Cameron.

Cameron laughed, then wrapped her in his arms. "Ye scared me when ye said *nay*. I couldna bear it if ye didna want me, too. I'm glad I mistook yer meaning. Let's find yer da. I have an offer from the Sutherland that should please him."

"We need to talk first," she told him.

Cameron seemed to finally catch on to her mood and sobered. "Is aught amiss?"

Mary nodded. She led him to a bench by the hearth and sat across from him. She needed to see his face when she delivered this news. A few people approached them, but she waved them away. "Do ye recall when I told ye about Dougal MacBean?"

"The man who didna wait for ye and married another." Cameron nodded.

"He is here. Widowed and seeking to renew what we had years ago."

"He's here now?" Cameron's gaze swept the hall, his brow tense.

Mary shook her head. "He's no' in the hall, but he's at Rose. I have...been taking time to get to know him again." She clasped her hands. "I didna ken if ye meant to return, and I thought he might be my only chance…"

"Ach, Mary, my love, I…I couldna promise, when I didna ken what my father would require." He reached out and laid his big hand over hers. "But I'm here now. Being away from Rose made me see how much I need ye." He took a breath as he tightened his hold on her hands. "What will ye do?"

Mary tilted her head, studying him, then smiled. Here was the man she had waited for. The one who loved her enough to respect her wishes. "I will send Dougal away and marry ye, if ye still want me."

Cameron leapt to his feet.

"And if Da will agree," she added.

Cameron smiled and took her hand. "Then take me to yer father, Mary, my love."

Mary stood, warmed by Cameron's pet name for her, one she now suspected he'd meant, all along. She put her free hand on his arm, slowing him as they approached the solar. "I must warn ye, Da hasna been well." The door was open, so she peeked in. Her father sat at his desk, staring off into space, piles of documents on the surface before him. "Da, we have a visitor." When he didn't move, Mary feared something was wrong. "Da?"

Finally, he turned his face toward her. "Mary. Come in."

He hadn't heard her. She took a breath in relief and did as he bade, Cameron following on her heels. "Cameron Sutherland has returned, Da."

"I can see that."

"And wishes to speak with ye."

"I've just arrived, Laird Rose, but what I have to say willna wait." He pulled a parchment from within his shirt, stepped forward and proffered it. "I've come a long way to give this to ye. 'Tis an offer of marriage from Earl Sutherland to Rose, between Lady Mary and myself. Since ye have corresponded so frequently in the past," Cameron said, fighting to keep from frowning at Rose's efforts to get him away from Mary, "Laird Sutherland sends his greetings and his hope that ye will find the offer of a formal alliance with him to yer liking."

Rose reached for the document. "He does, does he?" Dropping it on the desk, he used the same hand to wave toward the door. "Leave me to read it in peace, if ye would." He glanced at Mary. "Both of ye."

"Of course," Cameron replied and turned to Mary, his expression puzzled.

She clasped her hands in front of her waist, frozen with indecision. Should she be glad her da had taken the news so calmly, or angry that he appeared once again to be paying little attention to something so important to one of his daughters? Frowning, she nodded to Cameron and tilted her head toward the door.

Cameron put his hand over hers, worked his fingers inside her fists and lifted hers to his mouth. He kissed her knuckles, then led her from the solar without another word.

Mary pulled one hand free long enough to close the solar's door behind them. "Ach, Cameron, what will he do? I canna bear the thought of hearing him deny us. I've seen what his stubbornness did to my sisters. Now? To go through it myself?"

"Let's forget him for now. Take me somewhere private, lass. I've yet to greet ye properly—or as thoroughly as I need to." He caressed her cheek.

Mary's sense of doom eased at Cameron's teasing. Of course he'd find a way to make her feel better. And suddenly, with the prospect of time alone with him ahead of her, she did. No matter where it led. Cameron was back, asking for her hand. He was hers, and she would be his. "My chamber, then."

CHAPTER 12

*W*alking across the great hall with Mary, Cameron clenched his jaw, frustrated and angry with himself for letting Mary's father delay yet again. He should have known how a meeting with James Rose would go. True to form, Rose wouldn't commit, wouldn't accept his offer outright.

Cameron had another concern, as well. He'd been angry to learn Dougal MacBean was here trying to win Mary back. She had accepted him, not MacBean, so the man must leave before he got a chance to see her unpredictable father. He could have no part in Mary's life, yet Rose might agree to give her to him —eventually.

Cameron knew what else to expect. Rose wouldn't let Mary leave until his new bride was competent to take over Mary's duties. Until then, the betrothal agreement would sit on Rose's desk, gathering dust.

For now, he couldn't let Mary see how her father upset him. He stayed a pace behind her across the great hall and up the stairs. He hoped any who saw them would think she led him to a guest chamber. But he doubted anyone would be so obtuse. Both of their faces would reveal too much of Mary's nervousness and his eagerness to get her alone. The smiles they got from the people in the great hall confirmed his suspicion. A few even had the gall to wink at Mary. Two older lads elbowed each other and grinned, but the serving lasses were more circumspect, smiling and curtseying as they passed. At least no one seemed upset about his return to Rose, or to see him in Mary's company, despite MacBean's presence. How long had the man been here? Mary hadn't said. which gave him a moment's pause. Then he thought about how he'd been welcomed. The members of clan Rose approved of him with Mary, even though her father dragged his feet, or disapproved. Cameron had returned for her, and he had no intention of leaving Rose without her.

When they reached her chamber, Mary turned and met his gaze, then opened the door and stayed a pace ahead of him, backing up all the way inside. Her gaze never left his. He hoped she could see his desire for her in his eyes. She slid her hand along the heavy oaken barrier as if she thought she could duck behind it. He followed her to the stone wall at its end, into the shadows. A shaft of light leaked in from the high windows on the opposite wall and painted the outermost edge of her hem and the floor in front of her feet. Cameron stepped through the brightness and framed her face with his hands.

"Cameron, I've never..."

"I never thought ye have, lass. But ye will. With me. When I was sick, ye cared for me and ye learnt every inch of my body. I want the same. I want to learn every inch of yers. I burn to love ye, lass, as ye deserve to be loved. As yer da has kept ye from being loved for far too long." He grinned. "Though I suppose I'll have to thank the man for saving ye for me."

Mary blushed prettily, a temptation Cameron saw no reason to resist. He leaned in and brushed his lips across her cheek, the bridge of her nose, then took her lips. He did it gently. She was clearly unsure whether to permit such liberties, so he took his time, easing her into the idea of loving him. Her lips were as plump and delectable to touch as they'd been to imagine these past weeks. He nibbled and sucked, urging her to explore his in return. When she moaned and her arms slipped around him, he delved deeper. Her mouth was a hot, sweet well his tongue reveled in exploring. He was certain his groan of satisfaction reverberated through the entire keep. He didn't care. He could kiss her forever.

She arched against him with a little cry, and Cameron's thoughts turned to much more than kissing.

"I want ye, Mary, my love. I have returned for ye. I mean to have ye. I mean to marry ye, no matter what yer da says, and to make ye mine forever."

She pulled back and studied his face, then met his gaze. "Right now?"

"What do ye think I've been talking about these last minutes?"

"I thought ye wanted to bed me."

He grinned, his gaze going hot and feral. "Oh, I do, Mary, my love, I do." He glanced away and took a breath, fighting for control, for composure. "But I'll do it right, too. I'll handfast with ye if it's the only way we can get ye away from yer father. Handfasting seems to be a tradition among ye Rose daughters."

Mary smiled, but didn't nod her agreement.

Cameron persisted. "There's a kirk in our future, lass. Ye will be my bride. Never doubt it."

❧

AT CAMERON'S DECLARATION, MARY'S KNEES WENT weak. How could he promise to marry her in the kirk, knowing her father as they did? And her obligations. Cameron was right. She had an overdeveloped sense of responsibility. She needed to turn it off somehow if she ever wanted a future with this man.

How should she respond? Her mind was befuddled by his kisses. She wanted more of those sending fire down her limbs, making her ache with a need she didn't know how to satisfy. She wanted to shout her *aye* loud enough for the entire clan to hear it, and promise to love him the rest of her days, but that response would not be seemly.

Cameron's expression was utterly serious. He had her at a disadvantage, away from other members of the clan, pressed between his powerful body and the wall at her back. He watched her face, giving her time to think while waiting for her reaction, but his hands still caressed her, and his gaze fell again and again to her mouth.

"I would like that, Cameron. When the time is right..."

"What about now, Mary, my love?"

She sucked in a breath and shook her head. This was happening too fast. She'd waited longer than her sisters for the right man to come along, yet now he was here, she felt frozen with indecision. She wanted him. He wanted her. But he'd just returned after weeks away. "Nay, Cameron. Ye have been gone so long. Let's take some time to be sure..."

He pulled his head back. "What are ye afraid of, Mary, my love? Me? Ye already ken all there is to ken about me. I would never hurt ye. And I willna leave ye again, no' if I have any say in the matter."

He tempted her. With his body, his beauty, and his spirit. And she knew she tempted him. She could feel the evidence pressed into her lower belly, long and thick and growing more insistent. "I dinna fear ye,

Cameron. Ye ken that. I fear for ye. Ye canna promise ye willna leave. There's nay a man alive who can."

"Nor can a lass," Cameron chided. "Nothing is promised to us in this life. I want us to be together as man and wife, to live our lives together. I want ye to belong to nay other man, only to me."

Exultation and delight warred in her belly with dismay over having to deal with Dougal. Being desired by a handsome and powerful man like Cameron thrilled her. She would be daft to feel anything but happy to have Cameron Sutherland as her husband.

"Dougal has had a week to soften my anger toward him. Yet, all I could think about was ye."

Cameron shook his head and stepped back, his hands dropping to his side. "Has he also asked yer father for yer hand?"

"I havena given him the chance. Da has been ill, and doesna ken Dougal is here. I've told Dougal seeing him might make Da's condition worse."

Cameron barked a laugh. "Of all the—"

Mary held up a hand to silence him. "Da feels guilty over having ruined my one chance for happiness with Dougal—or so he says. I do fear seeing Dougal would upset him, or worse, cause him to betroth us out of hand. I didna want that. I hoped for ye to return. And there's more." She told him about the bargain Seona had offered. "If she pushed Da, he might have done as she asked. Ye might have returned to find me betrothed or married. How can I make ye see I wanted ye. I waited for ye?"

Cameron hung his head. "I deserve at least some of yer condemnation. I left confused in my own mind about ye, lass."

Mary could sense he told the absolute truth, and it scared her. "What convinced ye?"

"Being away from ye. Missing ye, day and night."

"Ye are daft."

"I am no daft, lass, except about ye."

She turned away from him, fighting sudden tears she didn't want him to see. "When ye left, I felt the same pain as when Dougal abandoned me. I grieved for ye." She gazed up at the windows, fighting the urge to turn back to Cameron. She couldn't look at him while she said the words that might send him back to Sutherland. "Now ye show up suddenly and rush to my father to demand we wed. Do ye no' see how ye might have confused me, too, just a wee?"

"I'm sorry, Mary. I didna mean to hurt ye."

Not *Mary, my love.* She pressed her lips together against the pain. "Please, Cameron, I need to think."

"I'll go to my chamber, then. Take the time ye need, and find me when ye are ready to talk."

She was tempted to look over her shoulder. But the chamber door closed, and she felt a sense of emptiness that told her no one else was in the room. Cameron had gone away.

❦

CAMERON PACED BY THE HEARTH IN THE GREAT HALL. He felt terrible about the way they'd left things last night. He'd thought Mary would come to him during the night, after she sorted through the choices she had and the emotions plaguing her. Instead, he found her at first light, working in the garden. She promised to break her fast with him after she finished, so he headed to the stable, where his Brodie escort was preparing to return home. By the time they rode out of the gate, she'd left the garden and he expected to find her in the hall, but she wasn't there.

Hungry, he resolved if she didn't arrive in the next ten minutes, he would fetch her. He wanted to be with her. Their argument last evening still stung; not because they'd fought, but because he knew it was his fault. He'd botched his reunion with Mary, assuming her need for him matched his own. But much had happened at Rose while he'd been away. He should have taken more time with her before demanding they wed.

He stood, tired of waiting, intending to find her, when a man he didn't recognize descended the stairs and joined him. "Ye must be Sutherland. Are ye waiting for Mary?"

This must be MacBean. "Ye are?"

"Dougal MacBean, an auld...friend...of Mary's."

Cameron introduced himself while he sized the man up. MacBean was shorter and slighter, but the hard glint in his eye told Cameron he might be a challenging opponent. "I am waiting for her, aye," Cameron answered. "Though 'tis none of yer business."

"Everything about Mary is my business," MacBean asserted. "We would have married, if no' for her stubborn father."

Cameron pursed his lips. "Perhaps James Rose is wiser than I realized."

"I saw ye arrive. Ye may think ye have her heart and the clan's acclaim, Sutherland, but I have a prior claim. She'll choose me when she has had time to come to her senses."

"Ye think so?" Clearly, Mary had yet to tell this man to leave.

"Wait and see, Sutherland. Wait and see." With that, MacBean stalked away and left the hall.

MacBean's confidence made Cameron uncomfortable. He rubbed his jaw. The man could cause trouble when he found out Mary didn't want him.

Annoyed that he'd let MacBean get under his skin, he decided to skip the meal, go to the practice field, and push himself harder. The first day he'd joined the other men on the field, before his trip to Sutherland, he'd meant to take it easy, but finally gave in to the urge to go at it. He'd felt a sharp pain as something gave way in his side and for the next day or two, he'd been in more pain. Mary had feared more damage but the healer advised waiting. Then it stopped and he realized his reach had improved and his ability to turn and swing a blade more easily surprised him. The Rose healer told him he'd probably broken loose some scar tissue. She led him to believe that was good. It certainly felt good to be able to swing a blade, and after seeing MacBean, it was just what he needed.

Something must have happened to delay Mary. If she wanted him, she'd know where to find him.

MacBean approached him on the field as soon as he got there.

"Care to see who's the better man?" he asked with a smirk.

Cameron considered taking him on, but if MacBean chose to make a real fight out of their sparring, Cameron would have to stop him—wounding or killing him—and Mary would be outraged. The lad Edan showed up at the edge of the field then, and Cameron saw his opportunity to avoid trouble. He waved Edan over, and before the lad reached them, Cameron told MacBean, "I promised this lad a lesson. Perhaps another time."

He spent thirty minutes with Edan, who impressed him with his willingness to try unfamiliar moves. Another of Rose's men came over as they finished, wanting to learn the same techniques, so he took more time with him. Had Mary seen him and gone about her day? He hoped so. She knew he needed this time on the field.

"Ye'll be back to yerself in nay time," the man told him. "Ye almost had me during the last few minutes."

Hearing the man's assessment, Cameron laughed, more glad than he expected to be. "I'll have ye on the ground in a day or two," he boasted, then winced, hoping he was right. If not, he'd spend a lot of time on the ground instead.

The man clapped him on the back and turned to a different partner. Cameron took a breath and surveyed the men in the practice ground. He wanted to do more, but recalled the healer's warning not to do too much too quickly. And MacBean still eyed him from the sidelines. He might be better served to return to the hall and break his fast. Mary might be there by now. The idea of seeing her decided him.

Inside, the hall was silent. People sat, many unmoving, some talking quietly. A few came in or left, but they moved as if through deep, rushing water, slowly and with great effort.

"What happened?" Cameron asked the first person who came near him, a lass he'd never met.

"The laird is ill. They say he can barely move."

"Lady Mary?"

"With him. And the healer."

"Where?"

"The laird's solar, last I kenned."

Cameron nodded and let the lass go on about her business. Mary must be devastated. She'd told him her father hadn't been well. If what the lass said was at all accurate, he'd taken a turn for the worse.

The door to the solar was open. Cameron slipped inside. Mary and the healer were standing over Mary's father and conferring in low voices. James Rose, slumped in the chair behind his desk, looked unconscious. Or dead.

Nay, he could not be dead, or Mary and the healer would not be conferring quietly. They'd have called the clan elders, or done something else to begin preparing the Rose laird's body for burial, and to notify the rest of the clan.

Mary glanced up then and saw him. "Cameron, thank goodness ye are here. We were just discussing how to move Da to his chamber. He needs to rest."

"What can I do?"

"Fetch some of the men to carry him upstairs, if ye would. He's too much a burden even for the three of us."

With help, they got Rose upstairs to his chamber and settled in his bed. Mary also sent for Rose's young wife, who took her time appearing, took one look in the room and retreated.

"That lass'll be nay help," the healer muttered, frowning at the empty doorway before turning back to her patient.

"She's young," Mary defended her. "Mayhap she's never dealt with illness."

"Then she'd best learn," the healer grumped. "She wed a man more than twice her age. What else can she expect?"

"What caused this?" Cameron had wondered since getting the news, but this was his first chance to ask.

The healer shrugged and looked worried, her brow crinkled and her eyes sad.

Mary's mouth pinched and her gaze dropped. "I dinna ken if this has anything to do with his collapse, but Da just received word one of the men he thought dead at Red Harlaw is alive and with the Earl of Mar's forces."

"A prisoner?"

"Nay, a captain in his guard. He…"

"Is a traitor. Is that what ye are saying?" Cameron tensed.

"Aye, Da got angrier than I've ever seen him, red in the face then suddenly…fell forward. When he came to sometime later, he couldna move the right side of his body. Look at his face."

Cameron had already noted one side of Rose's face had lost all expression and looked slack and loose, more akin to partially melted candle wax than how a man should look, even in sleep.

He shook his head, then turned to the healer. "What's to be done now?"

She shrugged. "There's naught I can do. He'll either heal and regain the full use of his body, or he willna. It may be well that his new wife is already with child. I dinna ken whether he'll retain the ability…"

Mary colored and her hand flew to cover her mouth.

"Sorry lass," the healer told her. "But ye may as well face facts. Yer da may never again be the man he was—in any capacity."

Cameron moved to Mary and put his arms around her, pulling her against his chest. "Whatever happens, we will handle it," he told her. "I'll be here to help ye."

She nodded, but he could feel her tears dampen his chest through the fabric of shirt. "I dinna ken what to do."

"Ye'll do as ye always have, and be a help to him," Cameron assured her.

CHAPTER 13

With her father's illness worsening, Mary knew more of her time would be spent caring for him. There was someone she needed to find. She dreaded the conversation, but now she'd seen Cameron's devotion to her fractious father, she realized how much he did care for her. And for Rose. He didn't deserve to have Dougal MacBean underfoot. It was time to tell Dougal she would never accept him. He needed to leave.

She found him out in the bailey, seated on a hay bale, watching some of the lads and lasses practicing archery. When he saw her coming, he smiled and stood, then reached for her hand.

"Mary, I heard about yer da. I'm sorry. Ye have been so busy, I despaired of seeing ye today."

"I'm sorry, too, but 'tis my lot in life, I fear. I need to speak with ye. Will ye walk with me?"

"Of course."

She led him around the keep, away from the noise of the practice yard while she tried to decide how to deliver her rejection. "Ye have been patient with me," she began, her gaze on the ground as they walked, "and I appreciate it."

"I promised ye I would do better this time."

"Aye, ye did. And ye have." She stopped and faced him. "But I must ask ye to honor yer other promise. I have made my decision, and 'tis time for ye to leave."

Dougal frowned. "Ye have decided in Sutherland's favor."

Mary nodded. "I have."

He spread his hands, beseeching her. "What we had was real, Mary. We can have that again."

She shook her head. "If we could, we would ken it by now."

"I do."

"I'm sorry, Dougal, but I no longer feel for ye what I once did. We've both grown and changed."

"And yer taste in men has changed as well."

"Perhaps it has. Still, I've spent more time with Cameron than I ever did with ye, and we've talked a great deal. I ken more about him than ye. And I see what kind of man he is more clearly the longer he is here."

"Because he helped yer with yer da? Aye, I heard about that, too. I couldha done the same, had ye called for me."

"But ye didna. It never occurred to ye to offer, did it? Ye have simply bided yer time, waiting for me to be available to ye. Cameron saw a need and did what he could to help. Without being asked. Perhaps that's the difference between the two of ye. Perhaps no'. But 'tis the difference ye have shown me."

Dougal reached for her arm. "Tell me what I can do to change yer mind, Mary."

Not *Mary-my-love*. Mary shook her head as she stepped back. "Ye canna. 'Tis time for ye to go. I wish ye a safe journey home, and hope ye will find another lass to love, one who loves ye more than I can."

This time, he did grab her arm. "I canna just walk away, Mary."

He moved closer, and she stepped back. But he kept coming and before she knew it, he'd backed her into the keep's wall. "Ye've never let me kiss ye. I'll wager he has. I think ye'll like mine better." He swooped in before Mary realized what he was about to do and pressed his mouth to hers. Mary tried to turn her head away, but he held it in place and forced his tongue between her lips while he ground his hips against her belly, his erection becoming more evident the longer he plundered her mouth. Mary struggled, but could not force him off. In the one moment he shifted enough for her to get a sip of air, she shouted, "Nay! Stop this!"

He ignored her protest, tunneled his fingers into her hair and grabbed her neck. He forced her head closer and sealed his mouth more tightly to hers.

This couldn't be happening! Never would she have imagined Dougal capable of this assault. Furious, she pummeled his shoulders, but he ignored her fists. With his other hand, he reached down and grasped her arse, squeezing and rubbing it, and pulling her tightly against his erection while he continued to bruise her mouth with his and to nip at her lips with his teeth. She couldn't get enough distance from him to hit his groin with her knee, but she kept trying, squeezing her eyes shut to concentrate. But that only made her feel Dougal's body more acutely.

Then suddenly, he was gone, ripped from her, the fingers he'd tangled in her hair pulling painfully. Mary opened her eyes in time to see Cameron's fist strike Dougal's face. The blow knocked Dougal onto his arse, but he rolled to his feet and came at Cameron with fists swinging. Cameron neatly sidestepped and knocked Dougal down again. "Is that how MacBeans woo a lass?" Cameron taunted. "Mauling her while she tries to fight ye off. Does that make ye feel like the better man?"

Dougal growled and got up again, his dirk in his hand.

Mary gasped.

"I wouldna, if I were ye," Cameron warned him. "Ye are nay match for me."

"I have this," he said, gesturing with his blade, "and ye dinna. I will have no difficulty killing ye," Dougal snarled. "Mary was mine. She will be again."

"Ye mean I was yers until ye abandoned me," Mary scolded. "I told ye I dinna want ye. If ye think this is the way to win me, ye are wrong. Accept yer loss and go home, Dougal. I've asked ye nicely twice now. If ye dinna leave, and I have to ask ye again, I will have Rose warriors escort ye off of Rose land. Is that what ye want?" No matter what, she'd never allow herself to be alone with him again.

Cameron's gaze remained on Dougal, but Mary knew he could see her from the corner of his eye. He might be spoiling for a fight, but he would never hurt her. She approached him and put a hand on his arm. "Let him leave, Cameron. Please."

Dougal snarled, sheathed his dirk, and stomped off.

"He'll collect his things and go," Mary said, watching Dougal march away and hoping what she said was true.

Cameron took her gently by the shoulders and turned her to face him. "Are ye well, lass? Did he hurt ye?"

She shook her head. "He didna. He just surprised me. I never expected him to become so aggressive. 'Tis no' at all like the lad I once kenned. He's been so patient since he arrived. I thought he'd changed..."

"It seems his patience came to an abrupt end, then, aye?"

Mary pressed her lips together, then winced at the

unexpected soreness. Cameron must have seen. He touched her cheek and gently ran his thumb over her mouth.

"Ye may be bruised."

"It will pass. And if anyone asks, I'll tell them who did it. The clan likes ye. I'll no' let Dougal spoil their opinion. I dinna want anyone to think ye capable of such brutality."

"Ach, lass, but I am."

She straightened and raised her eyebrows. "What?"

Cameron nodded. "And worse. If he'd done more to harm ye, if ye hadna asked me to let him leave, I could have killed him. Ye ken that, aye? I was ready to beat him to death. I willna allow anyone to hurt ye."

"Ye canna always protect me…"

"I can and I will. And someday, after ye heal," he said, lightly caressing her cheek, "I'll remind ye how a proper kiss is done."

"I'll look forward to it," Mary told him and smiled, then winced again at the pull on her sore mouth.

"I may have to kill him anyway," Cameron muttered at Mary's wince, then stared in the direction Dougal had gone.

❧

MARY ENTERED THE BUTTERY TO CHECK THE NUMBER OF empty ale casks stored there, determined to have nothing on her mind but putting the alewife to work replenishing their supply as soon as the grain harvest was in. Her father's illness, Dougal's assault—she wanted to forget all of it by concentrating on something she knew how to do. She could count casks, and in this state of mind, she didn't even care about the dust she'd stir up.

Instead of the alewife, she found Seona and her

Grant guardsman as close together as two people could be while still clothed, whispering to each other while they drank from cups they placed next to an open cask of ale.

"What are ye doing?" she demanded, tired of this cat-and-mouse game they were playing with her, and most important of all, with her father.

"'Tis none of yer business," Seona answered, stepping away from her companion.

"Aye, it is," Mary assured her, reaching for something to say rather than throttle the lass. "Ye are spoiling that cask of ale. And ye are married to my father, no' this man."

"Worse luck," Seona took a gulp and spat it out. "Grant ale is better. And if no' for yer invalid father falling in with my mother's schemes, we'd be married right now." She smiled at her companion.

The bile in Mary's stomach shifted upward and she swallowed hard to keep from spewing on Seona's slippers. "Ye make me ill," she announced. "Both of ye. If I could, I'd send him back to Grant…"

"But ye canna. I am Lady Rose, no' ye. And if ye say anything to yer father, I will tell him all about us. And assure him the babe is no' his. What do ye think such news will do to his fragile health?"

"Ye think he would be the only one harmed?" Mary tensed, furious that Seona would threaten her father in any way. "Do ye think he would refrain from throwing yer lover into the dungeon? That is, if he didn't kill him outright."

"He's no' capable."

"But he has men who are," Mary reminded her and was gratified to see Seona blanch. She would give much to slap Seona—or worse—this very moment.

Her guardsman noticed the change in Mary's

posture and stepped forward. "Ye'd best go now," he said.

His voice sounded deceptively mild, belying the violence Mary knew he was capable of doing if she pushed Seona much farther. He could kill her before her screams could bring help. Yet he hadn't threatened her. She took a breath and stepped back, then halted when he held up a hand.

"There is naught ye can do by telling yer father except make things worse for all of us," he said, looking at Seona. "I do love her. I have kenned she was mine since we were bairns together. How is it fair that I must now watch over her with another man? And someday, watch another man raise my bairn?"

His bairn? Mary's heart broke to hear Seona's betrayal confirmed, but also at the grief in this man's voice. "Ye couldha stayed at Grant," she told him, though she knew how unkind it sounded.

"Nay, I couldna." His fists clenched, then opened. "I've kept Seona safe my whole life. She is my whole life. And now she carries my bairn. Why would I ever stop?"

Seona turned into his shoulder.

"Perhaps because she belongs to someone else?" Mary hated to be so cruel, but it was the truth.

The guardsman glared at her for a moment, then dropped his gaze.

"The bairn truly is no' my father's?" Mary choked out, tears of rage or sorrow, she wasn't certain which, finally pricking at her eyes.

Seona glanced at her, then looked away.

Mary spun around and marched from the buttery, broken-hearted and furious, yet wondering if Seona was angry or relieved that her paramour had revealed so much. And wondering what she would do about it.

Mary didn't know what to do with their confession.

Seona had been right when she said the news could further damage her father's fragile health. Yet how could Mary keep this from him? He deserved to know.

❧

AFTER THE EVENING MEAL, MARY MADE HER EXCUSES and fled to her chamber, exhausted and sick at heart. She'd put a brave face on during the meal, trying to reassure everyone that Clan Rose was still in good hands.

The healer was at a loss for what to do for the laird. She claimed to have seen something similar before, and knew of no cure save trying to get the person afflicted to move. Or he'd die. That thought brought fresh tears to Mary's eyes. She collapsed onto her bed, wishing her sisters were here to hold her as she'd held them while they cried so many times over the years since their *maman*'s death. Instead, she'd have to send a *ghillie* to Brodie in the morning to let them know what had happened. She wished she knew whether to tell them to come and bid their father goodbye while he yet lived, or to tell them not to worry, he'd be fine soon enough.

A soft knock at her door startled her into sitting up. Who would seek her out now? It could be anyone in the clan with a problem they needed her help to solve. Mary dried her tears on her sleeve and called out, "Come in."

Cameron stepped into her chamber, and closed the door behind him. "How are ye, Mary?" He stayed by the door, his back against the solid oak as if he depended on its strength to support him. She knew he didn't. He was well, and nearly as strong as he'd been before being stabbed by a gallowglass mercenary.

"Honestly, I'm no' certain," she said as she walked

toward him. "If only we kenned how this would go...if Da will recover."

"Ye didna ken how my injury would go, or my fevers. Yet ye stayed strong, and helped me to regain my strength. Ye can do the same for yer da."

"Ye were nay my father. I hardly kenned ye at first, and tended ye because of a promise to my youngest sister. Seeing Da like he is now—'tis difficult. Worse, the new Lady Rose has no' bothered to put in an appearance anywhere. With Da. At supper. Naught."

"Did anyone ask for her?"

"Of course. I refused to cover for her, and simply said I didna ken Lady Rose's whereabouts. But her guardsman also missed the meal." Mary assumed her young stepmother was with him. Except for one brief appearance when they first moved Da to his chamber, Seona had avoided spending time with her husband. "If she feels any wifely concern for her husband's health, and after her threat in the buttery, I doubt she ever will, she hides it well."

"Threat? What threat?"

Mary sighed. She needed to tell someone, and if she could not tell her father, Cameron would understand. She repeated the confrontation she, Seona and the guardsman had that afternoon. "Da is so weak, I fear what such news will do to him."

"Ye must tell him, lass. Ye canna treat him like a *wean*. He is still laird, and the bairn isna his. He may choose to claim it, but he deserves to make that decision for himself."

"Ye are right. I wonder what he'll do to that guardsman."

"Have him marched out of Rose's gates?" Cameron offered.

"Throw him in the dungeon?" Mary thought that likely.

"Or hang him from the battlement?"

"Nay!" She would keep her father from doing that. "Ye shouldha seen the lad when he told me his side of it. He does love her, and always has. 'Tis no' his fault her mother made a devil's bargain with her future—and sent him along to witness it. 'Tis awful. For all of us."

Cameron wrapped her in his arms and held her close. "I shouldna be here, but I willna let ye suffer alone, Mary."

She let herself melt against him, needing his care. "If my sisters were here..."

"They'd be in this chamber with ye, and I wouldna dare set foot inside." He grinned at her. "I shouldha told ye this already, but Catherine is with child. Annie, too."

Despite his wonderful news, Mary couldn't find the strength to return his smile. Besides, her mouth still hurt from Dougal's rough treatment. "Ye never said why ye arrived with four Bodies. In truth, with all that has happened, I forgot about them."

"A storm came up, forcing a stop at Brodie. I saw them on the way to ye." He grinned.

"Catherine likes ye. I'm certain Annie did, too. Especially since Catherine surely told her all about the trip from St. Andrews and how ye kept her safe."

"Kenneth did most of that."

"Well, then, ye helped keep them both safe. Ye canna deny it. Catherine told me so. Of course, she also told me how ye flirted with her before ye left St. Andrews. She thought ye'd flirt with any lass."

He brushed her hair back from her face. "I'm no' flirting with ye, lass. I'm in earnest. All of me. And all of me wants to make ye feel better."

He bent his head and took her mouth so gently, the touch of his lips felt exquisite, not painful. Mary's despair lifted. She loved the taste of him, and the feel of his soft lips caressing hers. Her easy acceptance of his kiss always surprised her. She should not allow it, but she could not deny him. She wanted his kisses, and so much more.

He started gently, considerately, but his passion rose with hers and his kiss became more demanding, though still careful of her bruises. She slid her hands up his broad chest and wrapped them behind his neck, using one to pull his head down even more firmly to her. With her other hand, she stroked his neck and throat, then brushed her fingertips down his face.

Cameron groaned, picked her up and carried her to her bed, kissing her the entire way across her chamber.

When he stopped, she slid down his body until her toes touched the floor, surprising her. She suddenly felt so full of energy, she thought she'd float above it, anchored only by where she held onto Cameron, her arms still wrapped around his neck, and where his hands spanned her waist. One of Cameron's hands roved over her back and up to tangle in her hair.

"I want ye, lass. I dinna ken how much control I have left." Then he loosened his hold and stepped back, but didn't let go. "But I came here to comfort ye, no' to ravish ye."

A rush of warmth filled her. "Ye have comforted me." She stilled her caresses on his massive shoulders.

"What do ye need, Mary?"

Being in Cameron's arms made her bold. "Truly? Ye. But this is no' the time." She stepped out of his arms and clasped her hands together to keep from reaching for him. "I..."

He stroked her hair as he told her, "Ye are exhausted, lass, and hurt. Ye should sleep."

"I dinna ken if I can."

"Will it help if I sit with ye?"

As she had spent hours sitting with him while he was ill. "Only sit?"

Cameron pulled the chamber's simple wooden chair next to the bed. "Here. I'll be right in this chair. I'll hold yer hand, or talk, or recite poetry, whatever will soothe ye." He grinned. "But I willna sing ye a lullaby. I fear my voice would keep ye awake the night through."

Mary couldn't help it. Despite her exhaustion, fear, and grief for her father, she laughed. Then winced and lifted a hand to her mouth. "Ye must demonstrate—some other time, aye." She turned to the bed, then back again. "I must undress. Will ye turn away?"

Cameron gave her a wicked grin "I'd rather no'," he teased.

Mary answered his grin with a tired smile, throwing caution to the wind. "Then help me." She turned around. "And undo my laces, please?"

Cameron's voice behind her sounded low and sexy. "With pleasure." He gripped her shoulders, then ran his hands down her arms and slipped them onto her waist.

She fought the urge to lean back into his chest, knowing where that would lead. He made quick work of her laces, and she slipped off her dress, leaving her in her shift. Then she sat and offered him her boot. "Please?"

He gripped it and pulled it and her stocking from her foot, then did the same with the other. But instead of releasing that foot, he stroked it with both hands, then rubbed circles on her sole and across the pad under her toes.

Mary arched back and sighed with pleasure. "Where did ye learn to do that?"

"Ye dinna wish to ken, love," he told her. "Just enjoy it. Lie back and let me help ye go to sleep."

Mary knew she should tell him to stop, tell him to leave her chamber, that it was not proper for him to put her to bed. Her father would be livid. All those objections ran through her mind, then stilled under

Cameron's deft touch. Instead, she obeyed him, sliding back and stretching out on her bed, laying her head on a pillow. Cameron covered her with a sheet and woolen throw, then folded the covers above her ankles and returned to her other foot. He alternated from one foot to the other several times. But when his hands slipped up her calf, even under the covers, she knew it was time to deny him, or they'd never stop. "Cameron," she warned.

"I thought for a moment I'd succeeded in making ye drift off to sleep."

"Ye willna," she told him. "What ye are doing feels so good, I dinna want to miss any of it."

"I can make ye feel even better."

"No' tonight, Cameron. Please."

"Aye, I hear ye." He stood and pulled the covers down over her toes. "I'll leave ye be, as ye wish. Get some rest, Mary, my love." He bent and kissed her forehead.

Mary wondered then if sending him away was a mistake, but nay. Sick Cameron was one thing. Healthy Cameron in full control of his faculties and his body, wanting her, was quite another.

CHAPTER 14

"*H*e was my first love and he gave up on me," Mary complained to her maid as they carried baskets of bedding across the bailey to the laundress to be washed. She had started the conversation explaining the bruises on her face, determined that Cameron not be blamed for Dougal's actions. "He went off and married someone else. If he'd really loved me, he would have fought for me then, instead of trying to force himself on me now. Thank goodness, Cameron saved me from him." She could count on her maid to spread the word.

She just hoped Cameron was the kind of man who, when he found true love, would never give up on it. Or her.

"He was a fool, milady," the maid answered as they entered the laundry. "He's gone and ye must forget him. Cameron Sutherland is a different sort of man."

Dougal and his men had ridden out this morning, without a word to her or, as far as she knew, to anyone else. She was glad to see them gone so easily. Dougal could have made more trouble while he remained. She didn't know if Cameron's threats or her words had convinced him to go. She didn't care. He was gone.

After she had a chance to sleep on her decision to make Cameron leave her chamber, Mary regretted not asking him to stay. She couldn't imagine Dougal in Cameron's place last night, rubbing her feet, treating her so kindly, being solicitous of her welfare, and leaving without argument when she asked. She knew it would never have happened. Dougal lacked Cameron's innate concern for the welfare of others—even people he claimed he cared about. If he had an ounce of compassion in him all those years ago, he would have told her he'd tired of waiting for her, rather than letting her find out from others that he'd gotten betrothed, just not with her.

"A different sort of man?" She was eager to know how others in the clan regarded Cameron Sutherland.

"He came back. He did his duty by his clan and went home, and now he's back. For ye. Do ye fear the clan is waiting for him to leave ye again?"

How did she feel, knowing the clan was watching her relationship with Cameron develop? "When Dougal MacBean was here, who were they rooting for?" She meant it as a jest, but the maid answered seriously.

"Sutherland, of course."

Mary didn't know how to respond. Even after Cameron left, and Dougal was here, the clan had seen which was the better man? How has she been so blind? Cameron was different, and the maid was right. He had returned when he didn't have to. "I'm a fool."

"Nay, Lady Mary," the lass objected. "No' a fool. Just someone who has been hurt before. Ye have a right to wonder."

"Since when did ye become so wise?"

"Since I spent most of my life watching ye and yer sisters try to find yer happiness. Since I found my own. 'Tis never easy, but 'tis worth the struggle and all the doubts in the end. Ye will see. I wish I could say the same for yer poor father."

"What do ye mean?"

"'Tis plain as the nose on yer face. That lass he married is carrying on with one of her guards. Everyone kens it."

"Everyone but Da, I fear."

"Aye, well, 'tis no' my place to say, but I'm thinking he'd want to ken."

Mary pressed her lips together and winced.

The maid nodded in sympathy. She followed Mary out of the building and patted her shoulder. "Now go on with ye. Find that handsome Sutherland of yers." Then she turned back into the laundry.

Mary nodded and started back across the bailey. Out of nowhere, a horse charged right at her. Its hooves thundered on the straw-covered ground, kicking up tufts of dirt and grass. Mary froze for a second, then spun away and ran for the laundry door. Were the stables on fire? Were more horses coming?

It took her a second to realize she heard screaming. The horse had charged through the bailey and been stopped at the closed gates, rearing and screaming in distress.

Men ran toward it and fought to get it under control.

Mary's maid bumped into her as she rushed out the door, attracted by the noise. "What's happening?"

"I dinna ken. That horse nearly ran me down." She pointed to the commotion by the wall.

"My lady! Are ye well?"

"I'm fine," Mary replied. "Just a bit shaken up." She realized silence had descended in the bailey. "At least the men have calmed the beast." Mary left her and walked toward it.

One of the men pulled a sliver of wood the size of a

small blade from the horse's flank. Blood trickled down its hind leg. "From the stall?" the man asked the others with him. The horse shifted and rolled its eyes in distress. One of the stable lads took its head in both hands and talked to it softly, calming it.

"My lady," one of the men said as he noticed her approach. "Are ye well? This beast nearly trampled ye."

"It's injured?"

"Aye. This was stuck in its flank." He held up the triangular sliver of wood. Blood stained both sides of it. "I canna believe he did this to himself. This lad is usually as calm as can be in his stall."

Mary took the piece of wood from him. "Could someone have stabbed him with it?" She turned it over in her hand, then hefted it. Thick enough not to break, it had a point sharp enough for that purpose.

"I suppose so, but why? Who would do such a thing to an animal?"

"Why, indeed," Mary replied and tossed the offending piece of wood aside. "See that the horse gets good care. I dinna want his wound to fester."

"Aye, milady."

The stable lad led the animal away.

Mary watched it go as the others dispersed and her maid joined her.

"Are ye sure ye are well? Ye are pale as milk."

"Aye, I'm well, but puzzled. Who would deliberately harm that horse, and why?"

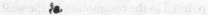

ONE OF THE MAIDS TOLD CAMERON MARY HAD GONE TO the laundry not long before he came downstairs. He decided to find her and interrupt her chores. In a most innocent way, he'd cared for her last night, then spent the rest of the night hard and aching, remembering the feel of her soft skin in his hands and the allure of her moans of pleasure. He wanted more. And he wanted it now.

On his way through the great hall, he heard the healer's voice echo angrily out of the laird's solar. "Ye canna wallow in yer grief, Jamie."

Cameron didn't like the sound of that. He changed direction and headed for the solar. In all the time the healer had cared for him, she'd never raised her voice

"Ye must walk, and move, if ye hope to regain what ye once had," she snapped.

Cameron could not mistake the anguished frustration in her voice. He paused at the doorway, unsure whether to interrupt. Rose sat slumped at his desk, head resting on his good hand, elbow on the flat surface. "'Twill no' help," he grumbled. "'Tis just yer way of torturing me, now ye have an excuse to."

Cameron stepped into the room. "I'm sorry to interrupt, but I overheard what the healer said she wants ye to do. She is right. I have seen it work at Sutherland." He lied, but the grateful smile the healer gave him made the lie worth the stain on his soul. Besides, if it helped James Rose, it would only be a small stain.

"See?" she challenged. "I'm trying to help ye."

"Ye canna."

"*I* will." The words were out before Cameron realized he'd said them. James Rose needed someone to push him, someone who could help him—physically as well as emotionally. He'd leave the man's emotions to the healer and his daughters. "I will walk with ye and help ye strengthen yer weak side," he offered. "I understand ye dinna wish to involve those of yer clan. I'm an outsider. I'm strong enough for ye to lean on when ye must. And I owe Rose my life for what the healer and Mary did for me. I would appreciate if ye would let me do this, to help pay my debt to ye."

The healer nodded. In a moment, so did Rose. "Very well. I'll take ye up on yer offer and we will see whether what she demands will make any difference." He gestured toward the healer.

"It will," Cameron promised. "Ye will get tired of my company, but it will." He glanced at the healer, who nodded again. "Most of the clan are at their chores, and there's nay a soul in the great hall. Come with me now and we'll walk around it. When ye are stronger, we'll walk outside. 'Twill appear as though we are deep in conversation about weighty matters of great importance to Sutherland and Rose."

With her lips pressed together, the healer gave him a grateful, wide-eyed smile, then turned to her laird. "Walk until ye tire," she said, "then use the weak arm to shove some chairs around. Cameron will make sure ye dinna fall. And none of the clan will be any the wiser."

"Hmmmph," Rose snorted, but he got to his feet with a lurching motion that hurt Cameron to see. "Very well. Let's go."

"On his weak side," the healer directed as Cameron approached him. "Only steady him if he needs it. He must do the work."

Cameron nodded and went with Rose toward the hall. Their pace was painfully slow and Cameron knew he'd regret his offer from sheer boredom, but his aggravation would be worth it if he managed to make inroads with the Rose laird. If he found out more about the reason Rose allied with Grant, the information would explain much for Sutherland, but mostly, he hoped to discover something that might help Mary. Such as whether her father knew his bride was unfaithful, and carrying another man's child. It was not his place to tell Rose. Mary would want to break that news. In the meantime, Cameron would support the man the best way he could, and thereby support Mary. He might suffer Rose's ire, but perhaps gain his trust and respect. Mary would approve. He hoped James Rose would soften toward him and the idea of him as a suitable husband for Mary.

MARY STOOD AT THE TOP OF THE STAIRS AS CAMERON kept pace with her father's halting steps away from her. The empty hall told her everything. He'd accepted Cameron's help, rather than from someone in the clan, because he didn't want anyone to see the condition he was in. Something twisted in her chest. Pity for her father? Or even more affection for Cameron. He did not have to do this. Yet there he was, offering a steadying arm when her father wobbled, but leaving him to make his own way as much as he could. Her heart swelled and her eyes moistened with proud tears. She couldn't deny how she felt about Cameron any longer. She wanted him. And by his devotion to her and her father, he showed he wanted her, as well. To prove it, he was willing to do whatever she needed. Unlike Dougal, who still thought poetry and flowers and reminders of what she'd once felt for him were enough.

They weren't. Not even close. Not when she could see the effort Cameron Sutherland made to help her difficult father get better.

"Damn it!" Her father's sudden oath as he tilted toward the side almost made her laugh aloud and she covered her mouth to keep from uttering a sound.

Despite his poor balance, he sounded more energetic uttering those two words than he'd managed in weeks. Whether the walking helped, or having

Cameron beside him in silent support, she didn't know, but something was bringing out some of his old fire. She was thrilled to see it. She only hoped it would continue. As they made the turn onto the far wall, Mary stepped back out of sight. If her father knew he was being observed, it would undo all the good Cameron was trying to do for him. Mary would talk to Cameron later and find out how the rest of their walk had gone. And thank him.

The one person who should be helping Mary's father had kept her distance since he fell ill. Even though she now knew why, Seona's actions made Mary's blood boil. Her father had loved Mary's *maman* so much, he'd stayed faithful to her and avoided remarrying all these years. It broke Mary's heart that the lass he'd finally taken to wife cared so little for him or his clan. Cameron was right. She must stop treating her father like a child and tell him the truth about his lady wife. Then he could deal with her however he saw fit.

CHAPTER 15

*M*ary waited until her father had a chance to rest, then went to his solar and closed the door behind her. "Da? Can we talk?"

"Of course, daughter." He set aside the document he was reading and regarded her across his desk. A cheerful fire danced in the hearth behind him.

He looked tired, but despite his physical challenges, he seemed more content than she'd seen him appear in months. Mary couldn't help but think the time he'd spent with Cameron today had done him a lot of good. She hoped Cameron's patience would last long enough for her father to make real progress.

Assuming the errand that brought her here didn't make him worse.

She sank into one of the chairs nearest his desk and clasped her hands. "I dinna ken where to start."

"The beginning is usually best," he offered.

"In this case, I must go straight to the conclusion." She took a breath, reluctant, yet determined to accord her father the dignity of the truth. "I'm sorry to be the one to tell ye this, but Seona has admitted to me that she and one of her guardsmen are lovers. The child she carries is probably his, no' yers."

Her father nodded and grimaced. "I ken it."

"Already? How?"

"I saw yer *maman* through three of ye, and two more we lost before ye came along. I ken what a breeding woman looks like. Seona was too far along, too quickly. And too friendly with one of the men Mhairi Grant left behind. I confronted her weeks ago."

"Da! I'm so sorry." Mary's throat closed as she fought tears. How had her father borne this secret on his own, all this time, and while faced with his illness? Cameron was right. She'd been treating him like a *wean*, and he never deserved that.

Her father leaned forward, reclaiming her attention. "Besides ye, who else kens this?"

Mary shook her head. "I fear 'tis common knowledge, or commonly rumored. Cameron kens, but he'll keep it to himself. I asked a few trusted servants and friends. The worst of it is that some are starting to feel between yer illness and Seona's lack of discretion, ye have lost control of the clan to her."

He pursed his lips, then flattened his good hand on the desk top. "I'm sorry this day has come. If the clan doubts me, then I must act."

"What will ye do?" Her father was capable of many things, but the fact that he'd accepted Seona's betrayal for the sake of the coming bairn made her think the penalty he contemplated would not be too severe.

"I'll throw the Grants into the dungeon for now."

"Da, ye canna mean to put Seona there, too."

"Nay, I'll confine her to her chamber, with a Rose guard on her door, and have the healer check on her every day. 'Tis no' unusual for a woman to spend her confinement in that way. Once the bairn comes, I'll decide what else is required."

Mary's heart lifted at the sudden strength in his tone.

He bent his head, then looked up again. "If ye'd do me the kindness of sending my arms master to me, I'll see this done before the rumors spread any further. And *dinna fash*, lass. I am still laird here."

❦

AFTER A FORTNIGHT OF WORKING WITH JAMES ROSE AND watching his condition slowly improve, Cameron's respect for the man had grown. He'd acted decisively to confine the Grants, separating his bride from her lover and pulling the teeth of any Grant guard who might be inclined to cause trouble. There was nothing they could do from the dungeon. He'd withstood Seona's curses and tears until she finally quieted down and settled into her confinement. Mary said she finally had the solitude she treasured, so she should be happy for now.

Rose had regained some of the use of his limbs, and when not consulting with Laird Sutherland's representative, as he called his time walking with Cameron, he had resumed spending most of the day at the desk in his solar. He wasn't yet able to ride out to inspect his territory. Cameron presumed he kept watch over the clan via the ledgers he kept on the clan's expenditures and earnings, and via any correspondence that reached him. Mary and Cameron had agreed his mind was still as sharp as a blade and his temperament as prickly as a thistle. His illness had done little to affect who he was, only what he could physically do.

With Rose firmly in control, despite his physical afflictions, Cameron deemed the time was right to approach the man again about the betrothal—and marriage—he hoped for. Cameron waited until after a meal, hoping a full belly would make Rose mellow and more amenable to listening.

Rose greeted him civilly enough after he knocked on the solar's door. "What brings ye, Sutherland?"

Cameron bowed his head, then met the laird's gaze. "I am glad to see ye so much improved," he began. His tension eased a bit when Rose nodded.

"I am, and I owe much of my improvement to yer efforts."

"I have done only what anyone else would have done if called upon to help ye."

"Nonetheless, I am grateful."

"I hope ye are well enough, then, to discuss Sutherland's betrothal offer." Cameron wouldn't presume on Rose's gratitude when it came to this subject. But he was ready to discuss the offer on its own merits.

Rose's mouth thinned, making Cameron's pulse spike and his muscles tense again. Still, Rose hadn't stopped him or yet said nay, so he kept going. "I love yer daughter, Mary, and I wish to wed her. Laird Sutherland has approved the match and looks forward to a lengthy alliance with clan Rose."

"He does, does he?" Rose leaned back in his chair, his gaze on the far wall.

The desk was too cluttered for Cameron to spot the betrothal agreement he'd given Rose over a fortnight ago. It must be buried under other documents. Cameron hoped Rose had at least read it and not simply let it disappear under a pile of other parchments. Or worse. Cameron glanced at the small fire dancing in the hearth behind Rose. His stomach sank as he noticed the remnants of several burned documents, still blackening and succumbing to the flames. Rose burning the betrothal agreement would be much more damning than Rose simply losing it on his chaotic desk. Cameron couldn't help wondering which was more likely.

"And what's in it for Sutherland?" Rose asked. "I am no' in any way capable of defending Sutherland right now, should yer laird call upon me to do so. After our losses at Harlaw in July, and with Grants in my dungeon, I havena the men to divert from protecting Rose from the usual troublemakers, much less the remnants of Domnhall's army."

"Ah, but in the future, ye will be stronger, and in the meantime, Sutherland can offer ye protection from... anyone...whose intentions toward Rose ye dinna approve." He'd almost mentioned Grant, but bit back the word before it escaped his lips. If James Rose didn't know what Mhairi Grant was up to, he was a fool. And it wouldn't help Cameron's suit to point that out to him. Besides, Cameron didn't think he was a fool at all. So he made his comment as generic as he could and hoped the Rose laird would not take offense. Grant didn't pose the only danger Rose might face, but was certainly the one of greatest proximity. And Grant guardsmen remained in the dungeon until Rose decided to send them back to Grant.

Rose regarded Cameron. "I heard the MacBean lad was hanging around hoping to offer for her, too. I held him off once. I've a mind to do it again, but I've yet to see him."

Cameron liked the sound of that, even if it didn't matter, since Mary had tossed Dougal out weeks ago.

"So tell me," Rose continued, "in this bright future ye hope for, ye see yerself as Mary's husband and consort to Rose's future laird."

Cameron heard it as more of a statement than a question and shook his head. "Honestly, I'd rather no'. Both of us would be pleased to see a son born to Rose— several of them, in fact. Being laird, or consort of a laird, is naught I've ever aspired to. I have older brothers to spare me from that. But for Mary, should she be called upon to become laird, I will gladly take on whatever responsibility she chooses to give me."

Rose inclined his head. "Words are easy. Deeds another matter entirely."

"I pay my debts," Cameron replied, rising to the challenge in Rose's words and tone, "and I take seriously what I owe Rose."

"So yer devotion to my daughter is simply a means to pay yer debt?"

"Nay." Cameron shook his head. "I didna mean that at all. I love her and would be pleased to take her to Sutherland and live there in peace. But I will remain at Rose with her if that is what she must do. We ask for yer approval."

"I must think more on this. Both her sisters were squandered to Brodie over my objections. I must make the best possible match with Mary."

"Sutherland is…"

"Powerful and all that, aye. I ken it. I must consider further."

Cameron's temper nearly got the best of him, but he held it in check, nodded and left.

❧

CAMERON STORMED INTO THE GREAT HALL, HIS expression fierce. He looked ready to spit fire, and coming as he had from the laird's solar, Mary could guess why, or at least who had put him in such a foul mood. "What's amiss?" she asked when she reached him.

He took her hand and pulled her into an empty chamber without saying a word, then closed the door.

Her heart beat faster, wondering what he had in mind.

"This is getting us nowhere," he told her. "Yer da

may be no more serious about ever letting ye wed than he was about Dougal."

"I ken it. Wondering what he intends to do keeps me awake at night."

"Would ye no' rather I kept ye awake?" Cameron's voice turned from irritated to husky and low. "If we handfast, 'twill unite us in a way we already ken yer father will have to accept."

"Even if he hates the idea."

"Do ye no' want to give Sutherland a stake in protecting Rose from whatever Lady Grant has planned?"

Mary nodded.

"So then, about our handfasting?"

"Cameron, are ye certain 'tis what ye want?"

He took her face in his hands. "Now is nay time for doubts. Ye ken what I want. *Ye.* Ye are what I want."

"But no' as consort to the laird."

"I never looked for the responsibility that comes with being a laird—or even married to one—but if ye become Laird Rose, I will stand by ye."

"Neither of us wants that to come to pass." But if it did, with Cameron at her side, she could handle it.

"Nay, we dinna."

"If we wait for Da's approval, we could be waiting forever." Mary knew that was likely. She also knew Cameron was not like Dougal MacBean, whose first thought was always for himself. "We must do this on our own."

"Verra well, then." Cameron stripped the Sutherland plaid from over his shoulder.

When he reached for her hand, Mary realized he meant to do this right now. "Should we have someone do this for us? Or be a witness?"

"Who would ye trust, lass?"

Mary considered. "The healer. Only her. Others might mean well, but they will talk."

"Then fetch her. Meet me in the wee kirk."

Mary's heart lifted, nearly making her float across the floor. As usual, Cameron had said just the right thing.

Mary didn't tell the healer why she wanted her company, but merely led her to the kirk. If Cameron wasn't there when they arrived, or failed to show up soon after, Mary could tell her she was worried about her father and wished for the woman to pray with her. If Cameron let her down after suggesting this, likely she'd fall to her knees before the altar anyway. So, it made sense. But, her heart told her he would not fail her.

Cameron was there, waiting, when they entered.

"Ye found her," he greeted Mary and kissed her cheek.

"What's going on?" the healer demanded.

"We are going to handfast," Mary told her, excitement bubbling along her veins now that they were here. "In secret for now. I dinna wish to make Da's condition worse..."

"And we need a witness," Cameron added.

The healer smiled. "I'm honored ye chose me. But I willna witness for ye."

Mary's heart sank. "Ye willna?"

"Nay. Well, I will, but ye need someone to conduct the handfasting, aye? I will do it."

"We can do it ourselves," Cameron objected.

"I dinna want ye in trouble with Da," Mary added.

The healer snorted. "He'll do nothing to me, no' if he wants to keep what fragile health he has left. Now, have ye what's required?"

Cameron pulled the length of Sutherland plaid from his shoulder and offered it to her.

"Excellent. Give me yer hand, if ye please."

Cameron let her tie the plaid around his wrist, then the healer reached for Mary's.

Mary's heart beat faster.

"This is as sacred as marriage by a priest, especially when done here in the Rose kirk. Ye are bound to each other."

She paused and looked from Cameron to Mary, meeting their gazes with a proud certainty that made Mary want to weep, or laugh. The emotions were so strong in her eyes, Mary couldn't contain her own.

"The custom says for a year and a day, but I've watched the two of ye for months. This is for the rest of yer lives."

Mary felt Cameron's gaze on her. Was he still worried she might refuse? She smiled at him and nodded.

"May yer lives be long and happy, with love, and bairns, and always, with each other." The healer concluded by wrapping both their wrists together with the rest of the plaid.

"Thank ye," Cameron told her, then cleared his throat.

Mary could see a sheen of wetness in his eyes. So her strong warrior could be brought to tears as well.

"Do ye have anything ye wish to say?"

Cameron nodded and turned his gaze to Mary, then placed his hand over their joined ones. "I love ye, Mary Elizabeth Rose. I will be true to ye all the days of my life. And nights." He grinned. "Ye saved my life...with help," he added with a nod to the healer, "and became the one person I want to spend the rest of my life with. Ye mean the world to me, lass."

Mary thought her heart would burst, it had swelled so with the emotions coursing through her. "I love ye, too, Cameron Sutherland. I will be true to ye. As much as I saved ye, ye have saved me. I'm proud to be yer bride. Even if we canna tell anyone yet."

"Kiss her lad, before I start crying," the healer sniffled, "and canna see ye do it."

Cameron's gaze never left Mary's face. He leaned in until his breath warmed her cheek, and the anticipation of his lips touching hers nearly had her dancing. His molten amber eyes stayed focused on hers, as if he tried to see inside her, to her soul.

"Aye, Mary, my love, this is real. With this kiss, ye are mine, and I am yers. For a year and a day, and I hope for the rest of our lives."

She could only nod, mesmerized. Then his lips brushed hers, lightly at first, then more firmly as she rose to meet them. When her cheeks dampened with happy tears, Cameron kissed them away. He captured her glad cry in his mouth and gave back a moan that reached Mary's toes and made them curl. Too soon, they broke apart, panting. "We did this!" Mary exclaimed.

"And about time," the healer said, fanning herself. "Ye two wouldna lasted another day, or I miss my guess."

Suddenly, everything changed. Mary was no longer her father's dutiful daughter. She was Cameron Sutherland's handfasted wife. Even if only for a year and a day, she was free of all the things that had bound her to Rose, all except duty. But she could bear that for a while longer if at the end, she got Cameron.

CHAPTER 16

*C*ameron waited impatiently while the healer unbound their wrists, gave them her good wishes, and departed. Finally, he and Mary were alone. Blessedly alone. He closed the kirk's door and turned back to her. She stood, hands clasped before her, a pensive expression on her face.

"Ach, Mary, love, ye are no' afraid of me, are ye?" The thought made his chest ache.

"What? Nay. I just—dinna ken what to do next."

Cameron chuckled in relief and moved toward her. *"Dinna fash."* He cocked an eyebrow. "I do."

She took a step back, then straightened her shoulders and held her ground.

"There's my Mary. Strong and resolute. I love that about ye, ye ken. And I willna hurt ye. If ye tell me nay, I will stop. I promise ye that."

"That's a pretty open-ended promise, Cameron Sutherland. What if I told ye to stop where ye are right now?"

Her tone was teasing, so Cameron played along and froze in mid-step. He didn't want to remain separated from Mary by more than the span of his reach, but he had made a promise, and if he meant to gain her trust,

187

he must stand by it. Even if it meant feeling foolish, standing as awkwardly as this, for as long as she wished. "Then I will stop, as ye see. But I would hope ye would soon change yer mind and allow me to move. I want to hold ye, lass."

"Then do so. I want ye to hold me, too."

Cameron gave her a reassuring smile, stepped forward and folded her in his arms. "Ye feel so good, Mary, my love," he told her, running a hand up and down her back, soothing her. "But the kirk is no place for what I want to do next. Let's go to yer chamber."

"Our chamber," she corrected.

They walked arm in arm back across the bailey and into the keep. Despite her wish for secrecy, apparently Mary had decided she didn't care who saw them. Once inside their chamber, Cameron barred the door and turned back to her.

She sighed and rested her head on his shoulder. "I canna think of another place I'd rather be," she admitted. "I've wanted yer touch for so long..."

Cameron inhaled air redolent with Mary's sweet scent, her body heat, and the banked fire in her chamber's hearth. He planned to stir her to life as he would that fire—and very soon. "Then ye shall have my touch," he promised, cupping her head. "And my kiss, and my love for as long as I live."

"Handfasting is only for a year and a day."

"I told ye once there was a kirk in our future. I meant it. Unless at the end of our year and a day ye wish to leave me, we will never part. I will never leave ye, Mary. I canna imagine my life without ye in it, now ye are mine."

"Then kiss me, Cameron. Make me yers in all ways."

"Are ye certain lass? We can wait. If I get ye with child..."

"Then what ye promised will come to pass, and we will be together always. I want that, too."

Cameron didn't need to be told twice. He kissed her, gently at first, but then she nipped his lip, her teeth firm but short of drawing blood, so he deepened the kiss. Her mouth opened to him, and her tongue met his thrust for thrust, soft moans sending thrills of need straight to his cock. Cameron couldn't help but groan when she pressed her breasts firmly against his chest. "Mary, my love, how I want ye."

In answer, her hands slid between them and fumbled with his belt. He eased back and let her unbuckle it. The metal clinked when it hit the floor.

"Undo my laces," she ordered, twisting around so he could reach the ties.

He made quick work of them, surprised when she stepped away, but gratified when she slid her dress from her shoulders and down her arms. Finally, she stood in her shift and slippers, gazing at him.

"Do ye need my help?" she asked.

He realized she waited for him to undress, too. The expression on her face told Cameron she recalled the many times she had helped him dress—or undress—while he was ill. And that bath... "Nay, lass. This time, ye only need watch." He kicked off his boots and freed the remaining yards of fabric clinging to his waist, pressed into place there by the belt. In moments, he stood before her, clad only in his shirt, his erection tenting the front, making his need for her as plain as any man could make it.

But Mary wasn't done. With her gaze on his lower half, she untied the ribbon at the neck of her shift and let it slip down her body, leaving her nude.

Cameron's cock jumped and beaded. She was the most beautiful woman he'd ever seen, and she was his.

And soon would be his bride in truth. He pulled his shirt over his head.

Mary's gaze went to the scar on his side, then flicked away.

"Ye needna concern yerself with that," he reminded her. "'Tis well healed."

When Mary's guilty smile lit her face, he moved to her, picked her up and placed her gently in the middle of the bed, her soft laughter urging him on.

"What are ye going to do?" she asked as he leaned over her.

"Make love to my bride," he replied and kissed her mouth, then moved to her ear, her neck, and her chest before licking and suckling each rosy nipple. Mary tangled her fingers in his hair, then tried to pull him back when he started moving lower. He kept going, kissing his way down her ribs and belly. He traced her inner thighs, then parted her intimate folds with one finger and stroked her until she writhed under his hand.

"Ach, Cam…"

"Aye, Mary, my love," he whispered and replaced his finger with his tongue. Her hips lifted and she cried out, but he didn't stop. She tasted so sweet, he couldn't get enough. All too soon, she shuddered, her release making her body quake under his mouth. He'd never felt anything so exquisite. His body was primed and rock hard, ready to take her, but he waited for her breathing to steady, then asked again. "We can stop now, lass, if ye wish. I will wait for ye."

"Ach, Cameron, I am ready. I want ye as much as ye want me. Now is nay time to think of waiting."

Cameron moved over her and found her slippery warm entrance with the head of his erection. "I will take this slow," he promised. "I willna hurt ye any more than I must."

"I ken it. Make me yers."

Cameron pushed into her welcome heat slowly, until he met the barrier of her maidenhead.

"Dinna wait," Mary breathed.

He pushed through and stilled when she gasped, but after a moment, she nodded.

"It has stopped. I'm ready," she said.

Cam penetrated further, then further still before pulling back.

Mary clenched around him and cried out.

"*Dinna fash*, lass. I'm no' going anywhere." He eased back in and out again until her body adjusted to his. Then he took his pleasure, carrying Mary with him to the heights he'd dreamed of finding with her.

❧

MARY SNUGGLED INTO CAMERON'S SIDE, HER HEAD ON his shoulder where she could watch his broad chest rise and fall with his breath. Her hand lay across his flat belly, just above his manhood, even now firming and filling out under her gaze, readying him to make love to her again. Like the rest of him, it was large. Long and thick and more than she thought could fit within her. Yet it did, and Cameron used it to bring about a marvelous result—for her and for himself.

They were wed.

She couldn't believe this day had finally arrived. She was a maiden no longer. A woman. A wife. With a man who loved her and wanted to make love with her. Who enjoyed seeing her body, touching her, tasting her.

Being loved by Cameron was more than she'd imagined, more than she'd ever understood being with a man could be. The physical part was wonderful, but no more so than the feelings he brought about within her—longing, but also comfort and joy. During his convalescence, he'd become her friend. Now he was her husband, and she felt stronger and safer with him by her side.

Instead of reaching for his manhood as she'd first been tempted to do, she let her thoughts lead her actions. She cupped Cameron's face with a trembling hand and gazed up into his eyes.

He met her gaze and held it, smiling, then traced a finger down her cheek. "If I'm dreaming, dinna wake me," he told her. "I've got the most beautiful, the most wonderful lass in the world in my arms."

"And I the bravest and handsomest man in Scotland. So dinna wake me, either. Today is a day I thought would never come."

"'Tis only because ye were waiting for me and didna ken it," he boasted with a grin as he rolled on top of her and supported his weight on his elbows.

Mary grinned back and wrapped her arms around his shoulders. "If only I'd kenned it, I wouldna spent so much time in worry."

"Ye were never going to be alone, lass. Had I no' found ye, some other lucky man would."

That made her frown. "I dinna want some other man, Cameron Sutherland. I've got ye, and I mean to keep ye."

"I'm glad to hear that, lass. 'Tis exactly what I want, too."

Mary arched her back so the tips of her breasts brushed Cameron's chest. "Is that all ye want?" she teased.

"Ye ken I want all of ye." He swooped down and took her mouth in a plundering kiss that set her body to humming again.

She spread her legs and wrapped them around the backs of his. "Nor is it all I want, husband," she goaded, tilting her hips to stroke his hardness against her thighs.

"Ye plan to drive me mad, do ye?"

"I do. Is it working?"

"Aye!" he exclaimed and shifted to enter her in one swift thrust.

Aye, Mary thought as she lifted her hips to match Cameron's rhythm. She'd happily go mad right along with this man.

※

A FEW DAYS LATER, MARY TOOK THREE OF THE YOUNGER lasses into the forest to show them her favorite spots for gathering herbs and berries. Since she and Cameron were now wedded, she would eventually leave. Someone needed to know what she knew about the useful plants in the area. Seona was in confinement, and if the child she carried was not her father's, Seona might not be Lady Rose for long. At least the younger lasses would learn and remember.

Mary bent to point out a well-hidden clump of coughwort in a damp depression when an arrow whizzed over her head and buried itself in a nearby tree with a solid thunk. She whirled, looking for signs of the hunter who'd let fly at a target he couldn't see and called out, "Stop shooting!"

She saw the next arrow coming as the words left her mouth. Shock held her immobile for a moment, then she fell to her knees shouting, "Get down!" The arrow buried itself in the tree at head height with another resounding *thunk*. The lass nearest her ran behind a bush. She couldn't see the other two and hoped they'd run away, back to the keep. "There are lasses here," she called again, fury and fear strengthening her voice. "Dinna shoot!"

Mary crawled to the lass still with her. "Come on, Lilias." She tugged and the lass got to her knees. Bent low, Mary led her deeper into the woods, then paused behind a clump of trees.

"I want to go back to the keep," Lilias whined, her voice trembling with fear.

"*Wheesht,*" Mary warned. "I'm trying to hear if anyone is still out there. If they move clumsily through the woods, we'll hear them."

"They shot at ye, no' at me. Let me go."

Mary hushed her with a wave of her hand and whispered, "'Tis no' safe." Then the import of the lass's words hit her. Had those arrows been meant for her?

"Kara and Fiona have gone," Lilias argued. "We can, too." The lass got to her feet.

"Ye wee fool!" Mary grabbed at her hand, but she slipped away, running from tree to tree in the general direction of the keep. At least she had sense enough to keep to some cover, but Mary feared the shooter would hear her. She quickly scanned the woods, seeing nothing but trees and bracken, shrubs and more trees, so she headed away from the route Lilias had taken, making as much noise as she could to draw the archer to her and away from the lass. "If ye want me, I'm here," she called as she ducked behind yet another tree. After a few minutes, she realized how quiet it had become. She was alone.

Mary couldn't blame the lasses for leaving her, though she still feared they'd made targets of themselves. But she hadn't heard any more arrows hitting trees, nor had she heard the anyone moving about. Perhaps her shout had made the archer realize the movement he saw through the trees wasn't a deer or a boar or whatever he hunted, and chastened, he'd moved on.

She didn't want to be alone out here, but she waited

a while longer, ears straining for any sound. If Lilias was right and someone had been shooting at her, if they meant to kill her rather than simply frighten her, they could come at her with a knife, too. The only sounds she heard were the wind and birdcalls. Finally, she slowly stood, fear making her breath come fast and shallow. Nothing happened for a moment. Then she heard hoof beats pounding through the woods and the distant sound of her name. At least one of the lasses must have reached the keep. Men were searching for her!

"I'm here!"

In moments, a horse and rider burst through the trees.

"Mary!"

Mary's heart lifted to see Cameron riding to her rescue. "How did ye ken?"

"Two lasses ran screaming into the keep." He jumped down and pulled her into his arms. "I passed a third and she pointed the way, but ye had moved. It took a few minutes to find ye."

More Rose warriors pounded up then.

"Fan out and search the woods," he told them. Then he lifted Mary onto his mount and threw himself up behind her.

"Cameron, your wound…"

"'Tis fine," he growled as he tucked her against him and spurred the horse into a gallop back toward the keep. They ducked branches until they broke into the open. Cameron folded himself over her, shielding her body while they raced for the gate. They burst through it before he reined in. People in the bailey scattered out of the way as the horse's hooves bit into the ground, throwing clumps of dirt and grass as it stopped.

Cameron swung down and reached up for Mary. "I can get down," she told him. He didn't listen. His hands went around her waist and hauled her against him before she could move. "God, lass, when they said ye'd nearly been shot, I thought I'd die. When they said they'd left ye behind, I thought I'd kill someone. I had to come for ye. I dinna want to let ye out of my sight ever again."

Mary melted against him and smiled. "I'm well enough, except for being thrown onto a horse, then lashed by branches and hauled off the horse again. How is yer side?"

"I canna feel a thing save ye in my arms. Come, let's get ye indoors, then I should join the search for the archer."

Mary nodded, reaction finally setting in. She was glad Cameron kept an arm around her waist. She was sure only his assistance kept her on her feet.

In her chamber, she made Cameron strip off his shirt and she inspected his scar. "Thank the saints, ye didna tear it open," she informed him.

"'Tis fine, Mary, my love. Healed and strong. Forget it."

"How can I? The healer wouldha skewered ye if ye had reinjured yerself. Then I wouldha finished the job." She placed a hand over it, as if to warm it with the heat of her palm. If only she could have healed him with her touch, he would not have suffered for so long.

Cameron groaned. "Ye could try, but if ye mean to kill me, I'd rather die another way."

"Aye? What way? So the next time ye try such a fool stunt, I'll see if I can arrange it."

"Ach, ye can. *Only ye* can. I wish to die of loving ye, in yer arms, a hundred years from now."

Mary crossed her arms and arched her eyebrows. "I see. It appears I have my work cut out for me." She looked him up and down, taking her time about it. Then she grinned. "Perhaps I should get started now?"

"I must go…"

"Ye must stay with yer poor frightened wife. There are men aplenty searching those woods. If they find the hunter, ye can deal with him later."

"We need to ken why someone was shooting at ye," he objected.

She put a hand on Cameron's chest and pushed him toward the bed. "*If* someone was, ye mean. They stopped after I called out."

He lifted his eyebrows and nodded. "Perhaps 'twas only a careless hunter."

She wasn't convinced he believed her, but right now, she didn't care. She had something else on her mind. When they reached the bed, she shoved harder. He fell back and she fell onto him. "A hundred years sounds about right to me," she told him and covered his mouth with hers.

Mary didn't know if it was because they'd handfasted, or a reaction to her near misses with an arrow, but she felt utterly free and daring, ready to do anything at all. To be anything at all. Especially to be Cameron's wife—and lover. He would not leave her now that she had her hands on him. She would not allow it.

Throwing her inhibitions to the devil, she kissed her way down Cameron's throat, then bit his collarbone. His groan of pleasure spurred her on and she moved down his body, kissing and nipping and licking her way down his chest and belly. When she reached the waist of his breeks, she glanced up and found him watching her. She couldn't resist teasing him. "Wondering what I'll do?" She went to work on the ties. When Cameron tried to help her, she pushed his hands away. "Be still, husband."

Cameron grinned and rested his head on his hands. With his elbows out, his broad chest looked impossibly broader, his normally flat nipples dark and tight above the corded bands of muscle defining his abdomen.

A trail of dark hair led her gaze down his belly. She was tempted to trace the rippled muscles with her tongue while she ran her fingers over his muscular chest, but decided she'd rather torture him where she was. A wealth of hard, heavy male flesh waited for her here, too. She pulled the fabric aside and Cameron's hips lifted in reflex, offering himself to her.

She grasped him in one hand, earning a groan that arrowed straight between her legs. He was fully erect, and she inhaled the musky warm scent of him. Not satisfied with using just one sense, she decided to taste and touched her tongue to his tip. Cameron cried out and reached for her. Mary took the hint and took him in her mouth, savoring the silky hot feel of him. He tasted of salt and musk, all Cameron, and she couldn't get enough. She licked her way down his length, enjoying the sounds her husband made with each stroke of her tongue, before he pulled her atop him.

"I'll finish too quickly if ye keep doing that," he panted. "And I want to be inside ye. I need ye, Mary, my love. I feared I'd lost ye."

Her heart filled her chest. "I need ye, too, Cameron." She rucked up her skirts and lifted herself over him, then slowly slid lower, taking him into her body while she watched his eyes glaze over. She loved the look of rapture on his face, reflecting the pleasure he felt. The pleasure she gave him. She would never tire of looking at him while they made love. And never tire of pleasing him this way.

Cameron gripped her hips, lifting and lowering her.

She quickly caught the rhythm and took over, putting her hands on his shoulders, silently telling him she had taken control. He was so big and so strong, she liked having such power over him. And most wondrous of all, he was hers. No matter what happened in the future at Rose, he would be by her side. She could face anything with him.

When they were done, Cameron wrapped her in his arms. "I meant what I said. I feared I'd lost ye today. Dinna ever scare me like that again."

"I didna mean to."

"I ken it. Ye never saw who shot at ye?"

"Nay. The first arrow came out of nowhere. I'd just bent down to show a plant to one of the lasses when I heard a thunk in the tree above me. I saw the second coming and dropped to the ground."

She felt Cameron tense then heave a breath. "So close. God's bones, Mary."

"Well, they missed."

"'Twould be simple to think Lady Grant was behind this through her daughter or one of the guardsmen she left behind, but they're all confined."

Mary frowned. "Could Dougal have remained nearby? He was certainly angry at being refused."

"Dougal? Nay. I can see him shooting at me, but no' at ye." He thought for a moment. "I have to wonder if Domnhall ordered it. He could anticipate that without ye and without another heir, yer father would be too weak to hold Rose. If Domnhall has designs on expanding Ross territory east along the Moray firth, Rose is the first territory he would need to control."

"Da willna let that happen."

"Yer father is in no shape to fight the Lord of the Isles, even with Brodie to back him, which they must, as they'd be the next to fall."

"'Tis a good thing for Rose, then, that Sutherland is also allied with us."

"It would be, if Laird Sutherland kenned it, aye." Cameron was glad he'd wed her, even if his clan didn't know about it yet. He'd write a letter to his father

199

today, informing him. And he'd protect Mary. If someone really meant to kill his bride, he'd find out who and put a stop to the threat. He was stronger than he'd been in months, and would keep getting stronger. Sparring was good training, but lacked the urgency that a true battle demanded. His wild ride today to find Mary and get her safe inside Rose's walls had done no harm. He could train harder.

CHAPTER 17

Cameron knew the stable lad had cared for his horse after he'd rescued Mary, but once he'd reassured himself she was well, and left her sleeping, he went to the stable. He enjoyed brushing down his mount after a brisk ride. The back stall was out of the way and quiet, the silence broken only by the rasp of the brush over the stallion's coat and the soft shuffling noises of the other horses in the stable.

Being here, doing this mundane but necessary task, seemed like a respite from the illness, shock over today's events, and the general sadness permeating the Rose keep. The laird's condition and his wife's betrayal had everyone on edge. The searchers had not found the person who'd shot at Mary. Not knowing whether the arrow was a stray or deliberate, and not knowing who let it fly, kept his nerves on edge.

Horses were simple creatures. Treat them well, and they returned the favor. Be calm around them and they remained calm. He used their quiet presence and his task to further calm his own anxieties.

When voices intruded into his solitude, he tensed and stilled.

"...failed...take care...soon."

The voices were coming from outside the stable walls. He didn't recognize the speakers, and strained to hear more.

"...too difficult."

"...change our plan..."

Cameron edged closer to the outside wall, but could only pick out a few words. He never heard a gender mentioned, or what the two were planning, but he heard enough to put him on guard. Something hadn't worked and they were plotting something new. Were they talking about James Rose or Mary? Were they getting desperate? If so, they might be sloppy enough to give themselves away.

He moved to the stable entrance, intending to identify and confront them. If they were responsible for the attack on Mary, he'd take them before Laird Rose immediately. But they'd moved away and blended in with the other people in the bailey. He had no answer, only an ambiguous bit of overheard conversation. With only that, he couldn't prove a thing.

%

"FIRE!" TWO LADS RUSHED INTO THE GREAT HALL, disturbing the evening meal.

Panicked shouts filled the hall as everyone leapt to their feet. Before Mary had a chance to speak, Cameron demanded, "Where?"

"The blacksmith's shed, but the wind is blowing cinders toward the stable," one of the lads reported.

The men ran for the door, while the women went to fetch buckets and pots—anything that would hold water.

Cameron wasted no time. "We've got to put out the fire before it panics the horses."

His longer legs gave him the advantage and forced Mary to follow him outside. She gasped when she saw smoke billowing from the blacksmith's shed. Sparks flew upwards from it, then skidded sideways as the wind caught them above the reach of the outer walls.

Cameron quickly organized the clan. "Ye lads get the horses out of the stable and move them to the other side of the keep, upwind of the fire. They'll calm if they canna smell it so strongly."

Three lads ran to do his bidding while Cameron got men and women lined up and passing containers of water along the line from the well. Then he ran to the head of the line. Mary stayed with him, on his heels. She handed him the next full bucket that came up the line and he tossed water on the flames.

"We risk cracking the forge," she shouted over the roar of the flames.

"I ken it, but we must get this fire under control." Cameron and others tossed more water, dropping each bucket for a lad to carry back to the end of the line to be refilled. When the fire was out and the blacksmith's anvil sat steaming, Mary called for the blacksmith.

"He's gone to visit his daughter until tomorrow," someone shouted.

"Then who is responsible for this?" Cameron demanded.

Mary spotted the blacksmith's apprentice in the back of the crowd. "There he is." She marched over to the lad, Cameron following her. "Where were ye when this fire started?"

The lad shook his head. "I only stepped away for a few minutes. I was on my way back, but the fire..."

"Ye could have burned out the keep and all the people and animals within it," Mary scolded. The lad glared at her and Mary didn't like the glint in his eye. Did the prospect of such suffering excite him? Annie had tangled with this lad about his treatment of the stable cats and mongrel dogs before she left Rose to marry Iain. Mary had hoped he'd grown out of such cruelty by now. Perhaps he had. Not *out* of it, but *beyond* it, to a larger scale.

Cameron spoke up then. "Ye'll get this cleaned up and repair anything that needs it before the smith returns tomorrow."

"And when he does return," Mary added, "ye will apologize to him before the entire clan for the damage. Right now, ye can apologize to the stable master for terrorizing the horses and to everyone who had to fight this fire for the fear and dismay ye have caused tonight."

The lad looked ready to argue. Mary raised a hand. "Ye will do as we bid ye," Mary said, silencing any objection the lad meant to make.

He lowered his head and muttered, "I'm sorry."

"Now go," she ordered. "Ye have much to do, even if ye have to work all night and all day tomorrow. Perhaps then ye will take more care with yer responsibilities."

The lad glared at Cameron, but he turned away and started pulling down the burned sections of the blacksmith's shed.

Mary caught Cameron's gaze and nodded. The punishment fit the crime.

Cameron took her arm. They went down the line, thanking everyone for their quick action and praising each person individually. As Mary spoke to them, she kept some of her attention on Cameron. For someone who professed no desire to be a laird, he certainly had the skills of a good one. Did he realize how well suited he was to lead the clan with her?

MARY DIDN'T KNOW WHO TOLD HER FATHER ABOUT Cameron spending the night with her, but he'd found out and was understandably furious.

"As soon as I can again wield a sword, I'll kill him," her father threatened.

"Ye will do no' such thing," Mary responded archly. "We are handfasted."

"Handfasted? Ye went behind my back, like yer sisters?"

"And for the same reason, Da. Ye willna kill my husband, a son of the powerful Sutherland clan. Ye may be ill, but ye are no' *tetched*. Ye should be glad to have Sutherland allied with Rose."

"I am *tetched*," her father snarled. "After raising ye three daughters, 'twill be a miracle if I have the wherewithal left in me to raise my son."

"If ye have a son," Mary muttered under her breath. "Nonetheless," she continued, loud enough for her father to hear her, "Cameron Sutherland is now part of the family for at least a year and a day. And if I get with child, forever. Besides, ye wouldha been proud of the way Cameron got the clan together to fight the fire in the blacksmith's shed. The wind blew sparks toward the stable. Thanks to him, all the horses were saved, and most of the blacksmith's tools, as well. Ye did ken about the fire, aye?"

"I did." He grimaced. "No' that I could do anything about it."

"The apprentice left the forge unattended. Cameron and I set him to cleaning up the mess he'd made before the blacksmith returns. The lad will no' soon shirk his duties again."

Her father nodded. "That was well done."

"Da, a wife's place is with her husband, and a husband's with his wife."

Mary fought the temptation to tell him about the attempt on her life—if that was truly what had happened. It could have been an accident. She hoped it was. The archer had never been found, and the arrows he left behind told them nothing about who made them. She didn't want to make her father's condition any worse by giving him something else to worry over. "I am happy with Cameron, but ye ken I willna leave ye yet."

Her father nodded and seemed resigned. At least he made no more objections. Mary would have to be satisfied with that.

Someone knocked on the door. A messenger entered without waiting for permission. "I bring news from yer daughter Catherine at Brodie," the man announced.

Mary's heart beat faster. If it was good news, it could be only one thing, but if bad, well, she could only hold her breath until her father gave the man his attention.

Once Laird Rose nodded, the man cleared his throat. "Yer daughter Mary Catherine bids ye ken she and Kenneth Brodie will wed in a fortnight in the Brodie Kirk," the man continued. "She requests the honor of her father's presence and the presence of her eldest sister, Mary Elizabeth, and Cameron Sutherland, a friend of both the bride and groom, among others of Clan Rose, to witness the nuptials. She advises that Mary Anne Brodie will stand in for Laird Rose if he is unable to…"

"Nay!"

Mary jumped at her father's outburst. "Nay? What do ye mean, nay?"

"Just what I said. Nay." He turned his scowl on the messenger. "Get ye back to Brodie and tell them we willna attend. I dinna give my permission for this marriage to take place."

"Da! Catherine is with child. She no longer needs yer approval."

"*Wheesht*, lass. I have spoken."

Mary abandoned one argument in favor of another that might be more successful. "Ye may no' be up to the trip, but surely Cameron and I can go to represent ye."

"Surely ye may no'. I dinna approve the wedding."

Mary lifted her chin and signaled with a glance for the messenger to leave the room. "I'll speak to ye in a moment," she mouthed. Then she turned to her father. "This is too much, Da. Catherine and Kenneth love each other and now they have a child on the way. They will marry in the Brodie kirk whether ye are there or nay. Whether ye approve or nay. But Da," she added, softening her tone, "she wants ye there. Dinna ye wish for yer youngest child to be happy?"

"No' my youngest child. A lad is on the way." He fell to muttering to himself.

Mary shook her head. He was hopeless when faced with a situation he didn't like and couldn't control. His illness had only worsened that tendency. She stood and quit the room, heartsick over her father's mental state. The messenger waited in the hallway. "I'm sorry for my father's rudeness," she said, drawing the man away from the door to the laird's solar and leading him into the great hall. "Please tell Catherine our father will no' attend. Cameron and I hope to, perhaps with others, as well. I just have to convince my stubborn father."

The man bowed. "I will carry the word to Lady Catherine."

"Thank ye. Do rest and have something to eat before ye go."

"I'd appreciate that," the man said, so Mary signaled for a serving lass to take care of him.

She turned, hands on hips, and frowned back down

the hall toward the laird's solar. Should she confront her father again? Nay, she'd be wasting her breath. A better course would be to tell Cameron. He'd help her.

CHAPTER 18

Cameron was in the great hall when he saw Mary bolt out of her father's solar and speak to a messenger. Once she sent him off with a serving lass, she turned back to glare toward her father's solar, then headed across the great hall. She hadn't seen him yet— her gaze was on her feet and she muttered under her breath. He intercepted her, concerned about the scowl marring her normally serene face. Mary had complained about her father many times, but when she told him her father's latest edict, cold fury tightened his belly. The man had gone too far. Her sister's happiness was too important to Mary to keep her from the wedding—for nothing more than spite. Cameron resolved to get them out of the keep and on the way to Brodie. The sooner, the better.

"Pack yer things," Cameron told her, fuming. "We'll leave as soon as ye are ready."

"Leave? And go to Sutherland?"

She misunderstood his anger. "To Brodie, of course. Ye want to stand with yer sister, aye? Yer father's wishes in this dinna matter. I am yer husband, and I say we will go. I will see ye happy—with yer sisters in Brodie."

209

Mary threw herself into Cameron's arms. "I kenned there was a reason I married ye."

He grinned. "Besides my irresistible good looks and my sense of humor?"

"Aye, well, those, too," she teased, lifting one shoulder.

"My touch?" He trailed his fingertips from her shoulder up her throat and along her jaw.

Mary shivered. "Aye."

His gaze bored into her. "My kiss?"

Cameron didn't let her answer. He covered her mouth with his lips and made love to her in the only way anyone could while standing up and fully clothed. And in the middle of the great hall, with people passing by. People who applauded and cheered.

Later, when Cameron saw what Mary intended to take with her, he gave up any pretense of leaving the Rose keep quietly. Instead, he carried her belongings to the stable and had the lads there secure them over the back of an even-tempered horse. It would enable them to travel faster than a using a cart. Then he set the lad to saddling his and Mary's mounts and went to secure an escort to accompany them. Finally, he returned to the keep to collect his few belongings—and his wife.

Mary stood in the center of her chamber, looking about and wringing her hands. Then she propped them on her hips, sighed and muttered, "That must be everything. There's little enough left in here."

Cameron chuckled, startling her into whirling to face him.

"Ye big oaf. How do ye move so silently?"

"Years of experience," he answered with a grin and a kiss. "And the horse carrying yer things would like me to inform ye she's full up. Ye canna bring one thing more. If ye need aught else, chances are one of yer sisters can supply ye."

Mary nodded. "Of course." She hesitated. "I should inform Da..."

"Ye shouldna. If anyone asks, yer maid and the stable lad ken where ye have gone. The healer is here should yer father need her care. Ye can go for a fortnight—or more—without the Rose keep falling into ruin."

"I'm no' so certain."

"Let's give it a try and see, aye?"

Mary nodded. "We must, or I'll never see my sisters." Cameron wrapped her travel cloak around her shoulders and escorted her out of the keep, half expecting someone to stop them, but the others they passed merely smiled and nodded in greeting. They met the healer in the bailey, and Mary told her where they were going.

"*Dinna fash*," the healer told her. "We'll manage, and I'll keep an eye on yer da."

Mary squeezed her hand. "Thank ye."

"Now get ye gone afore yer da finds out and orders the gates closed against ye."

Cameron was glad to see the notion of being stuck here got Mary moving even faster. They mounted up and headed out, their erstwhile pack-horse tied to his saddle, six Rose warriors riding escort in their wake.

❧

MARY NEARLY CRIED IN RELIEF WHEN THEY LEFT THE gates of the Rose keep behind them. She'd felt trapped by her obligations for years, but had never felt physically trapped until today. She didn't know if her father would have closed the gates against them, but she was perfectly happy not to find out. Instead, she needed to thank Cameron for reminding her she was no longer under her father's control, and for freeing her from Rose's walls, even for the short span of a visit to Brodie.

She took a deep breath and smiled at the serious expression Cameron wore as they rode along. She guessed he was on the lookout for trouble. His eyes moved constantly, taking in the woods and countryside around them.

She worried less about what lay before them than about the possibility of hearing Rose riders thundering after them from behind. "Do ye think the countryside is still overrun by gallowglass men, this long after ye were wounded?" Mary asked.

"Nay, I dinna. If they were about, we'd have seen some at Rose's gates long before now, counting on Highland hospitality to force us to feed and shelter them. Likely they've gone home to Ireland or settled in with Domnhall at Dingwall or on Islay."

"Then what are ye looking for?"

"Nothing and everything, lass. 'Tis a habit of long-standing and one that has spared my life many times. Even with our escort along, I willna be lax now, of all times, with ye here."

The hours passed quickly, and almost before she knew it, the Brodie keep rose before them and they passed through the gates.

"Mary!" Her middle sister Annie's voice rang out across the bailey as Mary, with Cameron's help, dismounted and gained her balance. She hadn't ridden for so long in months, and despite several stops along the way, the pins and needles in her rump, legs and feet told her she needed to get out of the keep more often.

She ignored the discomfort, and with a smile for Cameron in thanks, went to embrace her sister. "Surprise!"

"Da got my missive, then? Yet he is no' with ye?"

Mary shook her head. "He did, and nay. In fact, he refused to allow me...us...to come, but..."

"Us?" Annie interrupted and peered over Mary's shoulder. "Ah, Cameron!"

Cameron stepped forward then. "Cameron Sutherland."

"I ken who ye are..."

"Mary's...husband," he added.

Annie whirled, mouth agape, and skewered Mary with her gaze. "Husband?" She didn't wait for an answer, but turned back to Cameron. "Ye wasted nay time, I see." She studied him for a moment, grinning.

"The very same, and nay, I didna."

Annie stepped forward and hugged him. "Catherine and Kenneth will be so pleased with yer news."

With a bemused glance at Mary, Cameron returned the hug, then released Annie and moved to Mary's side.

Mary squeezed his hand. "Are they here?"

"Aye, of course," Annie answered with a grin. "And eager for the kirking, they are. They'll be even more eager, now ye are here. Come inside. Ye must be tired from yer trip."

In the Brodie great hall, Annie got them seated while sending for food and drink, her husband, their youngest sister, and Kenneth.

Before long, the hall filled with squeals and laughter as the sisters greeted each other. The men took their ales to seats near the hearth while Mary looked both sisters over.

"I canna believe Da let ye come," Catherine exclaimed, fairly vibrating with excitement.

"Da didna," Mary told her as she and her sisters chose seats at one of the dining tables.

"Then how..."

Mary grinned. "Cameron is my husband now. Like

both of ye, we handfasted in secret. So Da no longer gets to control…"

Catherine's shriek echoed off the rafters. She jumped up and ran around the table to Mary, then nearly knocked her off her chair, hugging her.

Annie looked on with a grin.

"Ye are free! I canna believe it!" Catherine exclaimed, dropping onto the chair next to Mary. "Are ye on yer way to Sutherland?"

"Well, no' entirely free, and nay," Mary replied and tugged her hair. "*Wheesht*, Cat. Ye are with child now, aye?" Her sister's gently rounded middle made that apparent. "Ye must no' jump around so."

Annie's brow drew down. "What do ye mean no' entirely and nay?"

Mary filled them in on the most recent state of their father's illness, Seona's pregnancy, and the fact that he'd confined all the Grants, including his new bride.

"Good heavens, we had nay idea it was that bad," Annie breathed. "Cameron told us some of this on his way back to ye. And it appears things have only gotten worse. After all these years, Da finally wants a son, marries, and had to pick a…"

"*Lamb-headed lass* is the term yer sister used," Cameron announced, coming to join them. He sank into a chair across the table from the sisters. Kenneth and Iain joined him.

Iain signaled for more ale while they settled. "Cameron has filled us in on some of yer news," Iain added. "Including that someone nearly shot ye in the woods."

"The arrows missed me," Mary insisted with a glare at her husband as her sisters paled. "And we canna prove I was the target. It could have been an errant hunter, for all we ken."

"Or the Grants want ye dead and out of the way, the

better to take over Rose and expand their own and Albany's reach," Iain said, softly. "I disagree with Cameron. I dinna think Domnhall is behind it— proximity and opportunity make a Grant conspiracy much more likely." He paused when a servant arrived with another pitcher of ale.

Annie asked her for something to eat and sent her away.

"Yer sisters are married into Brodie—or nearly so," Iain continued when they were again private. "With ye out of the way, and with this Grant lass married to yer da, especially if she gives him a son, Grant will have a strong claim to include Rose in its territory."

"Ach, but Mary is married into Sutherland—or nearly so," Cameron argued, with a smile at Mary. He took a sip and turned back to the others. "We handfasted in secret. Likely the new Lady Rose and her clan have no' heard the news."

Iain tapped the table top with his knuckles. "So Rose is vulnerable until they do." He looked grim. "And even after…"

Mary met Cameron's gaze, open-mouthed. She hadn't considered that when she agreed to handfast with him.

"Better Rose than Mary," he growled, taking her hand and kissing the palm, then turning back to Iain. "Despite yer theory, it might no' be Grant behind this. Domnhall would happily add Rose to his holdings, as well."

"There's another factor to consider," Mary said, her gaze still on Cameron. "Seona and a Grant guard who stayed after her mother returned home have been lovers. They both think the bairn she carries is his, no' our father's. Da kens and agrees. He says Seona is too far along in her breeding."

Annie straightened and shook her head. "Poor Da.

Though if the bairn is a lad, she'll have given Da a son he can claim and raise up as his own. He may no' care."

Mary nodded, possibilities and alternatives running wildly through her mind. "A lot hinges on the bairn."

Iain snorted. "Is it no' always so?"

The serving girl returned then with a platter loaded with bread, cheese and new apples. Catherine grabbed one of those and took a bite. "Let's back up," she said after she swallowed. "All of this is important, but too gloomy, and I'm so happy ye are here I dinna wish to dwell on clan Rose problems right now." She leaned to the side and hugged Mary yet again. "Ye said ye handfasted. So ye mean to marry, aye?"

Mary traded a smile with Cameron, gratified by his nod.

"We do," he asserted around a bite of cheese.

"Well, then." Catherine stood, an infectious grin on her face. "Here at Brodie we have a small kirk, too, and a priest coming, and a wedding planned in a week. Why no' marry at the same time we do? A double wedding—twice blessed and twice lucky, aye?" Catherine looked to Kenneth. "Ye dinna mind, do ye?"

"Nay, no' at all," Kenneth replied, turning a sly grin on Cameron. "I'll be happy to see Sutherland wedded to yer sister."

"Nay," Mary objected, setting aside the bread she'd just picked up and tugging on Catherine's hand. "'Tis meant to be yer special day!"

"'Twill be even more special to me if we share it," Catherine avowed as she sank into her seat.

"And 'twill keep ye safe from anything Da might do to keep ye at Rose," Annie added. "Or to keep ye from Cameron." She grinned and winked at him.

Cameron grinned back. "It sounds like the perfect solution to me."

Annie got to her feet. "Then that is what we will

do. Come, Mary, let's get ye and Cameron settled in yer own chamber, then we have preparations to make."

Heart in her throat, Mary stood and took Cameron's hand. "Ye are sure?"

Cameron nodded, his gaze steady on hers. "I've never been more certain of anything in my life, Mary, my love. Let's get married in the kirk."

🐝

MARY LEFT CAMERON WITH IAIN, KENNETH AND OTHER Brodie men she didn't know. He would be content for a while to sit by the hearth in the great hall, drink ale or whisky, and tell the sort of tales men told each other. Some true, some only exaggerated, some totally false. None of that mattered. Only the camaraderie they shared meant anything real and lasting.

She sat on Annie's bed, Catherine sprawled beside her. Annie took the window seat, looked around her chamber and announced, "This is exactly the way we used to gather in yer chamber at Rose, Mary. Only Catherine was much younger."

"We all were," Mary replied, tousling her youngest sister's hair. "But Cat hasn't changed her habits."

"None of us has," Catherine objected, "Annie is still over there where she can hear herself think—or so she says. Ye used to sit on the bed because it was yers. And I lay beside ye for the comfort. Ye and Annie may remember our *maman*, but I dinna. Ye are as close to a mother as I ever had."

"I'm sorry for that," Mary told her. "I did the best I could."

"Ye have naught to be sorry for," Annie interrupted. "Ye raised us and ye helped us find our happiness, even in the face of Da's disapproval. We owe ye a lot, Mary.

And we mean to help ye find yer own happiness any way we can."

"Like getting ye married in the kirk, so Da canna gainsay ye," Catherine put in. "I canna wait!"

Mary gave her an indulgent smile. The youngest sister, Catherine had matured, but despite what she'd been through with their father and Kenneth, her soon-to-be husband, her childish exuberance had not deserted her entirely. It still made itself known now and again.

Mary turned her gaze to Annie. If Mary was eldest and most responsible, Annie was next in age and in sense of responsibility. She also had excellent organizational skills, and seemed to be the perfect foil for her husband's more artistic and creative leanings. Annie kept Iain grounded.

And what did she do for Cameron? Were they too much alike, both duty-bound to their respective clans? Or had they managed to turn the urge to each other—not that Cameron was an obligation to her, or she to him, but that they were as strongly bound to each other. "Ye both seem so well matched, perfect complements to the men ye chose. I once thought I was, too, but Dougal didn't have the patience to wait for me, or the stomach to take on Da." She told them about Dougal's disastrous recent visit, and how he left.

"Cameron is no' Dougal. He is a good man," Catherine announced, sitting up. "Ye canna do better."

"I can tell ye he impressed Iain, and ye ken how seldom anyone manages to do that," Annie revealed.

"He knew trouble was coming and warned me to get out of St. Andrews," Catherine added. "Then when Kenneth and I left, he joined up with us, though he had no obligation to travel with us or protect me. Ye must give him credit for keeping us safe."

"I do. I have," Mary replied. "'Tis no' that there's

anything wrong with him. My doubts have more to do with me. I worry about our father and how he'll fare if I'm gone from Rose. How the clan will fare without me..."

"They will manage," Annie assured her. "Ye have trained them well."

"Ye ken Cameron has some interesting friends, aye?" Catherine interjected. "Like the man who gave us horses to cross the Highland mountains. Ye will never be bored around Cameron."

"But will he tire of me?" Mary shook her head. "I told him I thought he confused gratitude for his care with feelings for me. He says no', but I sometimes wonder..."

"Nay, Mary," Catherine said and put an arm around her. "I spent a lot of time with Cam, talking to him, watching him..."

"Ye mean ye took yer gaze from Kenneth?" Annie needled.

"Once in a while," Catherine replied with a smirk. "Cameron is a very good looking man, ye ken. And kind. There's a lot more to Cameron Sutherland under his charming surface. Anyway, I ken him well enough to be certain about the way he looks at ye, Mary. He loves ye. 'Twas no' gratitude driving him to return to ye from Sutherland, to stay with ye, and to stand up to Da alongside ye. The man is in love. With ye."

"I never thought it would happen again—though I suppose this is really the first time."

"Well, it has," Annie assured her. "First or second does no' matter. I see the same thing Catherine sees. Ye'd best accept the strong, handsome, powerful man who loves ye. Enjoy it. Ye love him, too, or ye would if ye'd let yerself. Stop worrying about Rose and Da. Let Cameron take ye off to Sutherland. Time away from Rose will do ye good, and might force Da to see what a poor bargain he made with Lady Grant in wedding her lamb-headed daughter."

Mary didn't share her sister's optimism. "None of that will matter if Seona gives him a son."

"Let's hope she does, then," Annie said. "That way, he'll get what he wants, and ye will finally be free of Rose."

Would she? Or would she always feel like there was more she could do, more she *should* do, to improve it?

CHAPTER 19

A week later, Cameron Sutherland and Kenneth Brodie waited nervously at the door of the kirk, the priest on the step above them. It was a fine late November day, and cloud-dappled sunlight filtered into the small stone kirk through the open door. The sun shone through colorful stained glass windows set high above the altar, throwing rainbows on the walls.

"Trust Catherine to be late," Kenneth muttered as a chill breeze carried a shower of dry leaves skittering by them.

"Mary is usually quite punctual," Cameron noted, hoping that was true. "And I suspect Annie can be counted on to get them here sometime today."

"Annie is up for the challenge," Iain assured them. "Ah—here they come." He lifted his chin in the direction of the keep, where the three women exited the door and started across the bailey.

Cameron nodded, but his gaze was fixed on Mary. Resplendent in a deep, wine red gown, she moved toward him gracefully, as if she floated above the ground. Gold and jewels around her throat and in her hair caught the sunlight, flashed and sparkled, making her appear a creature of magic. The image fit how he thought of her. Mary was magical to him. She'd saved his life, then changed it in ways she did not yet comprehend, making him a better, happier man just by her presence. He could only hope he'd done much the same for her.

He tore his gaze away and glanced aside at Kenneth and Iain. They stared at the approaching women, seeming as rapt in their attention to their ladies as Cameron was to his. Cameron barely noticed Catherine's pale blue dress or Annie's deep blue out of the corner of his eye. He grinned, then turned his gaze back to Mary and softened his expression into a smile of welcome. His heart soared when she caught him staring and smiled back.

"We are here and ready," Annie announced when they reached the steps.

Catherine blushed, but Mary's chin lifted, a touch of defiance Cameron approved. They all knew her father would not be glad of this news. Perhaps they'd send him a letter to inform him of what they'd done, and he and Mary would go straight to Sutherland rather than directly back to Rose. He knew they'd have to return eventually. Mary's sense of obligation and duty would drive her back to make sure Rose—the clan and her father—were well cared for before she could move away with a clear conscience. Still, he'd prefer they not return right away. They deserved some time to themselves.

For now, they were to be married. The priest cleared his throat and they all turned to face him. He kept the ceremony blessedly short, including both couples in the lessons and prayers rather than repeating the entire ceremony for each. Iain had confided that the man was little pleased at having to marry two couples at once—something he'd never done before. He'd made it clear he expected to be paid properly for officiating for both couples, Iain had added with a laugh.

When the time came to move inside the kirk and repeat their vows, the priest called Cameron and Mary, as the eldest couple, forward first. They made their vows, then stepped aside for Kenneth and Catherine. Cameron watched, fascinated by the love and hope in both their expressions. He wasn't a praying man, but he prayed for a long and happy life for them—and for him and Mary.

Finally, the priest declared them all man and wife and ended the ceremony with a last blessing. Cameron wrapped an arm around Mary, then had to release her so she could hug her youngest sister. "I canna believe we did this together," she exclaimed, "but I'm glad we did."

"I'm happy to share this day with ye and Cameron," Catherine said tearfully, reaching for Kenneth with one hand, the other in Mary's.

"Let's go to the hall," Annie said, ever the organizer. "Dinner is waiting, as is the rest of the clan, to greet the newlyweds."

The rest of the afternoon and evening were some of the longest hours Cameron ever spent. All he could think about was getting Mary back to their chamber. Yet she seemed so vibrantly happy with the celebration, he couldn't bear the thought of taking her from it. In fairness, he enjoyed it too. In addition to a wealth of food and drink, the hall rang with music and dancing. The entire clan crowded in and seemed bent on enjoying every last moment of the celebration.

Then, finally, the time came to leave the hall. Cameron took Mary's hand and stood while Kenneth did the same with Catherine. With a bow to Iain and Annie, another to each other, and a last to the friends and family gathered in the hall, Cameron and Mary took their leave, followed by Kenneth and Catherine.

⚜

AFTER THE WEDDING FEAST, AS CAMERON WALKED HER back to their chamber, Mary clutched his hand and marveled. She was married. Truly married in the eyes of the kirk and the king. She laid her free hand over her chest, feeling her heart beat under the cool satin fabric. At least she was dressed fit for court. She recalled Seona taunting her about her unsuitable clothes and fingered the edge of her silk chemise, then ran a hand down her heavy brocaded skirt. Not that the child king languishing down in England would care what she wore to be married, nor would he have any idea what being married meant. She spared a moment for an uncharitable thought—if only Seona could see her now.

In truth, she wished their father had forgotten his stubborn pride and come with them to see his eldest and youngest daughters wed—together. He should have been proud. Their *maman* surely would have been. Mary missed her fiercely on special days like this. But she could not let sadness mar her joy at marrying Cameron. For Mary, marriage meant freedom as well as love and companionship and care from Cameron. And the same from her to him. She felt different, but didn't know why. Was it the permanence of the vows they'd taken? *'Til death they do part.* She felt no guilt for no longer being her father's dutiful daughter. She felt justified. She felt like a new person. As wonderful as the handfasting had been, and as liberating as she'd thought it was at the time, this was so much more. "Do ye feel different?" she asked Cameron, wondering if he had similar thoughts running through his mind.

He pondered for a moment before answering. "I do.

'Tis odd, is it no'? Nothing has really changed, yet everything has."

"Exactly! I didna expect to feel so differently, but 'tis like we've turned a corner, and everything is new. A new country we've never seen before."

They reached their door and Cameron opened it, then scooped her up and carried her inside. He set her on her feet before closing it softly behind them, then pulled her into his arms. "Whatever the difference is, I like it."

"As do I," Mary answered, reaching up to brush her lips across his. "I can do this as often as I like now. Any time I like."

"And I can do this," Cameron answered with a grin, then kissed her back, softly at first, then with more ardor, his lips whispering over hers, then his tongue as he deepened the kiss. "And this." He pulled the jeweled pins—the ones Annie had loaned her—from her hair until, like cool honey rolling slowly from the lip of a jar, it tumbled down her back and swayed along her hips. "Glorious," he breathed, studying her before he untied the borrowed jeweled necklace and removed it from her throat. "And I can do so much more." He kissed his way down her throat.

Mary's breasts tingled, anticipating Cameron's touch. She didn't care if he used his fingers, his lips, or his tongue. All those possibilities made her blood rush hotly through her veins. Her body grew damp and hungry.

Instead, Cameron returned his attention to her mouth while he untied and loosened her laces, then tugged her dress from her shoulders. He followed the fabric, running his tongue down her neck and across her shoulder while he made certain the heavy satin pooled on the floor at her feet. Then he knelt and helped her slip off her fine silk slippers. Only when she stood before him in nothing but her silk chemise did he rise and trail his fingers down her throat and chest between her breasts. He cupped them in his hands and teased her nipples to fine, tight points. Mary let her head drop back, enjoying the frissons of excitement racing from them to the melting place between her thighs.

Deciding she couldn't take any more without reciprocating, she reached for the brooch holding Cameron's plaid on his shoulder and unpinned it. She set it on the bedside table, then unbuckled his belt and pulled the yards of his great kilt from his shoulder and around his waist until it made a puddle of fabric on the floor even larger than her dress. "I think I'm going to enjoy married life," she teased and reached out, cupping him through his fine lawn shirt.

"I already do," Cameron answered, his voice a gruff, low rumble Mary could feel even where her palm cradled his heat.

"Take this off," she commanded and lifted the bottom edge of his shirt to his waist.

He grinned and took it from her, then pulled the cloth over his head.

Mary couldn't take her eyes from the flex of his abdominal muscles, or the way his staff stood proudly away from its nest of brown curls. As the shirt cleared Cameron's head, his massive arm and shoulder muscles caught her attention as they bunched and flexed, then smoothed as he dropped his arms to his sides. He cocked his head, drawing her attention back to the wicked gleam in his eyes.

"I was right, all those weeks ago. Ye do like looking at me."

"I told ye then that I did. And I still do. I always will." She stepped closer, but he held her from him.

"Nay, lass. 'Tisna fair. Ye are still dressed. I'll have ye

out of yer silks, too." He tipped his head to the side, studying her. "So beautiful. I dinna ken whether I want to watch ye remove them, or help ye do it."

Mary smirked and stepped back. Without a word, she slipped the chemise off one shoulder and shrugged the cloth aside, turning and glancing coyly over it. Then she turned her back and let the fabric fall away. Holding it over her breasts, she shifted her hips.

Cameron groaned. "Ye are killing me, lass."

She looked over her shoulder at him and smiled, then let the fabric slip down to drape around her hips. "Shall I turn around?"

"God's teeth, I dinna ken. I like the view of your full, sweet arse so much, I canna choose."

He reached for her but she twisted away and turned to face him, then dropped the last of her clothing. Standing before him completely nude, her arms at her side, she felt powerful and liberated, the hunger in his gaze matched by the longing in her heart to hold this man to her for the rest of her life. "Can ye decide now?"

Cameron shook his head. "No' yet. Turn for me, Mary. Let me admire ye some more."

She rose up on her toes and pirouetted, flinging her arms over her head, her hair flying, then letting her hands drop to cradle the back of her neck before she turned to face him yet again.

Cameron's lips parted and he licked them. His erection, already massive when she stripped him, grew and purpled before her gaze.

In response, she arched her back even more and took a step back toward the bed. "Have ye no' decided yet? Perhaps ye need to touch, no' just look." She lowered her arms and kept going until she felt the bed behind her, then sat and leaned back, letting her thighs fall open.

Cameron groaned and stumbled forward, landing

on his knees before her. He took one foot in hand and kissed it, then stroked her arch with his tongue before he nibbled on each toe. Then he kissed his way up her calf and trailed his tongue around her knee.

Mary lay back, enjoying the sensations spiraling from her foot and leg. Cameron's tongue did magical things there. When he moved higher, trailing his tongue up the inside of her thigh, fire ignited and spread throughout her body.

Cam tucked her legs over his shoulders and parted her intimate curls with a finger. "So beautiful and so sweet. Mary, my love, I must taste ye."

His touch sent her flying. She thought she should be embarrassed by his regard, but he made her want him so, she didn't mind. He could do with her whatever he wished, as long as the sensations he gave her kept growing stronger and more delicious. When his lips followed his finger, Mary bucked, seeking more. Then he stroked her with his tongue, and Mary came apart, gasping and crying out his name.

❧

CAMERON HAD NEVER HAD A PARTNER AS RESPONSIVE AS his Mary. *His love.* She delighted him with her spirit, humbled him with her strength, and enchanted him with her lush body and her teasing. As she'd undressed, he couldn't believe her new confidence as she displayed herself for his pleasure, or how much he wanted her. He had gone from erect to hard as a steel shaft when she gave him one glance over her shoulder and a saucy twitch of her hips. It had been all he could do to stay still and let her enjoy seducing him.

And seduce him, she had. He'd never been so beguiled by a lass in his life. Once he felt her flying to her crest and floating down the other side, he stood and leaned over her, kissing and licking his way up her body, enjoying every taste, every scent he encountered. Her nipples, like ripe berries, begged to be plucked and tasted, savored and suckled. She writhed beneath his mouth, her thighs caressing his hardness until he couldn't take any more. He had to be inside her.

He stretched out on the bed and pulled her up alongside him, then moved over her and brought her hand to his cock. "Do ye feel how much ye make me want ye?" he teased. She stroked him and smiled, nearly making him come when she licked her lips. He pulled away and lowered himself to her thighs.

She parted them. "Take me, husband. I need ye inside me. Now."

He wanted to take her slowly, inch by inch, but as soon as his moist tip encountered her liquid heat, he couldn't hold himself back. He drove into her with a groan he felt to his balls, then pulled back and did it again. She wrapped her legs around his hips, and he forced himself to slow into a pace that would pleasure her while extending his endurance. But when she reached down and skimmed his buttocks with her palms, then squeezed them, he was lost. He came with a roar, driving into her and gathering her into his arms as tightly as he could while his body pulsed and shook with the ecstasy she'd given him. "My God, Mary, my love..." He rocked her, easing up to let her breathe, then rolled to the side, still within her, and rocked them some more.

"That was..."

Her words cut off as he covered her mouth with his and kissed her as if the only air he could live on came from her. Still deep in her body, his cock sprang back to life. "I need ye so, Mary, my love. Ye canna ken."

She clenched around him and chuckled. "I think I have some idea, my love. My husband."

Taking that for permission, he rolled to his back, keeping her impaled on him, then lifted and lowered her. She responded and he let her set the pace, enjoying the bob and sway of her breasts above him. He pushed up and took one sweet peak in his mouth, making her cry out and clench even more tightly around him until he felt the pulses of her climax. He licked and suckled while she calmed, then drove into her. When his own climax hit, he arched up calling her name. Holding him tightly to her, she wrapped her arms around his neck while he rode his release. He'd never felt so wanted, so needed, or so powerful. He'd searched for a long time, never knowing someone like Mary waited for him. But he'd found her and he would never let her go.

CHAPTER 20

*A*fter such a long time away, visiting Brodie, Mary was of two minds about returning to Rose, though she had talked Cameron out of going directly to Sutherland first. On the one hand, she missed the people and her father, but on the other, she needed to see all was well there, or as well as could be, given there were Grants in the dungeon. Seona's pregnancy would be further advanced by now. Somehow, Mary was certain, the girl would use it to wheedle privileges from her husband that she didn't deserve.

They'd heard nothing from her father, but that didn't surprise her. He had to be unhappy with the way she and Cameron had simply left. But Mary had written to him, a letter each week, telling him their news. The last advised him when to expect them home.

Home. Mary pursed her lips. Rose wasn't really her home any longer. She belonged with Cameron, wherever he chose to take them. At least with him, she had a say in those decisions.

They were greeted at the door to the keep by Seona, now much more visibly pregnant than when they'd left. What had happened to her confinement?

"I wonder that ye dare show yer face here," Seona challenged. "Leaving yer poor, ill da the way ye did and running off with a man." She wore an expression Mary had seen on Lady Grant. Seona had not only grown in girth, she'd grown in arrogance while they were gone.

"A man? Ah, ye mean my husband. Ye have met, I believe, though ye mostly ignored him before we left. This is Cameron Sutherland. Ye do ken the Sutherlands, aye?"

Her gaze dropped. "I do."

"So, we are on our way to our chamber, then I will see my father."

For a moment, Mary thought she would actually attempt to deny her access to the keep, but as Mary mounted the last step, Seona backed away and turned aside so they could enter.

The serving girls, when they saw Mary, brightened, but turned sullen and returned to their work as quickly as they noticed Seona pacing behind Cameron's broad form.

"Let's go up," Cameron murmured, also frowning.

He must know the sooner he got her away from Seona, the better.

"Aye," Mary agreed and headed for the stairs. Their chamber smelled of must and old dust. She doubted the window or door had been opened the entire time they were gone. Once they were safely behind a closed door, she rounded on Cameron. "What is she doing out of her chamber? Did ye see the way the lasses acted in the hall? Once they spotted her behind ye? She's been horrible to them, I can tell. How can I ever leave?" Tears pricked her eyes. Even married to Cameron, she could not escape wanting to take care of Rose.

Cameron gripped her arms, and his gaze bored into hers. "All that is secondary. Ye must see to yer father. Find out why he's allowing his wife the freedom of the keep. And also whether he's freed the Grant guardsmen."

"Perhaps she's been ill with the bairn." Mary kicked herself for making excuses for the lazy chit.

"Did she look ill to ye?"

She shook her head. "Nay. She looked like her mother—arrogant and irritated with the world. I'm sure she's eager for the bairn to come, to cement her place in the clan, but she has nay grounds and nay excuse for her arrogance."

"Except ye say her mother is the same. No doubt she learned it there."

"No doubt."

Mary found the healer, who said her father's condition was slowly improving, but he still had some paralysis on one side. And he had, indeed, released Seona from her confinement, but not the guards. "He took pity on her pleas and gave her the run of the keep. She spends little time with him, though I've asked her many times to help him move about. Instead, she spends her time visiting the dungeon."

"Yet she hasna dared release the man."

"Nay. Yer da's master of arms keeps the keys. He will only take orders from the laird."

"I fear…"

"I ken what ye fear, as do I. She will never be good for yer da, be the bairn a lad or a lass."

Mary grimaced. "I must go speak to him. Though I wrote to him while we were away, he never answered. He must learn I've returned—with my husband, Cameron Sutherland. We did marry in the kirk at Brodie."

"Ach, lass, what wonderful news!"

"If Da read my letters, he already kens it. But if no'…"

"I'll go with ye. If he didna read yer letters, this could come as another shock."

"Thank ye. I'll be glad of yer presence if he needs help."

The healer nodded.

"Ye will have mine, too." Cameron's deep voice at her shoulder startled her, then sent a frisson of pleasure coursing through her.

Mary whirled. "Ye really have to stop that."

Cameron grinned and nodded to the healer. "I'll no' send ye to face yer father without me," he told her. "Let's go."

The Rose was at his desk in his solar. When they entered, he glanced up, then pushed slowly to his feet. "So, ye have returned at last."

"Good day, Laird Rose," Cameron greeted him, speaking before Mary had a chance to.

"Is it?" Rose challenged.

"How are ye, Da?" Bees buzzed in Mary's belly, but she held her ground.

"I imagine ye already ken, since ye have her with ye," he replied, pointing with his good hand at the healer. "I am well enough for her to torture me every day."

"She's trying to make ye better," Mary reminded him.

"Well, it isna working." He collapsed back into his chair. "I havena improved since ye took my daughter away," he said, directing the comment to Cameron.

Mary hoped that was his way of saying he missed Cameron, or at least the help Cameron had been giving him. "Perhaps some happy news will make ye feel better," Mary tried. "I presume ye failed to read any of the letters I sent ye, aye?"

He looked away and a muscle in his jaw jumped.

"As I expected. Well, here it is, then. Cameron and I wed at the same ceremony as Catherine and

234

Kenneth in the kirk at Brodie. I hope ye can be happy for us."

Rose surged to his feet again, face red with fury. "'Twas bad enough ye went to Brodie against my orders —without my permission. And ye think this is good news?" He pounded a fist on the desk top and glared at Cameron. "Take yer wife and return to Sutherland. She is nay longer any daughter of mine. I have a wife and a son on the way. Perhaps my new family will provide me with greater satisfaction than three ungrateful daughters have done."

Mary quailed, hurt more than she expected by his ill-tempered reaction.

"That is no' fair and well ye ken it," Cameron objected.

Rose sank back into his seat. "Do as I say!" he barked.

His gaze stayed on his desk for so long, Mary feared he'd suddenly forgotten they were there. She took a step toward him.

Without warning, one of the serving lasses ran into the room. "Lady Rose is...healer, she needs ye. I think the bairn is coming!"

"Where is she?" Mary's stomach sank. She needed to clear the air with her father, not deal with Seona.

"In her chamber."

"Good," the healer replied. "Mary, can ye attend with me?"

"Of course. Give me a moment."

Rose looked up and frowned. "'Tis too early. Even with...'tis too early."

The healer narrowed her eyes at him. "Aye, 'tis. Perhaps ye'll need to mend yer ways with the three daughters ye already have."

With that rebuke, she left the room. Cameron gave Mary's hand a squeeze, then followed the healer out as well. Mary turned to her father, who remained at his desk, his gaze on his hands.

"Why, Da? Why have ye been so against the three of us marrying a man we love and being happy?"

Her father kept his gaze lowered. "I told ye why. Because each time I lose one of ye, 'tis like losing yer mother all over again." He looked up and met her gaze, his expression grim. "Ye all look so much like her. She was a great beauty, fair of spirit as well as face. She gave me the three of ye, the greatest gifts a man can ever receive. And now..." He's soft voice choked off.

Mary wanted to feel sorry for him, but the pain he had caused was too great. "Now it appears ye will lose another—even if 'tis no' yers." She covered her mouth with her hand—she had not intended to say those last words, but the thought was there in her mind, and they slipped out.

"Ye ken I would claim it if 'twere a lad."

"Da, I am so sorry."

His shoulders dropped and he looked away. "I have done my best to turn a blind eye, but it may all be for naught."

Mary went to him and laid a hand on his shoulder. "I'm so sorry, Da. I didna mean to make ye face something so painful..."

"Go on with ye and help the healer," he interrupted. "If there's anything to be done, I ken between the two of ye, it will be."

"We'll do what we can," Mary promised. "I love ye, Da. Ye ken I do, aye? So do Annie and Cat. They miss ye."

"And I miss them. I am sorry I missed yer wedding. Now go."

Her throat choked with unshed tears, Mary nodded and left the room. She couldn't bear to look back and see her father appear so defeated. It wasn't like him.

But she'd never imagined him in this position, either. Not just married again, but burdened with an unfaithful wife. Instead, she held his final words in her heart and went to try to help save the child he would claim as his.

❧

CAMERON SPENT THE FIRST HOURS IN THE GREAT HALL while Mary and the healer attended Seona's confinement. He hoped James Rose would at least leave his solar to ask about his wife's condition, but he never did. Cameron wanted to speak to him somewhere other than in the formal environs of the laird's solar. He hoped to build a better relationship with the man who was now his father-in-law. He'd made progress helping with Rose's physical ailment before he took Mary away—and wed her. Now, over an ale by the fire seemed a hospitable way to go about mending whatever rift that had caused. But it appeared he would not be given the chance. Finally, he set aside his ale and went to beard the man in his own den.

"What do ye want?" Rose challenged when Cameron entered.

Not the best beginning, Cameron supposed. Nonetheless, he forged ahead. "Now that the bairn is coming, I want to speak to ye about taking Mary to Sutherland permanently."

Rose shook his head. "Nay. She's needed here."

"She's my wife now. Ye canna keep her…"

"I can keep ye in my dungeon," Rose threatened, pounding his good fist on the desktop

"Even if she's in danger here?"

"Danger? Mary's in nay danger in her own keep."

"Then no one told ye about the horse that nearly ran her down, or the arrows that barely missed her in the woods?" He chose not to mention the fragments of conversation he'd overheard from the stable.

Rose gaped at him and shook his head. "I've heard nothing of this. What do ye mean?"

Cameron crossed his arms, trying to put into words his suspicions. "Both could have been accidents, but appeared to be aimed squarely at Mary. Someone may have stabbed one of the horses in its flank a few weeks ago with a sliver of wood from a stall, sending it bolting straight for Mary as she crossed the bailey. Only by her quick thinking did she avoid being trampled. Days later, someone shot at her when she and some of the lasses went to the woods to gather herbs."

Rose pushed to his feet, trembling. "Who did these things? And why has no one told me?"

Cameron leaned forward, ready to aid the man if he started to fall. His condition had improved, but not enough for Cameron to believe he could remain steady on his feet, especially after hearing this. Mary would be angry if he was hurt reacting to Cameron's news. "It all happened before we went to Brodie. 'Twas one reason I wanted to get her away for a while. As for who, we dinna ken. We never found the archer. And Mary wasna certain she was the target or merely in the wrong place at the wrong time. She didna wish to worry ye."

"I'll skelp that lass, I will." Rose sighed and sank back into his chair. "Have there been any other attacks?"

Cameron lifted his shoulders and shook his head. "None she has admitted to me. None that anyone else has mentioned. Ye can ask her. Perhaps she'll say more if she's aware ye ken."

Rose let out a sardonic chuckle and sank into his chair. "How well do ye think ye ken the lass? Nay, she'll have little more to say, except to complain that ye and I are inventing a danger she has dismissed. And she may be right. So perhaps only a panicked mount, stray arrows, and naught more. Coincidence."

"It's possible, but…"

"So ye tell me this to convince me to allow ye to take her away for her own safety, is that it?"

"Do these things no' worry ye?"

"Accidents happen. Hunters dinna always take the time to be certain of their target before they shoot. Horses injure themselves all the time. Since there have been nay other incidents, I choose to believe they were accidents, naught more."

"And if ye are wrong?"

"I am no' wrong." He jerked his chin toward the door. "Now go on with ye."

Cameron left the solar and returned to his ale by the fire. He didn't usually give up so easily, but he had no proof. Just a bad feeling in his gut, and that was not enough to convince Rose. Hell, it wasn't enough to convince himself. Rose was right about one thing—he'd tried to use the incidents as an excuse to get Mary away from Rose again. This time with her father's cooperation, he'd hoped. It hadn't worked.

When Mary finally appeared, she looked exhausted, and blood spattered her dress. Cameron stood. "How did it go?"

Mary shook her head. "I have a new half-sister, at least in name…but the healer thinks no' for long. She came too early. She's tiny and frail. She also has black hair, much like Seona's guardsman, and, I'd wager, his nose. My poor da. I must go tell him he'll no' get his wish of a lad, no' even one to claim. Even when they are no' his, he's cursed with daughters." Her mouth quirked up in a brave hint of a smile, then she shrugged.

Cameron thought he was sad until she uttered those

last words. Then his heart sank even farther. How much misery could one man cause? And to those who loved him the most? "No' cursed, Mary. Never that. Ye and yer sisters are the greatest blessing the man has. I believe he kens that, even if he canna admit it."

"He did admit it," Mary said, her voice choked. "To me, after ye and the healer left the solar. He said we were his greatest gifts."

Cameron took her in his arms and held her until her breathing told him she had regained some calm. He went with her to deliver the news. Mary spoke softly, then turned and left the room.

Cameron wanted to be angry at the man for the grief he caused Mary and his other daughters, but at the moment, he looked so miserable, Cameron couldn't find any ire within him. The birth of this small, weak lass would soon turn from a much anticipated event to a tragedy, and even James Rose appeared affected by the impending loss.

"Do ye want to visit the bairn and yer wife?" Cameron asked once Mary was gone. "I will help ye, if ye wish it."

Rose shook his head. "I dinna need to see another daughter. Certainly no' one that will soon be gone. My hopes for a son are doomed. I've taken a useless woman to wife."

Cameron left the solar. As his sympathy for the man faded and his anger resurfaced, he clenched his fists. He could feel sorry for Rose except for the way he treated his grown daughters. And it seemed Seona would fare no better. If her clan didn't represent such a threat to Mary, he might pity her, too.

But now, he needed to find his own wife. Mary would need him, and he meant to help her every way he could.

THE NEXT DAY, THE NEW BAIRN BREATHED HER LAST. Seona seemed numb, surprising Mary by neither crying out, nor shedding tears when it happened. She simply nodded and turned away. Mary watched in disbelief as she walked from the small chamber they'd used as a nursery.

"Let me get this wee one away from here," the healer said, scowling at the doorway Seona had disappeared beyond. "I'll prepare her for burial. Are ye certain yer da doesna wish to see her?"

"I'll ask him again and send him to ye if he has changed his mind, but he was quite clear with Cameron yesterday. He had nay interest in another daughter, especially one who would no' be here for long." Mary touched the tiny cheek with the tip of her finger. "How sad. She was so little wanted, she doesna even have a name."

"Say yer goodbyes, lass, and I'll take her away."

Mary bent and lightly kissed the tiny forehead, then left before her own tears could return. She found her father where she expected, in his solar. "She's gone, Da. The wee one. Do ye want to see her before the healer prepares her for..."

"Nay. I told yer husband nay yesterday, and I tell ye again now. I dinna."

"Can ye at least give her a name?"

"Why?" In a voice gruffer than usual, he added, "She was barely here and is best soon forgotten."

Mary finally saw a sheen of tears in his eyes and realized he hid his grief behind gruffness. She rushed to his side. "I'm so sorry, Da," she told him, bending down to wrap her arms around his shoulders. "I wish it could have gone as ye hoped."

He straightened and shrugged her off, but she

noticed he wiped one eye with the back of his hand. "It doesna matter. We'll try again."

Saddened even more by the hope he revealed, Mary left him to grieve. If he wanted to be certain any child of Seona's bore his blood, he'd best send the Grant guardsmen away. Though, even that might not matter. The healer had told her early on she feared he'd lost his ability to sire children due to the paralysis still affecting him. If that were true, he would never have the son he craved. Why had he waited so long to remarry?

That evening, he called her and Cameron into his solar. Seona was already there, wrapped in a warm robe, eyes downcast, expression grim. Mary went to her. "Ye shouldna be out of bed."

Seona shook her head and looked at Mary's father. He looked wan, but strangely determined.

"Sit," Rose ordered and gestured with his good hand at the round table. Mary glanced at Cameron, who nodded and pulled out a chair for her.

"Aye, Da? What do ye need?"

"An heir. An official heir. And since my wife has failed in her duty to provide me a son..."

"Da! How can ye say such a thing? Especially so soon..."

"Silence, daughter. Since I have nay son to inherit from me, it falls to ye, as my eldest, and yer husband." He frowned at Cameron. "If ye were no' a Sutherland, I would be left to choose that Brodie husband of Catherine's instead, but an alliance with Sutherland will be to Rose's best advantage in years to come."

"And Grant?" Seona's voice, though pitched low, penetrated.

Rose waved a hand. "As long as ye are here, Grant will no' interfere."

He turned back to Cameron, effectively silencing his wife, and picked up the document before him on the desk. "So, I am naming ye two as my heir," he announced with a glance at Mary before his gaze settled on Cameron. "As long as ye remain here and Mary continues to instruct my wife in her duties. She is more interested in jewels and fancy dresses than caring for the clan, solving disputes among the servants—or giving her laird a son." He frowned at Seona, who dropped her gaze to her hands. "She is a long way from providing the kind of care clan Rose is accustomed to from Mary."

Mary started counting how many years she'd been acting as chatelaine without ever hearing from her father a single compliment on the hard work she did every day—until now. Seona had no idea what she'd married into. Even when Da was well, much less now that he was ill and angry, he rarely praised anyone.

"And if something happens to ye? What are yer wishes concerning yer wife?" Cameron asked.

Rose snorted. "She can return to Grant. She'll be of nay use to ye here."

"And if something happens to Mary?" Cameron glanced at her, then locked his gaze on Rose.

Grant would take over, Mary thought, seeing a sudden gleam in Seona's eyes. Cameron, Iain and Kenneth had been correct in their suppositions—Grant was up to no good.

Then she realized what Cameron's words implied. So he'd told her father about what he believed were attempts on her life. Mary hoped her father had given some thought to Cameron's revelations. An accident was one thing, but they could've been deliberate and her father needed to consider that.

"Then that foolish girl Catherine and her Brodie can take over."

Cameron turned to Mary. "I must take Mary to Sutherland to meet my family."

She nodded. Her father had as much as told Seona she had no chance of controlling Rose unless she produced a male heir, so he would be safe. Cameron turned back to her father and added, "I trust ye can honor yer alliance with Sutherland by doing without her for a few weeks."

"A fortnight at most." Her father turned to her and frowned. "If ye stay away longer, I'll give Rose to Mary's youngest sister."

"A fortnight, then." Cameron stood and bowed to Rose, then reached for Mary's hand. "We'll leave in the morning."

"The burial…" Mary reminded them.

"Will take place at dawn," her father agreed stiffly. "Without ceremony." Seona frowned and Rose amended, "A simple prayer, then ye two may go on yer way."

CHAPTER 21

ary had enjoyed the week she and Cameron spent at Sutherland. The keep was even greater than Cameron had alluded to at supper—only weeks ago? So much had happened since then, it seemed forever.

Dunrobin was magnificent. She'd yet to see all of it, and wasn't sure how much more she could in the days left to her during this visit. Mary wished they hadn't agreed to her father's demand that they keep their visit to a fortnight. Cameron's brothers had yet to return and she hoped to meet them.

Tonight, Cameron and his father spent supper in the great hall planning the trip back to Rose. Yesterday, Sutherland's *ghillie* had arrived to tell them Albany's men were still in Aberdeen, not on the way to oust Domnhall from Ross lands. They could make the trip home without fear of crossing paths with either army.

A disturbance at the door caught her eye and her stomach sank when she realized the Sutherland seneschal led a Rose *ghillie* through the crowded great hall toward the high table where they sat. "This canna be anything good," she told Cameron as they stood to greet the man.

"Lady Mary, I'm sorry to bring ye such news. Laird Rose died suddenly early this morn."

Mary's vision hazed over and the platform tilted beneath her feet. She covered a sob with her hand while she fought for control.

Cameron put an arm around her and pulled her tight against his side. "Did his wife, Lady Rose, send ye?"

"Nay, the healer did. She said to tell ye it was the same illness that beset him before, only worse this time. He didna linger. She said Mary would wish to ken right away and to return quickly."

Cameron traded a glance with his father.

They had discussed every possibility around the succession, but despite Rose's illness, Mary had not expected to lose him so soon.

Cameron's father signaled to the seneschal. "See that this man gets food and drink and a warm place to sleep. He's traveled fast to get here so quickly."

"Cameron, I'm now laird," Mary gasped. "We are…"

"And we are outside the keep's gate with a potential enemy on the inside. I ken this is a shock to ye, but we must get ye home to Rose. We must leave at once."

"Ye canna go tonight," his father said. "In the morning will be soon enough. Gather yer things tonight and leave at first light. Take a *birlinn* and some men. Ye'll get back in a few hours over the firth. Even if the wind and tide are against ye, the men can row."

"Surely…" Mary started to speak but Sutherland cut her off with a wave of his hand.

"We have discussed this," Cameron interjected. "Ye must return and take charge of Rose as heir, or Grant will claim it through yer father's young widow."

"For the sake of yer people, ye dinna want that to happen," Sutherland added, then met Cameron's gaze. "They'll be under Albany's thumb by spring."

Mary shook her head, her body numb, her mind whirling with all she must do.

"Thank ye, Father," Cameron said, never taking his gaze from her.

"We'll do as ye suggest," Mary added, nodding.

"Come on, Mary, my love." Cameron took her upstairs and set her to gathering their things while tears streamed down her face. "I dinna expect packing our belongings to do much to distract ye, but it might help," he told her, his expression full of sympathy, his voice quiet.

"I canna believe he's gone," Mary said as she stuffed a leine in a bag, then a kirtle, punching them down to make room for more.

"Easy, lass. Yer maid will be cross with ye if ye ruin all yer garments."

Mary straightened and wiped her eyes. "If I'd known when we left I'd never see him again, I might have said something..."

"He kenned ye loved him and his people, lass," Cameron said. "Ye showed him yer devotion every day by the way ye cared for him and for them, for his keep and his lands."

"I didna tell him, or even say goodbye," Mary cried, clenching a shift in her hands and twisting it. "I was angry with him when we left."

Cameron took her tear-streaked face in his hands and gazed into her eyes. "Then promise me ye'll never leave me without saying goodbye and telling me how much ye love me and how ye canna live without me." He cocked an eyebrow.

She pursed her lips. "Ye are trying to cheer me up."

"Aye." He pursed his lips.

She studied him for a moment, then ran a fingertip down his cheek. His skin was damp, too. "Ye can do better than that."

Cameron pushed his fingers into her hair, framing her face. "I can, and I shall. Have ye finished packing?"

"All save what we'll need in the morning."

"Then," he said and leaned in to kiss her, "'tis time for me to do as I promised—and do *much, much* better."

Her arms went around his neck as Cameron deepened the kiss, then shifted to kiss the salt of her tears from her cheeks. "Ye ken I love ye, lass."

"Aye," she sniffed, then laid her head on his shoulder.

He stroked her hair, then picked her up, carried her to a chair and sat with her in his lap. "I could kiss ye for the rest of the night, but ye need to rest. So cry lass, if ye still need to. I'm no' going anywhere and I willna melt. Do yer worst."

Mary's response was part laugh, part sob, then she let go, and the tears flowed. Cameron held her close. She knew then she need never doubt how much she meant to him.

THOUGH HER HEART BROKE THAT HER FATHER WOULD NO longer be there, Mary was glad to see the walls of the Rose keep standing high and proud on its bluff over the Moray firth. People in the bailey hailed them as they rode through the gates. Several came up to embrace Mary and offer their condolences. Cameron's frown told her he could see she'd gotten teary. "Let's go in and get settled," he suggested. "Ye can talk to the healer and find out what happened."

Mary nodded and let him escort her inside the keep. "I should speak to Seona right away," she said when they reached the great hall. But Seona was nowhere in sight. The healer came out and patted Mary's hand.

"'Twas fast," she told her. "I dinna think yer da ever kenned."

Mary took a breath, willing herself to calmness. "Tell me."

The healer shook her head. "That...wife...of his. He finally confronted her, though I dinna ken what started the argument. The entire keep rang with the shouting. Finally she stormed off, back to her chamber, I'd guess. Several people had gathered outside the door to ensure no one got hurt. I was told yer da stood by his desk for a few moments, then collapsed. They rushed in to him and called for me. By the time I got there, he was gone. As I said, it was over before he kenned what happened. I'm certain of that."

"Thank ye," Mary told her. "Ye did everything ye could to help him. Where is Seona?"

"In the laird's chamber, most likely, with her lover. She had all four Grants released as soon as she heard she was widowed, and moved in there. And lass, ye need to ken she sent two of the men back to Grant with the news. Her favorite doesna willingly leave her side and has stayed with her since yer da collapsed."

Outraged, Mary objected. "My da is hardly cold yet."

"Aye. They snuck around before yer da had the last attack that was so hard on him. Since then, they've made no pretense of no' being lovers. I ken her poor bairn was his, no' yer da's. She was dark like the Grant, no' blonde like a Rose."

"I thought so as well," Mary agreed. "Though I didna want to say so at the time."

"Do ye want to confront her now?" Cameron asked.

"Aye, I do." She wanted that woman out of Rose.

"Then ye'll do it with me. We still dinna ken who spooked that horse or shot those arrows, or why. If they had anything to do with it, ye'll no be safe facing the two of them alone."

Mary nodded. "Ye speak sense."

Cameron grinned. "As ye well ken, I always do."

The healer snorted. "Except when out of yer head with fever, ye mean?"

Cameron rolled his eyes at her. "Ye would bring that up."

"Someone must keep ye humble," the healer taunted, then softened her remark with a pensive smile. "Take good care of our lass."

"Always." He took Mary's arm and led her to the stairs. "Are ye sure ye want to do this right away, Mary, my love?"

"I am. The sooner she goes back to Grant, the better for Rose."

"Then let's be about it."

Cameron rapped on the laird's door, then opened it, not waiting to be bid to enter. He went in first, Mary on his heels.

Seona, dressed only in her shift and a robe, sat by the hearth.

Her guardsman, shirtless, muscles bulging, stood behind her, his hands in her hair. He quickly removed them and stepped back as Seona gasped. "How dare ye!" he barked.

"I did no' invite ye in," Seona added. "So ye are rude as well as a disobedient daughter?"

"And ye," Mary answered, her gaze on Seona, "have dishonored yer marriage vows more times than I ken. For my father's sake, I turned a blind eye. And for the clan, so did he."

Seona gasped.

"Aye," Mary snapped. "I'm told ye argued before he collapsed, so I imagine ye ken he was aware of yer betrayal. Did he tell ye he wouldha claimed the bairn anyway, had it lived?"

"If it was male, aye." Seona sniffed.

"But ye werena satisfied. Ye had to flaunt yer affair, and eventually ye killed him." She turned her gaze to the guardsman for a moment.

Seona shrugged, and Mary saw her mother's arrogance reflected in her posture.

"Did yer mother put ye up to this once she learned ye were breeding?"

Seona shook her head. "She didna ken."

"I dinna believe ye."

At least the guardsman had the decency to look grieved at the mention of the his bairn. His daughter. Mary regretted he never got to see her before the healer prepared her for burial. She could sympathize with him—a little. He'd been trapped by his feelings for a lass he'd known since childhood.

Seona might have been a lovely child, once, long ago, but how could he continue to pine for her once she grew into the spoiled, arrogant brat she'd been since she arrived at Rose? Seona made Mary's blood boil. "Ye will pack yer things tonight and leave for Grant at first light," Mary commanded. "Ye dinna belong here any longer."

"Ye canna order me about," Seona objected, chin up. "I am Lady Rose."

"Ye lied in order to wed my father. Ye were no' untouched, and worse, ye already carried another man's bairn. I will have yer marriage to my father annulled," Mary snarled, "no matter how long it takes. And if ye dinna leave on yer own in the morn, my warriors will remove ye."

"*Yer* warriors?" Seona sniffed. She narrowed her eyes at Cameron.

Mary wanted to slap the smirk from the lass's face.

"She is heir," Cameron reminded Seona. "Ye heard her father declare Lady Mary and me heirs to Rose before we left for Sutherland. I have the document he signed." He fingered the pommel of his broadsword, a gesture likely not lost on either of the Grants. "Is that why ye tried to kill her? Why ye had someone shoot at her in the woods? So there could be nay challenge to ye and yer lover? Ye must have been furious when yer husband signed Rose's future over to Mary—and to Catherine after her."

Seona gasped. "How dare ye accuse me!"

"Ye'd already failed twice before he did that. Afterward, and after ye lost the bairn, I thought ye understood nothing ye did would keep ye here if yer husband died." Cameron's gaze shifted the guardsman. "'Twas no' ye. Ye were in the dungeon. So who?"

The guardsman froze, his gaze on Seona.

That was as good as a confession they'd conspired to kill her, as far as Mary was concerned, but Cameron wasn't done.

"Ye may as well tell us," Cameron cajoled. "Ye are leaving with her in the morning."

"Ye can marry her when ye return to Grant," Mary added. "'Tis a better outcome than ye deserve."

The guardsman's gaze dropped to the floor for a moment, then back to Cameron. "Lady Grant willna allow her daughter to marry a lowly guard."

The pain on his face saddened Mary, but she couldn't help him.

Seona sniffed and turned away from him to stare into the hearthfire.

How could she dismiss her lover's grief so easily? Mary pressed her hands over her middle, determined to remain strong.

"Anyway, it wasna him," Seona confirmed. "'Twas the blacksmith's helper did it all."

Mary recalled the injured horse that had nearly run her down. The lad had a history of harming smaller animals. She doubted he had any skill with a bow and arrow—perhaps that was why his arrows missed her. "The apprentice set the fire, too?" Mary hadn't believed he'd destroy the place where he worked, but since it was the one place where he had easy access to a hot fire, and a plausible excuse for the blaze, it made horrible sense.

"He had help," the guardsman agreed.

"We'll deal with them," Cameron said. "As for ye, as Lady Mary said, ye have nay place here. Ye never did. Ye are an adulteress in the eyes of the law and the kirk. And nearly a murderess."

"Dinna insult my lady!" the guardsman warned.

"Nothing worked," Seona fumed. "The damned bairn was a lass, and she died. If only I'd borne a healthy lad, my place with yer father wouldha been secure. At least he had the decency to die," she spat at Mary. "If ye were dead, if ye both were," she added with a glance at Cameron, "all would be well." She narrowed her eyes. "Ye must no' leave this room alive." She lifted an imperious chin at the guardsman.

He stared at Seona, disbelief written in his open-mouthed frown as he hesitated, then he pulled his dirk.

"Aye, kill them," Seona growled and stood, pointing at Mary.

Cameron was fast. His dirk was in his hand before Mary could blink.

Mary moved quickly, too. Seona's lover lunged at her, but she ducked out of the way.

Cameron blocked the guardsman's thrust, grabbed the man's forearm and twisted, turning out of the way of his blade as he moved.

The guardsman jerked his arm free and swung again, this time at Cameron.

Mary gasped as Cameron blocked him again, then attacked, forcing the fight away from the women.

Seona crept from behind her chair, her gaze on

Cameron's back. Mary noticed her movement out of the corner of her eye, then the *sghian dubh* in her hand. Too honorable to use it when his opponent wielded only a dirk, he hadn't pulled his broadsword from his back, but it offered little protection if Seona charged at him with her blade.

Mary dared not distract Cameron by calling out a warning. Instead, she rushed Seona and grabbed her around her knees, knocking her down. The wee blade skittered across the floor, out of reach. Mary sat on her, silently thanking her sisters for the hours of play fighting they'd done as children, trying to be more like the lads.

Seona tried to push her off, pummeling her back and grabbing at her hair.

"*Wheesht*," Mary commanded and slapped her. "I've had enough of ye to last me a lifetime."

Seona gasped in shock and quieted just as the guardsman rushed Cameron again, blade poised for a downward strike.

Cameron dodged and thrust his dirk into the guard's chest. The man fell to his knees, eyes widened in shock as his gaze turned to Seona. Then he lifted his hand to reach for her. With a shudder, he collapsed forward, onto Cameron's blade.

Seona screamed and thrashed, finally shoving Mary off of her.

Mary rolled to her feet and rushed toward Cameron.

Seona crawled to her bleeding lover, then cradled his head. "Ye killed him! Ach, nay, ye have killed him."

"He would have killed Mary," Cameron spat. "I willna let anyone harm her, least of all ye." He hugged Mary to him, then released her. "Lass, go out in the hall and call for help. Someone must remove the body, and I willna leave ye alone with *her*."

Mary nodded and went to the doorway. While she called for Rose guards, Cameron approached the man's body carefully, reminding her of how he was wounded months before. He'd learned caution that day.

Seona lay over the body, sobbing.

Mary kept her gaze on him and Seona. If Seona picked up the guardsman's blade, she could stab Cameron while his attention was on the body.

Instead, Cameron retrieved it, then pulled his from beneath the body, jostling Seona and making her wail even louder. He sighed and straightened, then his gaze met Mary's and he shook his head. Unlike the gallowglass man, the guardsman was indeed dead.

She nodded. She might feel sorry for Seona, except for all the misery the lass had caused. The sooner all Grants were gone from Rose, the better.

Hours later, the body had been removed, the blood cleaned up, and Seona had been given a sleeping draught and put in another chamber under guard. At Cameron's direction, the blacksmith's apprentice and his helper Seona had bribed had been consigned to a cell in the dungeon. Mary and Cameron finally retired to their chamber.

"Rose needs a new beginning," Mary told him as they readied for bed. "We'll start by burying my father in the morning." She pressed her hand to her mouth, her throat tight, yet surprised when tears failed to come. Cameron's gaze was on her, and she sighed, then told him, "I canna find the strength to cry right now."

He nodded. "When ye do, I'll be here to hold ye, Mary, my love."

She went to him and gave him a grateful kiss, then climbed into bed. "The next thing we must do," she continued, "is ask yer father for more men to help keep us safe from retaliation by Grant."

"A wise decision, Laird Rose," Cameron told her as

he joined her. He pulled her to him and wrapped an arm around her.

Mary snuggled against him. She laid her head on his shoulder, inhaling his scent and melting into his warmth. "I will also have everything removed from Seona's chamber and my father's," she promised. "We will furnish the laird's chamber anew 'ere we move in there. And use hers for storage, I suppose. If I learned one thing from Lady Grant, it's that appearances make an impression. I want this clan to be able to see all trace of Seona's betrayal removed."

"That suits me."

The next morning after seeing her father laid to rest in the kirkyard, Mary bid Seona and her remaining Grant guard goodbye. "Do tell yer mother to forget about Rose," Mary bade her. "Unless she wishes to go to war with the clans of the Moray firth, backed up by Munro, Erik Ross, and, aye, Sutherland, she'll turn her territorial ambitions in another direction. Rose is in good hands and will remain so."

&

CAMERON WATCHED THE TWO GRANTS RIDE OUT OF Rose's gates with his heart in his throat. The people of clan Rose filled the bailey, and the din of their cheering echoed from the walls of the keep to the fortress walls around it, and back again. Suddenly, everything about his new situation hit him. In the gut. In the head. But mostly, in the heart. Mary was now Laird Rose. And his wife. He was consort, tied to this place, this clan, and these people for the rest of his life. He felt wonderful. And terrified. Despite the chill, sweat rolled down his spine.

Mary, standing beside him, watched the Grants go.

Once they were out of sight, she turned to face her clan —*her clan*—and spoke.

"Clan Rose is once again in Rose hands. My father named me laird before he died, along with my husband, Cameron Sutherland, whom ye ken."

Cheers broke out afresh, and Cameron took heart that Mary's words—and his position in the clan—were well received. He raised her hand over her head, a sign of victory, and of gratitude the clan stood with her.

Mary smiled up at him, then leaned close. But instead of whispering something to him, she kissed him. In front of everyone.

"Well, Mary, my love," he told her when they broke apart to more cheers and good-natured catcalls, "if anyone had any doubts, ye just removed them."

"Good. I need ye, Cameron Sutherland," she continued, speaking softly, just to him. "Without ye by my side, I canna do this. I feel terrible about Seona's lover, even after all the trouble he caused on her behalf. And sorry for her, despite what a liar and schemer she turned out to be. Though not too sorry. If she'd had a son, she would have married her lover and ruled Rose for Grant. I'm certain that was what Lady Grant intended, to have Seona in charge until her brother attained an age to take over Grant and us. Yet ye ruined it all by keeping me safe and bringing Sutherland into what she saw as Grant business."

"Nay, lass, ye needna feel guilty. They earned what they got."

"As did that lout in the dungeon. Annie said he was trouble years ago. She was right. I shouldha paid more attention. We must banish him and his helper."

"Ye could hang him for what he's done, perhaps both."

"Nay, I dinna want us to begin that way. The clan will be watching—and judging—us."

"*Dinna fash*, ye can do this. Ye have done so for years now. I will be with ye, whatever comes."

She bit her lip. "I ken ye never wanted to be laird, and how difficult a choice this was for ye to make. I'm sorry."

"Ye are wrong lass," he told her, cupping her cheek. "Ye ken fine, I never wanted it, but I did want ye. And I will do what I must to be with ye and to support ye."

"Will ye be my war chief?"

Cameron's heart stuttered. "I will."

"And my consort."

"Aye."

"My protector."

"Always, Mary, my love."

"And the clan's."

Cameron nodded, sensing how seriously Mary meant the question, even though she asked it lightly. "Ye can count on me, lass. I'll never abandon ye."

She took his hand from her face and raised it over his head, as far as she could reach. The cheers got louder, so Cameron pulled her arm down and wrapped his around her, then kissed her soundly for everyone to see.

EPILOGUE

*M*ary stood with her back to the hearth, enjoying the warmth of the yule log burning there, and observed the great hall with satisfaction. Despite a heavy snowfall making travel difficult—even dangerous—for two pregnant women, Mary's sisters, their husbands, and Annie's first bairn had made it safely to Rose three days ago. The scent of pine boughs filled the air. Ropes of holly with bright red berries bound together with red ribbons draped the windows. Mistletoe hung in each doorway, making perfect spots for lovers to pause and kiss, to revel in the magic of the Druid's herb. Members of the clan came and went on their own errands, some remaining at the long trestle tables, cups of ale or cider in hand, awaiting the evening meal and the celebration to follow.

The blaze at her back couldn't match the warmth filling her heart at seeing her sisters with husbands and children of their own. And seeing her own husband sharing an ale with them and listening to the tale of their trip to Rose.

It meant so much to have her loved ones with her for their first Yuletide without their father.

"I wish Da could see us," Mary murmured to her

sisters, but loudly enough for their men to hear. "He did love us. He told me so before Cameron and I left for Sutherland."

"He was a sly man, for all of that," Iain said and grinned at Annie. She grinned back, then set her cup down to chase their son, who was headed for the door out to the bailey at a fast crawl. "Ewan, come back here, ye we scamp," she called. "'Tis too cold for ye to go out there." One of the serving lasses helped her round up the lad, and Annie marched back to the hearth with the shrieking babe on her hip to join the rest of the family.

Catherine handed him his favorite toy horse and he immediately put it to his mouth, gumming its back.

"He's developed a fascination with horses," Annie said, "and he saw where the Rose stables are. If he's no' riding before he walks, I'll be surprised."

"We did," Mary reminded her. "Da made certain of that, though seeing us riding frightened *Maman*. He indulged us shamefully when we were wee."

"One could wish our father had been a wee less difficult once we grew up," Catherine complained and raised her glass to her husband, Kenneth. "We missed out on so many years together," she added softly, a glint of tears in her eyes.

"Now, lass," Kenneth said, "we've decided none of that matters. Only the years to come. Remember?" He leaned over to kiss her cheek, laying one hand possessively on her growing belly. "And our child, come spring."

"Aye, I do." She laid her hand over his and gave him a shy smile.

"He told me he made it difficult for us to wed because he couldna bear to lose us," Mary said, her voice dropping as sadness welled in her chest. "He said it was like losing *Maman* all over again, each time." She wanted her sisters to get a glimpse of him he'd given only to her.

Annie and Catherine traded glances, then turned back to Mary and nodded. "He meant well."

Mary didn't think they believed her, but she refused to let that deter her. She would tell them stories about their father until they understood him better. She owed them that—and him.

Cameron cleared his throat, his gaze on his wife. "And whether he meant to or nay, yer father gave his life to protect Mary's inheritance. Iain is right. He was a sly man. He had Lady Grant's and Seona's measure from the beginning." He raised his cup, as if making a toast. "All is well," he insisted. "Ye are all together. No matter that ye have wed, ye will always be Mary Elizabeth, Mary Anne and Mary Catherine Rose."

Mary loved that Cameron was the one to make then see what they had, not what they'd lost.

After they chorused, "Aye, aye!" and took a sip, Cameron continued. "Clan Rose remains in Rose hands, and it has strong alliances to protect it, including its closest ally, clan Brodie."

"For as long as ye men keep Rose and Brodie—and we three Marys—safe," Catherine agreed.

"Here's to Da and all of us!" Annie cried as she raised her cup.

"Here's to Da," Mary said, raising hers and taking another sip. "He made us fight for what we wanted, so we were sure to get only the very best."

Her sisters turned their smiles on their husbands as Cameron pulled her into his embrace. He kissed her, his lips soft and warm, then his breath warmed her cheek and he murmured in her ear, "Ye, Mary, my love, are the very best part of me."

Joy and contentment filled her. "I'm so grateful for ye," she told him, then laid her head on his shoulder and breathed in the scents of ale, wine, roasting meat, and woodsmoke, along with Cameron's own.

Soon, the clan crowded in, and the hall rang with conversation and laughter. Once everyone was seated, servants carried out huge platters laden with the winter feast. From her place in what had been her father's seat at the high table, with her loved ones all around her, Mary lifted her voice to be heard throughout the hall and wished, "A happy Yule to us all!"

START A NEW SERIES

HEART OF STONE

Riding home after two years away, Gavan MacNabb encounters a lass and her deerhound in a moonlit circle of standing stones. Little does he know the garland of bluebells she weaves and the spell she sings will change the course of his life.

Marsali Murray doesn't really believe the old wives' tale that making a chain of bluebells by the standing stones under a waxing moon will bring true love, but she's desperate to try anything to escape the boring, everlasting sameness of her life. Anything except marrying a man her father chooses for her. When her deerhound, Corrie, insists on following Gavan, Marsali decides that's the excuse she needs to have the adventure she craves. She'll go where he goes, whether or not he is the man promised by her spell.

Gavan has already seen much of the world denied to Marsali. He's ready to settle down. She is eager to spread her wings. Can they find what they need with each other?

Keep reading for a sneak peek…

HEART OF STONE (HIGHLAND TALENTS SERIES PREQUEL)

*H*e needed the distance, but it appeared she did, as well. Her shoulders had dropped when he moved away. But after she picked up the chain of flowers she'd been weaving and ran a fingertip over a few of the bell-shaped blooms, he could see tension reflected again in her stiff posture.

"'Tis a harmless thing I do." She paused, eyeing him, as if wondering whether she dared continue. A frown marred the smooth expanse of her forehead, but only for a moment.

Her reluctance made Gavan wonder what harm a woven strand of bluebells could harbor. Was she embarrassed or uneasy to tell him? "Aye?" he prompted, curious now.

She exhaled, glancing skyward, then met his gaze. "'Tis said if under a waxing moon a maid weaves a chain of bluebells within the stone circle, the next lad she sees will be her true love." She held up her handiwork. "'Tis no' quite finished, so I believe ye are safe from me. Corrie tells me I am safe from ye."

Gavan gave her his most innocent smile. "I dinna believe in such things, but if ye do..." Not in the magic, and not in the illusion of safety her dog gave her.

265

Buy Heart of Stone

ACKNOWLEDGMENTS

As I wrap up this series and look forward to new adventures in writing, several people stand out in my mind as having played a major role in making it a success. My heartfelt thanks go out to my Beta readers and to my editor, Maureen Sevilla, for your critique, ideas and encouragement. And to Tamra Westberry, cover artist, for your gorgeous interpretations of my stories.

And last but never least, my eternal gratitude to my husband, Laird Peter, who encourages my love for writing, even when deadlines approach.

His Highland Heart

His Highland Rose

His Highland Heart

His Highland Love

His Highland Bride

Highland Talents

Heart of Stone

Highland Healer

Highland Seer

Highland Troth

The Healer's Gift

When Highland Lightning Strikes

Sweetie Pie (A Candy Hearts Novella)

Waiting for the Laird

When You Find Love

ABOUT THE AUTHOR

*Willa Blair is an award-wining Amazon and Barnes &
Noble #1 bestselling author of Scottish historical, light
paranormal and contemporary romance filled with men in
kilts, psi talents, and plenty of spice. Her books have won
numerous accolades, including the Marlene, the Merritt,
National Readers' Choice Award Finalist, Reader's Crown
finalist, InD'Tale Magazine's RONE Award Honorable
Mention, and NightOwl Reviews Top Picks. She loves
scouting new settings for books, and thinks being an author
is the best job she's ever had.*

Willa loves hearing from readers!
Contact her:
www.willablair.com
authorwillablair@gmail.com

Sign up for my Newsletter
Find links to the rest of my books

CPSIA information can be obtained
at www.ICGtesting.com
Printed in the USA
LVHW10125803012Z
707736LV00022B/404

9 781648 390999